Ricochet

Ricochet

by p.m.terrell

Published by Paralee Press
USA

ISBN 0-9785632-0-4 (Soft cover)

Library of Congress Cataloging-in-Publication Data applied for

Printed in the United States of America

10 9 8 7 6 5 4 3 2 1

Author's website: www.pmterrell.com

OTHER BOOKS BY
p.m.terrell

KICKBACK

THE CHINA CONSPIRACY

ACKNOWLEDGEMENTS

This book would not have been possible without a number of people who provided technical assistance and who shared law enforcement knowledge to lend credibility and authenticity to this book. Special thanks to:

Bob B. Andrews, M.D., retired pathologist;
Master Detective Kevin Bacon, Chesterfield County, Virginia Police Department;
Special Agent Steven Barry, National Press Office Supervisor, Federal Bureau of Investigation;
Lt Colonel James Bourque, Chesterfield County, Virginia Police Department;
Officer Mark Kearney of the Waynesboro, Virginia Police Department;
Pamela June Kimmell, author of *The Mystery of David's Bridge;*
My good friend and thriller expert, Karen Luffred;
Mary Ann Masters, O.D., of Lumberton, North Carolina;
John Neelley, retired FBI Special Agent;
G. Mitchell (Mickey) Reed, Chief of Police;
Georgia Richardson, author of *A Funny Thing Happened on the Way to the Throne;*
Major Bill Rohde, Petersburg, Virginia Police Department;
Captain Gregory J. Seidel, Petersburg, Virginia Police Department;
And most of all to my husband, Don Terrell, without whom this book would not have been possible.

1

I awakened in a cold sweat, my breathing labored and coarse, the way it had been in the explosion.

And now I see where decisions I made placed me on certain paths heading in specific directions. Sometimes, I knew my life would be altered the moment I'd made up my mind, such as when I chose to major in computer programming at Vanderbilt University instead of working on my family's tobacco farm. Or when I sold the farm after my parents died from carbon monoxide poisoning. I knew my path would change again when the FBI recruited me as a Special Agent. Those choices are ones I refer to as "life intersections", sometimes lovingly and sometimes not, because I was consciously making a ninety-degree turn at the time. Those are the kinds of decisions I laid awake at night and mulled over, knowing my life would be changed because of them.

Then there are those quirky little turns that I never saw coming and sometimes didn't specifically recall making… what to wear, when to leave for work, where to go for lunch. The kind of choices that I don't give much thought to, and certainly would never have believed such a small decision could alter my life forever.

I was soon to learn differently.

I'd arrived in Virginia after an extended summer hiatus at my Aunt Jo's house in Sunnyside, Tennessee, where I experienced a much-needed rest from a stressful job that I was thankful was over.

Fall was in the air—a beautiful crisp November day with clear, pale blue skies—the kind of day that's best spent watching the leaves slip away from their branches and flutter to the ground on puffs of wind.

That evening would be one of those turning points in my life, my first glimpse of the FBI Academy at Quantico. I was scheduled to report there before nightfall where I would be assigned a dorm room and a roommate. The next day would be my first official day as an FBI employee.

I'd originally expected to join the New Agents Class scheduled for September, but it was already full. Normally, I'd have had to wait until the winter class began, but because of the high terrorism alert, the FBI was building up and building up fast. They placed me into a special group of computer and foreign language experts that would run simultaneously with the other class. My foreign language skill was limited to Spanish, a necessity as my parents often hired Latino laborers to work their tobacco farm. But my computer skills were the best they could have hoped for, even if I did say so myself.

My best friend and roommate from Vanderbilt University was settled into a wonderful little house in Richmond's Fan District, a mere fifty miles or so from Quantico, so naturally I stopped by Margaret's house to visit for awhile. And naturally, she suggested we go shopping. Shopping for clothes and particularly shoes was Margaret's favorite pastime, and used to be one of mine, too, until that fateful day.

I was anxious to get to Quantico but I had a few hours to kill, so I agreed to go shopping and delay my arrival primarily because I knew once the Academy started, the last thing on earth I'd have time to do was relax.

So I followed Margaret's BMW in my Honda Civic, up Interstate 95 to a point a bit more than halfway between Richmond and Quantico, to a nice new mall on the outskirts of the Washington suburbs.

We shopped until late afternoon. Having not eaten since breakfast, I was famished by then. By the time we made it to the food court, I had a new pair of Nikes in tow, along with at least a half dozen of Margaret's shopping bags. Not that she wasn't carrying her share; she was so burdened, she would've looked like a bag lady had she not been so beautiful. I still remember her outfit—a bright yellow sweater that had guys turning their heads as she passed, her blue jean jacket tied fashionably around her waist. She towered above most guys—when she put on those three-inch heels, she was over six foot.

The odd mixture of odors reached our nostrils even before we reached the food court—fried chicken and oriental rice, pizza, tacos, and freshly baked cookies.

The food court was packed. We had too many shopping bags to go through a line and come out with a tray full of food, so we opted to wait until a table was available. Then two tables were emptied at once—one right beside the door and the other one smack dab in the middle of the room. For some reason I can't put a finger on now, we both lunged for the one by the door. As we piled the shopping bags and my worn leather aviator jacket into two of the four chairs, I glanced back at the other table. A young mother with two children, one in a stroller and the other clinging to her mother's tunic, had descended upon it. I see the three of them to this day, every time I close my eyes and try to sleep, and I wonder—I wonder.

We didn't flip a coin to decide who stayed with the packages and who went for the food. I tried later to remember how we decided something so mundane, but the memory never returned. Margaret went to Popeye's to get some good fried chicken and some New Orleans-style rice for us while I sat at the table, grateful to take a load off my feet and watched her in line, twirling her hair and looking as if she didn't have a care in the world.

The door to the mall was opening and closing on a regular, if somewhat brisk, basis, letting gusts of autumn wind inside as shoppers struggled to straighten their windblown hair and shed their coats.

I spotted the man as soon as he walked through the door. He hesitated not four feet from my table; looked around as if he didn't quite know what to do. Medium height, black hair, olive complexion. He looked foreign, but it was difficult to tell. The Washington area was a melting pot. It was his coat that grabbed my attention: a faded green parka that appeared to have a thick layer of down, and a band of fur around the thrown-back hood. It was more in line with what one would wear in the middle of a Midwestern winter than a mid-Atlantic autumn.

His hands grasped it tight around his abdomen as if to fit over a bulky physique, but his head appeared too small to match the wide chest and wider abdomen.

He moved away from me, through the crowd, to a point halfway between the table with the young mother and Margaret, who was still standing in line. She turned and half-waved to me, a wide grin on her face. She was talking to a handsome fellow in line behind her.

At that moment, the man moved his arms and his coat gaped open. It was then I saw it: something rigid under his coat: vertical sticks of dynamite strapped side by side around his middle.

He turned and stared directly into my eyes. His face was expressionless, his eyes a gunmetal black. Then he clasped his hands together and raised his head toward heaven.

I opened my mouth, a scream on my lips, when the world collapsed around me.

2

In my confusion, I don't remember what I noticed first: that the brightly lit food court was so black it was impossible to see my hand in front of my face, or that the pleasant odors of cooked food was suddenly replaced by the reek of acrid smoke, or that I could no longer breathe, as if my lungs were rapidly filling with cotton candy.

I don't know when I fell. The wind was knocked out of me and I was lying face down with something protruding into my belly. I struggled to turn onto my side to prevent myself from lying face down or face up, and I pushed my hands out in front of me, blindly groping to move debris.

Liquid was pouring into my eyes, and as I swiped my grit-filled hand across my lids, I realized I was bleeding. I fought the panic that threatened to sweep over me as I fought my worst fear: that I'd been blinded.

I tried to call out, to cry for help, but I didn't have enough air to make a sound as drywall dust streamed into my lungs.

It was then that I heard the screams. They were everywhere—a child's cries for a mother, a man's for his wife, a woman pleading for God not to let her die.

I fought the terror that threatened to engulf me. My legs were pinned underneath something long and weighty. I thought of the heavy metal beams that crisscrossed their way above the food court. No, it couldn't be that. They would've crushed my legs. Painstakingly, I succeeded in reaching my hand to my legs where I pinched each one, breathing a sigh of relief as I felt the pain.

It was still as black as a shark's eye in front of me. I managed to work up enough saliva to spit. It cleared the God-awful taste from my mouth, even if it was only temporary. And it gave me the chance to determine which way was really up and which way was down, as I let the gravity pull the spittle down the side of my face. It was then that I realized I was lying at a forty-five degree angle, head down.

The screams were growing stronger and more numerous. My nose was plugged with a fine dust. I struggled to blow out and to regain my sense of smell as I inhaled. And as the screams grew more intense, I realized the building was on fire, and there were people around me burning.

There was a pocket of air directly in front of me, and I fought to keep my face inside that pocket like a drowning victim struggles to stay afloat.

I tried to remain calm, reminding myself that drywall was an insulator. I'd seen my dad tape whole strips of it around pipes. And when I'd sold their house after they'd died, I recall the inspector commenting on it. But as doubt crept in, I found myself wondering what he meant by that; was it an insulator in that it kept the pipes warm or cool, or would it insulate against fire?

I wondered where Margaret was, and tried to calculate the number of feet between us. The explosion occurred far closer to her than to me. I strove to hear her voice in the maelstrom but didn't know if I would recognize it in the growing chorus.

I tried working each leg, bit by bit, trying not to shift the debris. I don't know what I was most afraid of—losing my little pocket of air and suffocating, or lying there paralyzed until the flames lapped at my body.

Eventually the voices subsided, leaving me surrounded by silence that was even more terrifying than the pandemonium.

Everything was still pitch black, and as hard as I tried, I couldn't figure out if my eyesight was gone, or if I'd been plunged into some black hole.

From somewhere in the distance, the muffled sound of sirens reached me. When I thought help was only a moment away, there was a massive creaking and the world around me shifted. I was squeezed like an accordion and plunged deeper under mounting debris as my world came crashing in around me.

3

That evening found me huddled in a hospital room, holding my head while trying to will away the throbbing that had me on the brink of nausea. Occasionally I found myself staring across the room at my best friend's still body. Had it not been for the steady green beat on the heart monitor coupled with the rhythmic sound from the respirator, I would have wondered if Margaret was dead. My heart cried out for her to wake up and say something—anything—so I would know she'd be all right.

The nurse finished checking the equipment, and started toward the door.

"Can you tell me—?" I started to ask before stopping abruptly.

The nurse, a middle-aged woman with the kind of stout physique and squared shoulders of one accustomed to bearing others' burdens, squeezed my arm. "She's in a coma," she said softly. "She could come out of it in another minute, or…" her voice drifted off and she shook her head. Then her eyes drifted upward to my forehead. "You know," she said, "you really do need to be examined."

I caught a glimpse of myself in the mirror beside her. Sandy blond hair lightened by fine drywall dust, dazed blue-green eyes, and a petite frame covered in rumpled, dusty

clothing. Instinctively, I reached up and felt the dried blood
smeared across my brow as I watched my reflection.
Miraculously, it was the only bit of blood on me. "This is
nothing," I said.

She nodded as though unconvinced but quietly left the
room.

I made my way to Margaret's bed and grasped her hand.
I spoke to her softly, letting her know I was there, but she
didn't respond.

It had been several hours since we were brought here.
Although each second felt like an eternity, the rescue workers
had extricated me rather easily from the depths of a
blackness so complete that I will never forget it.

Despite my objections, they'd insisted on loading me
into an ambulance beside a small boy. I was in awe of the
paramedic and nurse and how swiftly and efficiently they
used the defibrillator to jump start his damaged and
weakening heart. They repeatedly ordered him to remain
conscious and not to fall asleep; they asked his name so
many times their words were etched on my brain, but he
never responded.

My vitals were good, and the only external injury I had
was the cut across my forehead. Judging from how quickly
the blood stopped flowing, I figured it wouldn't even need
stitches. I felt guilty for taking up space in the ambulance
when there were so many who were seriously injured.

When we reached the hospital, additional medical
personnel helped to whisk the young boy inside. As the
paramedic left the ambulance, he sternly directed me to
remain as I was until he returned, which would presumably
be only a short time.

Once he was out of sight, I unlatched the straps that
had kept me immobile on the stretcher, and I climbed out

of the ambulance. My father was fond of saying we were from tough pioneer stock, though the days of our European ancestors settling in middle Tennessee occurred at least eight generations before his birth. Still, he would have expected me to walk as long as my legs could still carry me.

I quickly got caught up in the growing crowd; then before I knew what was happening, I was caught in the glare of white lights and a microphone was thrust into my face.

"Where were you when the explosion occurred?" came an urgent voice.

I looked up to see a woman in perhaps her mid-twenties with straight blond hair and almond eyes, her press pass clipped to her suit jacket. "Were you inside the mall?" she pressed.

"I was in the food court," I said.

"What happened? Did you see anything?"

"A man with dynamite strapped to him," I answered. "He looked right at me—"

"Can you describe him?" she interrupted breathlessly. "Did you recognize him?"

"I'd never seen him before," I said. "But I'll never forget his face. Ever."

"So how did it feel when the bomb exploded?"

"Excuse me," I said, a sudden throbbing pain beginning to course through my head. I extricated myself from the reporter, made my way past a horde of others and into the hospital. Thank God they were prohibiting the press from entering the emergency room. Before I knew it, a nurse had me cornered, then seated, while she took my vitals and asked for information: my name, date of birth, and other personal data, interspersed by a short quiz on current events to make sure my mental faculties were intact.

She examined my head, where thankfully the bleeding on my forehead had stopped. And by now I knew I hadn't been blinded, simply pulled into the black womb created by the collapsed building. I was covered with dust ranging from a fine, talcum-powder consistency to rock-sized pieces of drywall lodged in my hair. But I was alive, and it didn't appear that I'd broken anything.

The nurse told me to stay in the waiting room and someone would be with me shortly, but I knew I'd be at the bottom of their list. Watching the steady stream of ambulances arriving, it was obvious I was one of the more fortunate.

I came to my feet, a bit more unsteadily than I would have preferred, and started through the throngs of people, looking for Margaret's bright yellow sweater.

It would be more than an hour before I would find her amidst the pandemonium.

Oddly, it was the same paramedic and nurse who'd been with the young boy who returned with Margaret several trips later. And like the young boy, she was unresponsive, her face bloated almost beyond recognition, an oxygen mask covering her nose and mouth, her swollen eyes closed.

I followed them through the doors and into a curtained area where a doctor was immediately summoned. I stared in morbid fascination as her clothes were cut away. Then the medical personnel surrounded her amidst the doctor's barked orders, and I was unceremoniously ushered out.

I remained beyond the curtains listening intently until several nurses and a doctor left some time later. Then I cautiously parted the curtains and peered inside where a matronly nurse was checking intravenous fluids that hung over Margaret's body.

Another nurse soon joined the first and they discussed room availability. My heart was hammering in my chest as I followed them, Margaret's pale body completely still on the stretcher. We meandered through the emergency room and into an elevator. I vaguely recall the nurse talking to me, and dimly remember answering, though I can't recall now what was said. I caught my reflection in the cold stainless steel walls and saw tracks of tears streaming down my face, but I was so stunned that I hadn't even known I was crying.

I didn't want to call Margaret's parents until she woke up, until I knew she'd be all right. But when a nurse came in to interview me and determine who would be making the decisions for Margaret while she was incapacitated, I realized I couldn't wait.

As much as I hated to admit it, even to myself, Margaret could be dying. And the longer I waited, the less chance there would be of her parents being with her when she passed on.

I'd lost my cell phone and my purse, and assumed they were now buried beneath the rubble. I used the hospital room phone to call Margaret's parents. Mrs. Reed answered on the second ring.

"Mrs. Reed, this is Sheila," I started.

"Sheila, are you alright?" she said, her voice rising.

I felt my heart drop into my shoes. "I'm fine. But something's happened to Margaret—"

"Tell me you weren't at the mall!" she shrieked. "You couldn't have been in the explosion!"

"Yes, we were, but—"

The phone must have been dropped. I could hear Mrs. Reed wailing hysterically. I tried to hear what she was saying, but I was unable to decipher her words.

Then Margaret's brother Harper picked up the phone. "Hello?"

"This is Sheila—"

"Sheila, are you okay?"

"I'm fine, but Margaret—"

"Where is she? Is she—?"

"She's at INOVA Fairfax Hospital," I said. "She's in a coma."

"We'll be there as fast as we can," came his breathless voice.

After we hung up, I paced the floor, one eye trained on Margaret. The Reeds lived in a house large enough for a small army in Richmond's historic Fan District, over two hours from the hospital. I'd met them during my first year of college, when Margaret and I became dorm mates through a simple twist of fate. We'd become fast friends, but I'd had no idea how important she would become to me until my parents died suddenly, leaving me with one living relative: my great-aunt, who I refer to as simply Aunt Jo. Margaret took me under her wing, and her parents and brother treated me like a member of their own family. Though we came from very different backgrounds—me from a tobacco farm in rural Tennessee and Margaret from an upscale urban family—we became as important to each other as the air around us.

In my mind's eye, I saw them speeding up I-95 in their black Lincoln Continental, Mr. Reed's Ambassador license plates ensuring they wouldn't be stopped.

I held Margaret's hand for some time. I ran cold water over a washcloth, and gently wiped her face, noting the dozens of razor-like cuts in her lips and across her cheeks. I listened to her rattled breathing that sounded as if her lungs were filled with water balloons.

Nurses moved in and out in a steady stream constantly checking vital signs and occasionally pushing the bed elsewhere to get more x-rays or perform more tests while I was left to pace the room.

Eventually, I turned on the television set. Every channel was focused on the explosion. Eyewitness accounts pointed to a suicide bomber, but whether he acted alone hadn't yet been determined.

There'd been no calls from extremist factions claiming credit, which was a bit odd. Homeland Security was on the scene, already trying to piece together the event.

I caught a glimpse of a jacket with large white letters emblazoned across the back: FBI. I gasped and looked at my watch. It was after nine o'clock, but it seemed like a lifetime ago when Margaret had stood in line waiting to order dinner for us both. In less than twelve hours, I was due in a classroom at the FBI Academy in Quantico.

The Reeds arrived after ten. Mrs. Reed's eyes were bloodshot, her nose red, her hands clutching a partially destroyed tissue. They hugged me tightly and asked about my own welfare, though I knew they were aching to see Margaret. Then they converged on her, stroking her hair, grasping her hands. Harper eventually broke away and came to stand beside me.

"Are you okay?" he asked.

I nodded.

"Are you sure?"

"Yeah, I'm sure." I ran my fingers through my hair and came away with a handful of drywall and a nail. I stared at the nail for a long time before sticking it in my pocket.

"You're staying at our house, of course…" he was saying.

"Thanks, but I can't. I'm starting the FBI Academy tomorrow." I looked across the room at Margaret. "I really want to stay here—"

"We won't leave her," Mr. Reed interjected. I hadn't even realized he'd left Margaret's side and joined us.

"But certainly you can't start in the Academy in your condition—" Harper insisted.

"Sure, I can," I answered. "I look worse than I feel. A hot shower, and I'll be ready for anything."

We spoke for a few more minutes; I answered their questions as best as I could, and they attempted to reassure me, though I knew they were doubtful themselves.

When they eventually left my side, I quietly made my way out of the room and left the hospital.

4

I took a cab back to the mall. One end was totally unrecognizable and cordoned off from the public. The place was teeming with first responders and rescue dogs swarming over the gaping wound that had been the vibrant mall's center. Though fire trucks and firefighters surrounded the area, there was no sign of smoke or fire; everyone appeared to be concentrating on rescue efforts.

The cabbie drove me to the opposite side of the mall, where my Honda Civic was parked, all shiny and new with a keyless entry system. And once inside, I'd dug my hand into one of my suitcases to grab the extra set of keys and money for the cab.

It was after midnight when I approached the gate at Quantico. The young Marine sentinel was clearly stunned at my appearance, and I wished I'd had the forethought to at least comb my hair or run a damp washcloth over my face. Once he verified my name on the list, I was directed to pull over to the side, step out of the car, and open all the doors for an inspection.

I was exhausted and wanted nothing more than a firm bed and a soft pillow, but when I tried to explain my unfortunate set of circumstances, he wanted to hear all about it in macabre detail, even going so far as to pull another Marine over for a repeat explanation. It was clear they both thought they would've been Rambo had they been there, single-handedly putting an end to the terrorist's plans before he had a chance to act. Their excitement made my head hurt worse, which was compounded when he asked for identification.

I hesitated, caught between irritation because he obviously hadn't understood the rescue workers had rescued only me, not my possessions, and sudden panic that for the first time in my adult life, I did not have a purse.

Then I realized I had copied all of my identification for my in-processing. "I have my birth certificate and a copy of my driver's license," I said, walking around to the open trunk. "And all the papers I was asked to bring with me to class." I dug out a suitcase and rifled through the papers. "Here—this is everything I have."

I watched him inspect the papers. That was everything— my whole life. Right there in the palm of his hand. A dozen papers that showed every school I'd attended, every reference I had, every club I'd ever been a member of, every relative I had. All right there, signed and notarized. I began to feel empty inside.

He folded the papers and handed them back to me. Without a word, he proceeded to my car, where he opened each suitcase and each carton, inspected the new laptop I'd gone into hock for, opened the glove compartment and even ran a mirror under the car.

"Do I look that dangerous?" I joked.

He gave me a stern, humorless glare. "Heightened security."

I glanced at the gate, where a bright orange security notice was posted. Of course we were at a heightened state of alert. After all, there were terrorists who wanted to kill us.

At last I was directed to the Administration building, which was easy enough to find. But by then, I was seriously considering sleeping in the car. Somehow, I managed to put one foot in front of the other and make it to the front desk.

After explaining why I looked the way I did for the third time, I was given directions to what would become my home for the next sixteen weeks.

I thanked the man at the desk, who I assumed was an agent, and turned, abruptly running headlong into the handsomest man I think I'd ever laid eyes on.

He must have been a six-footer with warm brown hair cut short as if to announce his involvement in law enforcement. His eyes were a strange kind of green—almost emerald—and absolutely piercing. It was downright difficult to look away. But when I did, my eyes fell on broad, football player shoulders and biceps that threatened to rip through his shirt.

Then he opened his mouth and all my fantasies dissolved right then and there.

"It looks like Dorothy's house fell on your head!" he said with the slightest hint of a drawl.

The man at the desk bellowed. I knew my face was turning ten shades of red as I tried to sidestep this incredible moron, but he blocked my exit.

"Do you mind?" I said in my iciest voice.

"Yes, I think I do," he answered, lazily stretching his arm across the doorway. He pointed to the floor with his other hand. "I think you're littering the floor."

I glanced down and a piece of drywall fell from my head onto the floor, joining a steady line of drywall pieces that looked like Hansel and Gretel's trail of breadcrumbs.

I could feel my cheeks burning as the Moron and the desk agent burst into laughter.

I straightened my backbone to a full height of—at least—five foot three, and looked him square in the eyes. "How dare you poke fun at me, when you have no idea what I've been through!"

"Spunky little thing, aren't you?" he said, his lip curling.

I realized I was so mad my hands were balled into fists. "Get out of my way," I hissed. "I might be small, but these fists pack a wallop."

He laughed again, his voice echoing down the hallway, but he stepped aside. As I pushed past him, he called out, "I've never heard of packing a wallop before. Is that anything like a Smith and Wesson?"

5

I was dog-tired by the time I finished unloading the car. My new roommate was an incredibly deep sleeper; as hard as I tried to be quiet, I knew I was making enough noise to have awakened her ten times by now, but she didn't appear to move an inch in her bed across the room from mine.

I showered in the bathroom connected by two dorm rooms, washed and combed my hair, tended to the cut above my eye, and briefly checked the bruises that were sprouting all over my body. When I finally slid beneath the covers, I knew even before my head hit the pillow that I wouldn't be able to sleep. As tired as my body was, I had a serious brain buzz.

I lay in bed for awhile, flat on my back and staring at the ceiling, then trying each side in turn to see if some magic position would ease my aches and cause me to grow drowsy, but in the end I gave up. I couldn't stop replaying the explosion, Margaret standing in line smiling and waving at me, and the young mother with her children just feet from the bomber.

I pulled the covers back and turned on the light beside the bed. On my nightstand was a box of pictures Aunt Jo had given me.

I placed the box in my lap and opened the lid. I hadn't looked at pictures of my family in months. I could only speculate my yearning now to be close to them had everything to do with the ordeal I'd been through.

We used to be close: Mom, Dad, and me. When I was younger, I wanted a sister but as I aged, I gradually got used to the idea that they weren't going to have another child. And by the time I reached high school, I was content to be the center of their affections.

Mom had been ill off and on through the years, but always with minor ailments. I only remembered her going to a doctor once or twice. And Dad—Dad never got sick. He just didn't.

I figured they'd be around forever.

I flipped through the pictures: standing on the steps of the James K. Polk home in Columbia, Tennessee; Mom and me excitedly watching the Mule Day Parade, her soft brown hair looking reddish gold in the sunlight; the picture of me with my first fish; and me on Dad's lap on the tractor, plowing the tobacco fields.

I was at college when they died. I was in shock at first, then denial. After the funeral, I had too much grief to face it. So I didn't. I buried myself in my schoolwork and finished college the following year.

When I sold their home, Aunt Jo was pretty darn upset. The land had been in the family for generations. But a working tobacco farm was more than I could handle, and the neighboring farm was eager to expand. So I sold the house, the land, and even the furniture and equipment, and prepared to turn my back on middle Tennessee.

Then I got a job offer in Washington, DC, and if Aunt Jo could get even more upset with me, she did. She couldn't understand why I didn't want a life of farming. Why I needed to do something else, something I hoped would utilize my computer science degree from Vanderbilt.

There were pictures of my father when he was young. I was particularly fond of the one where he was seated in an oval cauldron of some sort; someone had written on the back of it "John Carpenter was hatched"—how I missed him!

I rummaged through the pictures, recalling memories I'd thought long forgotten when I ran across an odd picture. It was taken at a discount warehouse of a man with swarthy skin and short black hair placing cartons of cigarettes on a flat cart already overburdened with tobacco products.

I pulled the picture out of the stack and then realized there were more underneath—a dozen in all.

I leaned back. Why would my father have taken pictures of someone buying cigarettes?

It didn't make sense. Here, in the middle of family pictures was a man obviously not related to us, not only filling a cart, but also going through the register and then loading his car. With the bombing fresh in my mind, he looked similar to the man I'd seen at the food court. I blinked my eyes several times, trying to distinguish between the two, but they kept merging together.

I peered closely at each picture. In the background of one, I could almost make out the store number and location at the customer service counter located behind the man. And in another, I could swear the license plate was from New York; it looked like the Statue of Liberty in the center between the letters and numbers.

I climbed out of bed and booted my laptop. I could scan in the pictures, enlarge them, and perhaps identify when and where they were taken. But one question still remained: why did my father have these?

Once the laptop was ready and the printer/scanner warmed up, I opened the lid and started to position the pictures on the glass when I felt my fingers turn to ice.

On the back of one of the pictures was the handwritten message: "beginning of the trail."

And it wasn't in my father's handwriting. My mother had written it.

6

I awoke with a start.

I was groggy and disoriented; my head and heart pounded as I peered around the unfamiliar room. Slowly, the events of the last few hours came tumbling back, and I realized I had fallen sound asleep with pictures scattered between my bed and desk.

The lights outside the window crept through the darkness of the night, casting the walls into the color of passionflower with intermittent streaks of muted off-white. My eyes wandered sleepily around my unfamiliar environment—two beds, two desks, the lampshades that rose out of the darkness like thin bodies with bulbous heads. A tree outside the window swayed in the wind, causing shadowed tendrils to scrape across my surroundings like a ghostly reflection.

I lay back in bed, the movement causing sharp pains to shoot unmercifully through my body. My back felt as though I'd been put on a rack and my arms were like leaden weights. Then I realized my eyes were swollen and my head was pounding like a jackhammer. I groaned inwardly. It couldn't be morning yet.

I fretted about my condition and my ability to complete the physical portions of the Academy, something I'd been training for all summer. I drifted in and out of a fitful sleep until the alarm sounded the start of my new life.

There were more than thirty recruits in my class, apparently considered large enough to warrant two assistant counselors. Four recruits were women, and all four of us shared the same bathroom.

I learned the moment my hand hit the button on the alarm clock that my roommate was a New Yorker named Maria Alejandra who preferred to be called Alex and who thought, much to my chagrin, that *my* accent was the funniest thing she'd ever heard. She was taller than me with eyes the color of amber and chestnut hair that cascaded over her shoulders almost to her waist. The daughter of a Puerto Rican businessman and a Panamanian doctor, she was fluent in several Spanish dialects and techno-savvy to boot.

I learned about the other two females just before our swearing-in ceremony: Christiane was as tall as any man in the class, with shoulders suited to a linebacker's, leaving no doubt she could kick butt and take names. I wondered if they would pair us up on the defensive tactics class, and I hoped to God they wouldn't, or I'd end up butter on her toast. Oddly, she was a mathematician who most likely would be assigned to work in Intelligence.

Adiva was dark and sultry with brown eyes that drooped at the outer corners. It was immediately apparent why the FBI recruited her; she knew more about the Middle East than the current Administration and spoke several languages. She'd become a code breaker, for sure, if she didn't go into the Terrorism Task Force.

The men were just as varied; some studious and slightly built, while others appeared more at home in a sports arena.

I sized up the others as I'm sure they were appraising me. As I looked around the room, I could see the recruiters' heads spinning with all the languages that were suddenly needed to make the FBI into an intelligence-gathering force, and not one that simply solved crimes. They obviously had done their homework: there were a number of swarthy guys with heavy accents that might be able to infiltrate some suspect organizations. But this morning, with their almost perfectly matching blue suits, they looked like an advertisement in GQ.

Our first item of business on the first day of training was to take the oath as a FBI Special Agent. We all stood and repeated the oath in unison:

"I will support and defend the Constitution of the United States against all enemies, foreign and domestic; that I will bear true faith and allegiance to the same; that I take this obligation freely, without any mental reservation or purpose of evasion; and that I will well and faithfully discharge the duties of the office on which I am about to enter. So help me God."

With that, I was presented with my FBI Special Agent Badge. It was now official. On my first day at the Academy, I became Special Agent Sheila Carpenter.

After our swearing-in ceremony, we were escorted to a room where we began the sixteen-week-long training that would culminate most likely in an assignment to a field office, though we could also be assigned to a satellite office, headquarters, or international office.

The instructor was Supervisory Special Agent Philip Pippin, a tall, wiry man with sandy hair, pale sharp eyes, and a rigid jaw line, whom we were all expected to call Phil, which immediately made me feel like part of a team. He spent the morning announcing what they had in store for us NATS—New Agent Trainees, which consisted of exactly 643 and a half hours of instruction.

The course would be divided into a dizzying array of academics, firearms, operational skills, and integrated case scenarios. We'd be expected to score no lower than 85% on 11 academic exams, ranging from legal, behavioral science, forensic science, and national foreign intelligence to interviewing, ethics, white-collar crime, organized crime, informants, and interrogations.

As if that weren't enough, we'd all be getting our first physical training test tomorrow, which for now remained conspicuously undefined. We'd get another PT test in our seventh week and our final test in the 14th week.

And that didn't include the defensive tactics tests—boxing, handcuffing, control holds, disarming, and grappling. Now I knew I'd be teamed with the Amazon woman.

Phil was finishing his discourse when the door at the back of the room opened. He introduced the two assistant counselors making their way to the front of the room as the people we would depend upon to help us through a successful completion of the Academy.

As I turned around in my seat, my face started burning like a car dash in summer. My eyes locked on the first counselor's emerald eyes as he reached the front of the room and introduced himself as Special Agent Steve Moran.

The name would have been fitting, were it not for one letter. For now, standing directly in front of me, was Agent Moron. And I knew that somewhere, somehow, I would blurt out that name without thinking, and I'd have the shortest career in FBI history.

7

It was close to lunch time when I was called out of class to meet with an agent assigned to investigating the mall explosion.

As I was ushered into a conference room, I was pleasantly surprised to see Agent John Davidson, whom I'd met this past summer when I was working at my first full-time job. It had been with a computer consulting company; I'd been recruited to perform programming services for their clients. When their programming requests had fallen into a category of questionable ethics and illegal activities, I'd contacted the local FBI office. Agent Davidson had led the investigation, and it had been Agent Davidson who had suggested that I apply with the FBI. I suspected he helped push my paperwork through the chain.

He was hunched over some notes, his dark brown hair cut so short it didn't come close to brushing the collar of his somber suit jacket. The crow's feet around his eyes made him appear as though he'd spent a lifetime staring into the sun.

He stood as I entered and offered his hand. "Good to see you again, Sheila."

"Same here, Agent Davidson."

"Call me John." He motioned for me to be seated. Once I was situated, he sat across from me. "I hear you were in the wrong place at the wrong time yesterday."

"I'll say."

"Care to tell me about it?"

I hesitated. "Where do I begin?"

He flicked on a tape recorder. "At the beginning."

And so I did. I started with our arrival at the mall, glossed over the amount of shopping we did, and quickly progressed to the food court. I ended with a detailed, minute-by-minute account of Margaret standing in line, me seated at the table, and my observance of the bomber. John listened intently.

When I finished, he sat pensively for a long moment before speaking. "Where did you say he was standing?"

"Near the center of the food court; I remember a table with a young mother and a couple of children... You don't know what happened to them, do you?"

He shook his head. "A casualty list will appear in the paper; it's probably already online. The media will probably write stories about every victim they can find information on."

"I guess."

"Where was your friend?"

"In line."

"Which fast food place?" He drew a diagram, and I pointed to the approximate location.

"Where were you seated?"

I pointed again to the diagram, and he made a notation. Then he drew a line from my position to the bomber's and another one to Margaret's position. He followed with a barrage of questions about the bomber: his exact position, his physical attributes, and anything else I could remember about him or the people he was standing close to.

"What's going on here?" I finally asked.

"What are you talking about?"

"I've already answered these questions, but you keep asking them. We're going around in circles."

He stood. "It's part of the job, Sheila."

He flipped off the tape recorder and extended his hand. As I rose to shake it, he added, "It's part of the job."

We chatted for a moment about the Academy and the grueling weeks ahead of me. Then as I turned to leave, he said, "Oh, Sheila. One more thing: don't talk to the media, okay?"

"No one's even contacted me."

"No, but they might. And I'd just as soon you not say anything."

His eyes were narrowed, and I took his statement as a directive and not a request.

"You got it," I answered.

8

I hung up the phone as Alex breezed into our dorm room.

"Bad news?" she said.

I nodded. "My best friend's in the hospital."

"Does this have something to do with last night's terrorist attack?"

"How did you know I was—?"

"Who *doesn't* know? You were on the news last night." She plopped down on her bed, kicked off her shoes, and started unbuttoning her oxford shirt.

"I was?"

"You were interviewed, you don't remember?"

"I guess not."

"Anyway, your friend—is she expected to make it?"

"Harper—her brother—said she hasn't regained consciousness. They ran a battery of tests on her today…"

I fell silent. Alex had finished undressing and was now pulling an oversized t-shirt over her head. I didn't know what else to say. Margaret was standing in line to get fast food chicken one minute, and fighting for her life the next.

"So, anyway," Alex was saying as she pulled on a skin-tight pair of jeans that must have been a size zero, "we're

going to a wholesale store to pick up some sweats for PT.
You want to go with us?"

"No, thanks. I have a lot of studying to do." I pulled up
a chair and opened one of my course books. It was obvious
from the amount of homework assigned that the FBI
expected their trainees to live and breathe the Bureau.
Though I had to admit, it was a pleasant surprise to learn
that we would not be restricted to Quantico during our
training. Maybe I'd expected a boot camp mentality, but it
wasn't like that at all. I was already beginning to feel like
part of a professional organization.

"Suit yourself," Alex shrugged. "We won't be gone long.
We have the same assignments you do."

I caught a glimpse of her in the mirror, checking the
contents of her purse. "Does this store sell aspirin?"

"I suppose so." She glanced up. "They sell just about
everything."

"And you won't be gone too long?"

"We'll be back in less than an hour. Promise."

Alex was right; it did look as if they sold everything.
The store was larger than the Wal-Mart SuperCenter back
home, a store of which Aunt Jo was fond of saying, "If
they don't have it, I don't need it." This store could give the
Wal-Mart a run for its money on a Sunday afternoon.

As Alex, Christiane, and Adiva headed off to the sports
clothes, I wandered past office supplies, computers, and
software, and eventually found my way to the pharmacy. I
debated awhile on the merits of aspirin versus ibuprofen,
finally decided on plain old Bayer, and reluctantly picked
up the smallest size they had, a package of two bottles
containing five hundred tablets each.

I had just turned around when I ran headlong into a
rail-thin man with a hooked nose and angular jaw. His

weathered hands instinctively raised as if to push me away. I mumbled my apologies and slinked past him. As I continued down the aisle, I had the disturbing impression that he was watching me. I stopped and turned back. He had continued to the other end of the aisle, his frame bent with the weight of a flatbed cart he pulled behind him. He hadn't been watching me at all.

I was walking toward the front of the store when I felt an eerie sensation, as if someone's eyes were boring into the back of my head. I hesitated, and then I slowly turned around. The man I'd almost run into was a short distance away in front of a wall of cigarette cartons. He was busily loading his cart, the stacks so high they threatened to topple.

I glanced at the sign above the cartons. In large, bold print—highlighted in yellow in case the characters weren't large enough—was a sign that proclaimed "For Personal Use Only." I looked at his cart. Cigarettes of every description—regular, light, ultra-light, extra-long, Marlboros, Newports, Camels, Winstons, Virginia Slims—menthol and regular… Cartons of them, stacked precariously on his cart as if it were food and he was headed to a desert island. And with that many smokes, he wouldn't need food. He'd be dead in a week.

I thought of my mother busily taking pictures of a man like him, and wondered again why she did it and how she was able to do it undetected.

He labored past me, the sweat popping out on his brow while he struggled to turn his cart into one of the register lines. I fell in behind him.

He reached the register as I watched, fascinated. The clerk never questioned the quantity as she painstakingly counted the cartons. People in line behind me made guttural noises as if their sounds could speed up the process, and then finally moved to different registers. I stood transfixed.

There were a hundred and thirty cartons in all, and the bill was over twenty-four hundred dollars. The man pulled a wad of hundred dollar bills out of his pocket and began counting them out. When he was finished, his purchase had barely made a dent in his roll.

The clerk handed him his change. "Thank you," she said. "See you next week."

He heaved the cart away from the register and I quickly paid the seven bucks for my one thousand aspirin.

As I was exiting the store, I saw him again, loading his purchase into a van with a single window on each side and none in the back. The New York plates stuck out like a sore thumb amidst the myriad of Virginia plates.

I wandered over to Alex's Toyota Camry. The others hadn't returned yet. I opened one of the bottles, rifled through five pounds of cotton, and pulled out two aspirin. I stood there chewing them while I watched the man with the strange purchase. They tasted bitter, and as I stood there in the sweltering sun, I wished I had some water. The parking lot began to swim in front of me, and I steadied myself against the car, finally slithering down to sit on the bumper. I was used to heat and accustomed to humidity, and this sign of weakness didn't sit well with me.

A soda machine caught my eye, and I unsteadily came to my feet in a sudden quest to quench my thirst. My eyes were riveted on the giant picture of a soft drink can drenched with droplets of condensation as the white van backed out of its parking spot and slowly passed by me.

9

It had been four days since we started the Academy. In some respects, it felt as though it had whizzed past. But looking at the amount of information we'd been given this week, it also felt like one of the longest four days of my life.

I sat at my desk in the dorm, my mind reeling with case law, criminal profiles, organized crime, terrorism, and foreign intelligence. I wondered how I would ever remember all of the information thrown at us. But remember it, I would—I'd have to, if I expected to graduate.

I grabbed another slice of cold pizza from the box under Alex's watchful eye. "I thought my last year at Vandy was tough," I observed as I pulled up *The Washington Post's* web site. "It was nothing compared to this place."

"How's your trigger finger?" Alex asked.

"I'll survive," I said, examining the swollen member. I actually enjoyed going to the firing range and was looking forward to the day when they permanently issued me a weapon, versus the one I had to check in and out for designated classes. But when we went to the firing range, we definitely made up for lost time. We fired those weapons until I thought my finger would fall off. "I hear Adiva's wearing a splint."

"I'm afraid she's not gonna make it."

"Why do you say that?"

"Have you been paying attention to her scores?"

"She only needs fifteen points to pass. She'll make it." I slid open my desk drawer and whipped out my mega-bottle of Bayer and popped a couple of aspirin.

Alex reached for another slice of pizza. For a diminutive gal, she sure could pack the food in. "Any plans for the weekend?"

I hesitated. The FBI Academy ran from Monday through Friday, leaving us with every weekend off. Though we had to report where we were going or leave a number where we could be reached, we were under no other restrictions. "I'm going to stay with my friend, the one in the hospital I told you about."

"Is she conscious?"

"No," I said, my voice sounding fainter than I would have liked.

"Why don't you come to New York with me?"

"What are you doing there?" I asked, more out of politeness than interest.

"My cousin's getting married Saturday. Come with me. It'll be good for you after all you've been through."

"You're right, but I can't. I have an obligation—"

"Listen," Alex said, leaning forward intently, "I'll go with you to the hospital Friday night and we'll check on your friend. If she's conscious, you can stay. If not, I think she'd want you to go. We'll grab a flight to LaGuardia. Take a day off; enjoy yourself. We'll be back on Sunday."

I shrugged and turned my attention to my computer. On *The Washington Post's* home page was a picture of the mall where the explosion had occurred. Investigators were combing through the wreckage, presumably searching for clues.

According to the accompanying article, it didn't take the authorities long to identify the bomber. They'd even followed the trail back to the Pakistani-Afghan border, to a remote village still under the control of extremist fundamentalists.

The article was continued on an interior page and I clicked on the link, my attention now riveted. I wanted to look at the suicide bomber's picture, to look in his eyes one more time, as if his picture could answer the myriad of questions that were on my mind.

The text popped up on the screen, followed a few seconds later by a large color picture. I gasped.

Looking back at me were the enormous ebony eyes of the suicide bomber, the head covered in a dark turban that concealed the hair and forehead down to the eyebrows, the skin fair, the lips full. I was staring at the face of a woman.

10

It was almost ten o'clock when we arrived in New York. It had been a long day of studies, followed by a drive to the hospital to check on Margaret, who was still unconscious.

As we exited the terminal, Alex exclaimed, "There he is!" She waved at a man of medium height and a slight build wearing a dark blue windbreaker and khaki slacks, weaving his way through a line of taxis. "Ricky! Over here!"

"Alex!" he called out as he drew near.

She dropped her overnight case onto the sidewalk and wrapped her arms around him in a bear hug.

He glanced over her shoulder at me with olive eyes under perfect black brows, the kind of chiseled face generally seen only in fashion magazines.

"Sheila, I want you to meet my brother, Enrique," Alex said with a flourish.

"Call me Ricky," he said smoothly.

Before I could respond, Alex asked, "Where are you parked?"

He nodded to his left as he grabbed her bag and my gym bag. We walked past the line of taxis and to my dismay, trudged along until I was sure we must be in New Jersey before he finally pressed a remote control that unlocked a sports car. I wondered if I'd be able to fit in the tiny back seat.

"I need to stop before we get to the house," Alex said to him across the roof of the car as I climbed in back. "I forgot to pick up a wedding card."

"You got a gift for them, didn't you?"

"Yes. A beautiful crystal figurine."

I glanced at the bags beside me and let out an audible groan. If we started out with one figurine on that flight, it had probably turned into Snow White and the seven dwarfs by now.

As we left the airport, I wondered where he would stop at this time of night, and wished Alex had the forethought to get a card before we left DC. My bones were begging for a nice soft bed and a good night's sleep.

Their voices droned on in the front seat. Sitting behind them with the roar of the engine and the road lulling me to sleep, I barely snatched a word of their conversation here and there. I gazed out the window, my lids growing heavier as we left the city behind.

When at last we turned off the highway, we found ourselves on a narrow, winding road. The lack of street lighting made it appear as if the very blackness was reaching out to grab us, and I shivered from a chill that inched its way down my spine.

The headlights made it appear as if the trees came from nowhere. They were suddenly there, bending over the road with skeletal branches that appeared strong enough and capable enough to snatch the tiny car right off the pavement. I could spot spider webs in the trees, their intricate webs appearing white with moisture almost like the dew of morning. There were dozens of them in each limb that reached over the roadway, the headlights bouncing off them, giving them a ghostly appearance. They began to wave on currents of air that foretold of a giant oncoming storm.

We came to a stop sign and turned to the left. Up ahead, I spotted isolated lights looming out of the darkness. As we approached, Ricky slowed the car and then turned into a parking lot.

"Coming?" he asked as he hopped out, pulling his seat forward.

I glanced at the store, its ancient walls leaning a bit too far to the left, decades of aging once-white paint now faded and peeling on the bent and sun-scorched wooden boards. It reminded me of the old general store near Sunnyside. I hadn't intended to get out. I didn't need to buy anything, and I hoped Alex was planning on finding a card quickly. Then I heard myself saying, "Sure!" as I scrambled out of the tiny sports car.

Inside, the lights that swung from the ceiling felt too bright. In contrast, the air inside was frigid as if the building lacked heat.

I bought a soft drink and was putting the change into my purse when Ricky appeared and asked for a pack of Marlboro Lights. Funny, he didn't strike me as a Marlboro Man.

"Ouch," I said as the clerk behind the counter quoted the price.

Ricky looked at me with a puzzled expression and forked over a ten-dollar bill.

"That seems like a lot," I whispered while the cashier counted out his change.

"State tax," the cashier said in the same monotone, pointing to a sticker on the underside of the pack.

My mind jolted hundreds of miles away to the man at the wholesale store, purchasing a hundred cartons of cigarettes. If he bought them in Virginia and sold them here, he could make close to two hundred percent profit.

Had my mother discovered a cigarette smuggling ring?

I followed Ricky away from the counter. He held the door open for me, and as I passed through, I asked, "How much is the state tax?"

"I don't know exactly," he muttered. "Maybe a buck fifty?"

His voice and sidelong glance didn't exactly invite conversation, so I fell silent. We were both in the car with the engine running when Alex came out. The next stop would be our last for the evening, and it wasn't coming a moment too soon for me.

11

It wasn't exactly the perfect day for an outdoor wedding. The clouds were churning overhead like the beaters on an old mixer, tossing any dead leaves that still remained on the trees onto the expansive, well-manicured lawn. Servants in crisp black and white uniforms fought with tent poles that precariously floated romantic white cloth above perfectly coifed women and tuxedoed men who shivered in the cold. As I made my way down the wide marble steps from the house to the lawn, I found myself wrestling with a billowing skirt that threatened to rise and wrap itself around my head. When I finally reached the tent, I found the skimpy overhead cover did nothing to shield us from nature's onslaught, and I wondered how the wedding could possibly take place as planned. What had appeared romantic from the comfort of the house now was conspicuously flimsy and foolhardy.

I was seated on the heavily occupied groom's side but I saw no sign of Alex or Ricky. Her cousin's family was obviously of financial means, for they readily housed at least two-dozen overnight guests under their roof and there appeared to be enough room for more.

I felt a bit out of place, as everyone else appeared to be in a group or at least were half of a couple, while I sat completely alone like the lump of pork in a can of baked beans. And though Alex had said she'd meet me here she was nowhere in sight.

I scanned the surrounding terrain—the gently rolling lawn that touched the beach and reached out toward the ocean, the people milling about, and the driveway filled with arriving guests.

A muffled noise caught my attention, and I watched a small private plane struggling against the shifting air currents. I wondered who would fly a plane in this weather, especially one that looked so small against the growing storm. It disappeared beyond some trees. I was about to turn back around when I spotted something moving along the tree line.

Two figures were walking toward each other. One was dressed in a tuxedo, while the other was conspicuously underdressed in light-colored slacks and a plaid shirt.

The man in the tuxedo glanced about as if checking to see if they had drawn any undesired attention. This in itself interested me. As he looked my way, I diverted my gaze toward the other wedding guests. When I felt it was safe, I peered back in their direction.

Something about the man in the tuxedo appeared vaguely familiar, but I couldn't be sure with the distance between us. I strained to see his face, but the clouds were thickening and were quickly consuming any light this Saturday morning might have brought.

The men appeared to be arguing. The man in the slacks was gesturing wildly, at one time throwing both of his hands in the air as if in disgust. There was something sinister about him. Maybe it was the way he kept running both hands across his jet-black, slick hair, or the way he intermittently punched the air.

I tried to see the other man's face, but he remained with his back to me. In a quick movement that caught me off guard, he pushed the other man against the tree and grabbed his throat. For a moment, they were lost in the shadows, and I strained to see them, to find out what was happening. I thought I saw the glint of metal, but I couldn't be sure, and I debated with whether to sound an alarm.

In another second, the two men emerged from the trees, neither looking mortally wounded. The man in the tuxedo was disheveled, his bowtie askew. He stopped momentarily to light a cigarette, the flame from his lighter jumping unsteadily in the wind, which only seemed to increase his agitation. He reached in his pocket and pulled something out and threw it on the ground.

The other man was a step behind him; his shirt was pulled partway out of his slacks. His hand was wrapped about his own throat, as if he were soothing a pain. He reached to pick up what the other had thrown, but part of it sailed into the gathering storm. From the movements of the man trying to capture each paper drifting away on the wind, it looked as though he was chasing money.

The tuxedoed man straightened his bowtie and walked toward the wedding guests. I glanced about me, studying the faces of the others. No one else looked as if they'd witnessed the incident.

I pulled out my purse and pretended to be engrossed in its contents. I could feel the man approaching, could sense his rage still boiling. I pulled out my compact and studied my eye, as if I had a stray lash irritating the surface. In the corner of the mirror, I saw the pants leg, then the jacket. I tilted the mirror upwards to his face.

It was Ricky.

I sucked my breath in so rapidly that I almost choked. I fought the shock that engulfed me as I saw his face, contorted in rage, his cheeks flush and his hand shaking as he struggled to keep his cigarette against his lips. He turned toward me and looked into the mirror, his eyes meeting mine.

Then the linen that had only moments ago symbolized romance and gentility was ripped from the poles and flung into the sky. The clouds opened with a vengeance, the downpour beginning in one solid wash of water, like a riptide bellowing down on us. There was a simultaneous shriek as women and men alike raced for the cover and safety of the house.

12

I've never been one to lay awake at night listening to the creaks and groans in a house and worry that it's the boogeyman. I've been known to sleep just about anywhere—a hotel room, a dorm room, or in a chair at the library… But tonight was different. Tonight I tossed and turned and studied every object in the room as the lightning flashed and thunder boomed just outside my window. My brain was buzzing with the bombing, Margaret lying still unconscious, and my new career.

Around two a.m., the tiny night-light beside the bed abruptly darkened, blanketing the bedroom in total blackness. The hum of the heater ceased, leaving a silence so distinct that it was deafening. As I lay there wondering how long we would be without electricity, I heard the faint creak of a door opening down the hall.

I tossed back the bedcovers and slipped out of bed. I tiptoed across the hardwood floor, praying the boards wouldn't creak. I put my ear to the door and listened. I heard a faint *click* as another door closed. I couldn't be certain, but I thought the sound came from the room next door to mine. I tried to recall if I knew who was staying there, but I didn't recall having seen anyone.

I was just about to return to bed when I heard the footsteps. They were hesitant at first, as if the person were creeping stealthily down the hallway. I could hear a separate, distinct noise, too, that I was hard-pressed to identify until it reached my door. They were running their hand along the wall, and now it stopped just outside my door.

I fought the impulse to pull back from the doorway, afraid to move lest I reveal my presence. I held my breath and hoped the person could not hear my heart pounding. I focused on the doorknob, unsure of what I would do if it began to turn. I wanted to search for a weapon but I remained frozen in place.

After a moment that was entirely too long, I heard the hand sliding across the door and along the wall. The footsteps continued past my room; when I was sufficiently certain it was safe, I slowly opened the door and peeked out.

The hall was long and dark, although there were floor to ceiling windows peppered along the way. A wicked flash of lightning came simultaneous with a thunderous boom, lighting up the hall momentarily. I caught a glimpse of a figure dressed in a long hooded rain slicker. I couldn't tell whether it was a woman or a slender man. I wondered who would wander through the house with the hood pulled up, unless—unless it was someone who didn't want to be recognized.

I closed the door and groped my way to the chair beside the bed, where I quickly donned my clothes from the evening before. I carried my shoes as I returned to the doorway. I pressed my ear against the door and listened for any sign of activity, but I heard nothing. Then I slowly opened the door and peeked out. The hallway appeared empty, though it was too dark for me to be certain. I decided to take a chance. I stepped outside and softly closed the door behind me.

I stood still for a moment and listened. Still hearing nothing, I crept down the hallway in the same direction the hooded figure had just taken.

From outside, the house appeared to be a turn-of-the-century Victorian. Inside, it reminded me of a medieval castle. The hallways were a labyrinth, occasionally coming to circular intersections, where other hallways would branch off in various directions. It was difficult to see more than a few feet ahead of me as I wandered deeper into the bowels of the house. I knew at any moment, someone could be standing just an arms-length away and I wouldn't know it until it was too late.

I lost track of the hooded figure and realized how reckless I'd been in leaving my room. I didn't have anything more than the heels of my shoes to use as a weapon, if I were attacked. The house was so quiet that it seemed deserted, void of the people who, just a few hours earlier, had partied at a packed wedding reception. I started to chastise myself for my over-active imagination.

I stopped at a landing and peered through the darkness at the floor below, trying to recognize something from the day before so I could at least get my bearings. There was a rustling near me, and I froze. Someone was opening the door closest to me.

I searched frantically for a place to hide. How would I ever explain why I was wandering through a stranger's home in the middle of the night, during a blackout, with my shoes in my hands?

I raced for the stairs. I'd never make it to the bottom. I stopped at the first loop and ducked to remain just out of sight.

It was then that I heard Alex's voice.

"Do you know what this could do to me? To my career?" she was saying in a high-pitched, trembling voice.

I held my breath and prayed they wouldn't begin descending the staircase. Their footsteps stopped when they reached the landing where I'd stood just a moment earlier. I peeked from behind the balustrade. There was a swath of light filtering through an adjacent window, casting two shadows onto the floor.

"No one ever has to know," came Ricky's voice.

"What if you get caught?" Alex was saying.

"I won't."

"You need to think about what you're doing."

"I don't need a lecture from you," Ricky spat.

There was a sudden buzz, the lights flickered on, and the house came alive. I ducked lower and peered below me. There was no way I could descend further without being detected from up above.

"Thank God," Alex sighed. "I hate walking this house in the dark."

Don't we all, I thought grimly. I remained crouched until their voices faded down the hall. Then I got to my feet, hurried down the staircase, and tried to find my way back to my room.

It didn't occur to me that I hadn't solved the mystery of the hooded figure until I reached the safety of my room and closed the door silently behind me.

13

It was after ten o'clock on Sunday night and in less than ten hours, I'd be fully engrossed in the start of my second week of training. I was sitting in Margaret's hospital room hunched in a corner underneath a lamp that put out too little light, my Academy books piled into my lap. The rhythmic sound of the ventilator threatened to lull me to sleep even as I struggled to focus on my studies.

The hospital room had seen a constant stream of people until just over an hour ago, after the nurses had satisfied their paperwork requirements and Margaret's family took a much-needed break, retreating to a local restaurant for a late-night dinner. She'd been moved earlier in the day via helicopter from INOVA Fairfax Hospital to the Medical College of Virginia in downtown Richmond to be nearer to her folks. Ironically, it was the very hospital where she worked. I could see her in days past caring for patients with her ready smile and genuine love of people.

I glanced at her, lying so still with her beautiful long blond hair cascading across the pillow, an IV taped into her hand and its tube extended overhead.

I was angry. Angry that someone could snuff out so many lives in an instant. Angry that so many more could be fighting for their lives now, so many like Margaret, who'd done nothing to deserve this fate. She'd simply been in the wrong place at the wrong time.

I'd printed out the article from *The Washington Post* website and now I pulled it from under my books and read the article for the umpteenth time. It was all there—the details surrounding the suicide bomber, her past, and her movements on that fateful day. The reporters, and presumably the intelligence community, had identified her within days of the blast; they'd gathered every shred of information about her from the time she was born to practically every person she'd ever encountered. I imagine by now they even knew every date and time she'd ever sneezed.

There'd been another picture online today—a different one, showing the same young woman with a gently flowing scarf that covered her hair, framed her face and crisscrossed her neck. Two enormous eyes stared back from under perfectly arched brows like two dark pools in an Arctic tundra. Her full lips were curved in a delicate smile, showing just the slightest bit of perfect white teeth.

She was someone's daughter. Someone's sister. Someone's friend. She was only eighteen years old, and now she was dead, along with four innocent Americans.

There was just one problem.

She wasn't the bomber.

As long as I lived, I would never forget his face. The memory of him turning to face me just seconds before the blast, of his deep-set eyes vacantly staring at me moments before detonating the explosives. How can someone kill and injure so many, and remain so emotionless?

I had to tell someone.

I pulled out the phone book and dialed the local FBI office before realizing John Davidson wouldn't be in the office at ten o'clock on a Sunday night. I was just about to hang up when someone answered.

"Federal Bureau of Investigation," the female voice answered as if it were ten o'clock on a Monday morning. "How may I direct your call?"

"Agent Davidson, please."

"One moment."

I stayed on the line, incredulous that he could possibly be there. A moment later, the familiar voice answered.

"This is Sheila—"

"Sheila! How are you?"

"Fine, thanks, but I need to talk to you."

"What's up?"

"I've been reading the stories about the suicide bomber—"

"Don't believe everything you read."

"Then you know it wasn't a female? That the description I gave you was the real bomber?"

"What makes you think he was the bomber?"

"Oh, please, let's not play games. I saw the outline of the explosives under his coat."

There was silence on the other end of the line. After an awkward moment, I asked, "Are you still there?"

"Yes," he said. "But I can't discuss it with you. Not over the phone."

"You know it wasn't her, don't you?" I said excitedly. "You just don't want the media to know—"

"I'll be in touch, Sheila. I'm getting together some pictures for you to look at."

"Maybe I can identify him."

"I'll be in touch. Until then, be quiet about it, understand?"

"Yes." I swallowed. "My phone number's—"

"I know how to reach you."

With that, I heard a soft click and a dial tone.

I tried to go back to studying, but the bomber's face kept popping into my head like a pesky fly that wouldn't go away. I turned to a chapter on investigative techniques and tried to apply the strategy to the bombing. Suppose I'd been the agent on the other end of the phone and I was given information about a male bomber? What would I— could I—do?

And maybe this woman *was* a bomber. Not *the* bomber, but part of a team. A team that at a precise, predetermined time, they would both detonate, ensuring maximum damage.

14

It sounded like a single gunshot, fired only a foot away from me. For a moment, my heart stopped. I jumped up even before my eyes were open and my brain was functioning. In the process, all the books that had been stacked in my lap tumbled to the floor with a clatter.

It was then that I realized I was still in Margaret's hospital room. I'd fallen asleep in the corner chair and what must have awakened me was the sound of the uppermost book, a monstrosity over four inches thick, sliding off my lap and onto the floor.

I tried to shake the cobwebs from my head as I picked up the textbooks, piling them neatly onto a table, where they really should have been in the first place. The nurse, who bore a prominent badge proclaiming her name as Agnes Ackman, stuck her head in briefly to see what the ruckus was all about. From her pursed lips and narrowed eyes, I surmised it was a real faux pas to make noise in a hospital in the middle of the night. I fully expected her to inform me that visiting hours were over and I should leave immediately. Then just as quickly, I wondered where Margaret's folks were and why they hadn't returned.

I glanced at my watch. It was approaching one o'clock. In less than seven hours, I'd be starting another week at the

Academy. I groaned. I knew at least one big test was headed toward me like an oncoming train. I felt undeniably unprepared.

By the time I had everything piled together, I decided I'd better get back to the Academy, grab as many hours of sleep as I could, and wake up ready to go, even if I felt like I'd slept in a trash bin.

I slipped across the room to Margaret, and grabbed her hand. "I'll be back," I whispered. "I promise."

Her fingers tightened around my hand.

I stared at her. Was it just my imagination? I shook my head, trying to clear it. Her eyes were closed, her face still swollen. Her eyelids seemed to be moving, like someone in deep sleep.

"Margaret?" I whispered. "Can you hear me?"

Her fingers tightened around me again.

I felt my heart leap into my throat. "Margaret, I'm here. It's Sheila." My words tumbled over one another. "You're in the hospital. You were in—an accident. You're going to be okay, Margaret. Your parents and Harper have been here with you the whole time."

I fought back tears. I'd be of no use to anybody if I started bawling. I looked back at her hands. They were still. Maybe I imagined the whole thing. I started to pull my hand away when she grabbed me.

"My God," I cried, jamming the Call button with my other hand. "I'm here, Margaret. I'm right here."

Nurse Ackman appeared at the door a moment later with an even more agitated look than she'd had earlier. "Listen—" she started to say, but I cut her off.

"She's conscious!" I cried out. "Margaret's conscious!"

She raced to Margaret's side. My friend's face remained expressionless, and Nurse Ackman glared at me as though I was purposefully lying. Then she saw Margaret's fingers grabbing mine, holding on as if for dear life.

I spoke to my friend, tried to tell her where she was and how long she'd been there, but above all else, I tried to convince her that she would be okay. She was still alive. And now she was regaining consciousness.

Nurse Ackman rang for assistance. "Call Dr. Francis," she shouted as she checked Margaret's vitals. Margaret's mouth moved, the lips barely parting, as if she were trying to speak. Her lips were cracked and swollen.

I pulled my hand away from hers, explaining all the while that I would be right back. Then I rushed to the bathroom and grabbed a face cloth. I ran it under cold water and wrung it out only slightly, then returned to Margaret's side. It hadn't been all that long ago when the tables had been turned and I was in the hospital and Margaret was watching over me. And when I would have sold my soul for one drop of water, she had been there dripping it into my mouth through a washcloth.

"What are you doing?" Nurse Ackman demanded.

"I'm just wiping her face," I said, dabbing at her lips. When the nurse's attention was focused elsewhere, I put a piece of cloth against Margaret's lips and squeezed the water into her mouth. I thought I detected a slight smile.

"What happened?" she whispered so low that her voice was barely audible.

"You were in an accident," I answered.

"Is she talking?" Nurse Ackman said, pushing her way past me.

"No—no accident," she said, her breathing labored.

She appeared to be fighting to open her eyes. I didn't know enough about the liquids they kept pumping into her, to know if she was heavily sedated or if she was in danger of slipping away again.

Things were happening fast. I tried to stay with her, to keep the cloth on her mouth, to soften her lips, but I was eventually pushed back.

"A woman—" she whispered.

"What about a woman?" I asked.

Before she could respond, a doctor rushed in and began checking over her records, barking orders as he did so. Perhaps it was all orderly to the medical professionals, but it looked like mayhem to me, and in the midst of it, I was ushered out of the room. I stood in the hallway for what felt like an eternity, until Harper and his parents joined me.

Then it was pandemonium again as they rushed into her room, where she was drifting in and out. Eventually, it was determined that she had fallen back to sleep, and her family decided wisely to stay with her in the event she awoke again, which we were all confident she would. It was just a matter of time.

I gathered my books and made my way out of the hospital and into the cool night air, found my car, and drove back to Quantico.

15

I was standing outside a building at Quantico in one of the glass-enclosed hallways that connected one building to another. My new cell phone was cradled against my shoulder. I'd hung up not thirty seconds earlier after getting a status report on Margaret, who was still moving in and out of consciousness. Now I anxiously listened to Aunt Jo's phone ringing. The sun was high overhead, beating down on the glass enclosure so strongly that it caused perspiration to break out across my forehead.

I looked once more at the photos my mother had taken, now scanned and enlarged, even though they were firmly etched in my brain. I could clearly see the New York plate on the back of a Volvo station wagon; could see it so clearly, in fact, that I could easily make out the letters and numbers. Two other pictures plainly identified the store location in Chesterfield, Virginia.

I glanced at my watch. I had only a thirty-minute lunch break. I'd hoped to talk to Aunt Jo and still have time to eat before we launched into our afternoon studies and physical fitness. I was really starting to hunger for a fresh fruit platter and a tall glass of sweet iced tea.

Just as I was resigning myself to hanging up, she answered.

"Aunt Jo, it's Sheila," I said breathlessly.

"Why are you calling me in the middle of the day?" came her familiar, rapid-fire voice with the southern lilt. "Are you alright?"

"I'm fine. I'm on my lunch break... I know this is going to sound bizarre—"

"What in heaven's name are you up to now?"

I pictured Aunt Jo standing in the center of her house, her corded phone on the telephone stand as it had been for decades, the long, thin fingers of one hand wrapped around the black handset while her other hand was placed with an air of authority on one slender hip. She was tiny—not much more than five feet tall and eighty pounds soaking wet—but she was feisty. Maybe that's where I got my spunkiness.

I swallowed and then dove right in. "Aunt Jo, do you know if Mom was working on anything right before she died?"

"What're you talking about?"

I could feel my heart pounding in my temples. "The photos you gave me—there were some of a guy buying cigarettes at one of those wholesale outlets. I was wondering if you knew why Mom would have taken them?"

There was a pause and I hoped she was gathering her thoughts. I was tempted to blurt out more, to coax her, but I bit my lip. Despite my most valiant efforts, my foot tapped impatiently and I found myself wanting to reach through the phone and shake her into a faster response. When she finally answered, I felt my heart sink into my feet.

"I don't recall having seen them."

I tried another approach. "Did she take any trips before she died?"

"Out of town trips?"

"Yes... To Virginia, maybe?"

There was another pause. I could feel the seconds slipping through my fingers.

"Yes," she said abruptly. "I believe she did."

"Do you remember why?"

"It was a tobacco grower's meeting, held in Richmond or thereabouts, I believe."

"When?" My heart was beginning to beat in my temples.

"She passed in late January," she mused as if thinking out loud, "so it must've been around October, November... early November, I think."

The same time of year as it was right now. The mere thought made me feel as if someone was breathing down my neck.

"Did she say anything to you about her trip, when she got home?"

"Not really..." her voice faded.

I glanced at my watch and wrestled with my thoughts. My stomach told me I had to grab a bite to eat. The heat would make the run this afternoon difficult; on an empty stomach, it would be unbearable. But now I knew I was onto something.

"I'll call you back later," I said. "I have more I want to talk to you about, but now isn't a good time." I gave her my love and hung up.

"Why aren't you getting some lunch? It's gonna be a long afternoon."

Turning, I bumped right into Steve, my nose actually grazing his chest. As the photographs fluttered to the floor, I was grateful his attention was averted elsewhere. I knew my face had to be the color of a woodpecker.

He bent down immediately as if to pick them up, but he stopped abruptly and studied the pictures as if he were assessing a crime scene.

"It's nothing," I said, stooping to retrieve them. Before my fingers could touch them, he scooped up the pictures and stood.

"Oh, I wouldn't say that," he said.

I watched his eyes narrow as he studied the pictures, his dark brows knitting together.

After a moment, he handed them back to me. "Cigarette smuggling."

"How did you—?"

"It's not exactly a secret," he said, one side of his mouth turning into a slightly lopsided smile. "They come to Virginia, Tennessee or North Carolina—tobacco states— buy the cigarettes cheap, and transport them to Chicago, Detroit, New York… take your pick. They raise the prices, and pocket the difference."

"But if you—if the FBI—knows this is going on, why don't you stop it?"

"And just how do you propose we do that?"

The tone of his voice made me feel like I was back in the classroom and taking an oral exam.

"You sit in the parking lot in an unmarked car," I said, stretching my spine to give me just a little bit of extra height—and confidence. "You probably wouldn't have to wait long. When a vehicle shows up with out of town plates, you follow the driver into the store. You take pictures with a hidden camera or even seize the store's surveillance film. Wait until they check out, follow them back to wherever it is they came from, and arrest them. You'd have the evidence from where they bought the goods, and you'll have followed them across state lines."

He was grinning now.

"Better yet," I continued like a prosecuting attorney trying the case of my life, "Set up surveillance at his place of business. Come in and seize the goods. They'd have fake tax stickers on them, probably done with a high quality inkjet printer. Now you'd have them for counterfeiting as well as tax evasion."

"And if you're lucky, *real* lucky, you'll get a misdemeanor conviction. Unless, of course, you happen to seize at least sixty thousand *and one* cigarettes—roughly three hundred cartons—and can prove they were all obtained on the black market. Then you might be able to get a federal conviction. Meanwhile, you'll have spent thousands out of the Bureau's budget on an insignificant case."

I was so dumbstruck, it took me a moment to respond. "So, what do you do? Look the other way while they break the law?"

"Number one: it isn't Bureau jurisdiction. The data would go into an 'O' file, meaning you'd have referred the info to another agency. In this case, it might be ATFE. Or the IRS, because it might only be tax evasion.

"Number two," he said as he turned to leave, "You look for bigger fish to fry. Follow the money, see where it leads. It could be just the tip of the iceberg. If terrorism, kidnapping, or extortion is involved, *then* the FBI would have a case. Otherwise, you'd be wrapping up a case while you're still at the beginning of the trail."

16

The sun bore down on my Academy class as we ran like we actually had someplace to go. Though it was early November, I began to see flickering lights and gray spots more in keeping with a summer sun that was high overhead like a bright yellow orb cutting through a haze.

Steve came alongside me.

"You okay?" he asked.

"Sure," I said. "I'm used to running a lot further than this."

"You don't look too good."

Great. There's nothing better than a hunk telling me I don't look good. I avoided his eyes, preferring instead to stay focused on the ground in front of me. "I'm okay, really. It's only a two-mile run."

He sprinted ahead of me, and I found myself staring at the middle of his back, where his gray t-shirt was slightly stained with sweat, until he grew smaller and blended in with the rest of the pack.

I wasn't used to coming in last. Though I'd never been the dedicated type that ignored ice or snow or a hundred degree heat wave just to get that runner's high, I'd never much minded a good run, either.

But today was different. Today the pavement refused to stay level, preferring instead to rise up at the oddest moments, grabbing my feet before they were ready to come down. Today the air felt so thick it almost gurgled in my lungs as my body cut through a wave of humidity so solid it caused my muscles to ache.

Alex was falling back. In another moment, we were even.

"I need to talk," she said.

"So start talking." My head was throbbing and I was having trouble concentrating.

"Ricky has me worried," Alex said.

"Oh?" I tried to appear a bit disinterested, but red flags were beginning to wave in the distance like a matador baiting a bull. Between Margaret's ordeal and the mysterious pictures, I wondered how much more I could handle.

"If I tell you something, you won't tell anyone else?" she asked.

"Who would I tell?" I puffed.

She nodded toward Steve. "Him. Or anybody else at the Academy."

"Ricky's not doing anything illegal, is he?"

She didn't answer, which was an answer in itself. I thought my head was going to explode. My right eye felt as if someone were piercing it with an ice pick, which was made worse by the unforgiving and unrelenting heat, and my labored breathing threatened to drown out Alex's voice beside me. My face was turned toward her, yet somehow I knew I was propelling myself forward with one foot in front of the other, putting yards behind me.

I turned to focus on the building up ahead that marked the end of our run. Various colors danced and swam in front of me—grays and greens and an occasional yellow.

I could barely see the outline of a white van parked alongside the road and several people milling about. I was almost beside them when I realized it was a television news van. Steve had stopped running and was chatting to the news team as if he were narrating a slice of life at the Academy. A cameraman turned toward me, a red blinking light on the front of his recorder signaling that he was filming.

I straightened my spine. I would breeze right past them as if this run was simple child's play.

Steve turned, waving his hand in our direction. Then he pointed his finger at something in front of us. He seemed to be saying something, but it sounded like Aunt Jo's old phonograph player when we lowered the speed.

"Are you okay, Sheila?" Alex was saying. "You have sweat pouring off you."

"It's nothing. Just this heat wave," I answered.

"Heat wave?" Her voice was shrill. "It's barely fifty degrees!"

As I came alongside the news team, the ground bolted up in front of me, as though the pavement had suddenly come to life. My knees slammed against the asphalt and I caught sight of a stream of blood spurting outward in front of me. I was falling in slow motion, my arms flailing about like a string-puppet out of control, my knees smashing against the hard surface with a cracking sound that filled the air.

My torso hit the pavement with a whoosh of air expelling from my lungs. When I tried to gulp in more air, my mouth was filled with granular black pebbles. The last thing I remember was my face striking the asphalt and blood bursting from my nostrils.

17

I don't know what awakened me. It might have been the lights shining so brightly overhead that they seemed to burn straight through my closed lids. Or it could have been the smell: that strange combination of odors that are simultaneously reminiscent of floor cleaner and strong medicines. Or the voice that wafted through the air, reaching my ears as if we were at opposite ends of a tunnel, droning on in a one-sided conversation.

Then I was running with my eyes closed, and the sun was penetrating my eyelids like a torch burning through metal. And then I realized I wasn't running after all.

I struggled to open my eyes. I tried to raise one arm to shield them against the light. Then I realized something was stuck in the back of my hand, like a weight that grew heavier with my labored movements.

Then I recognized the odors that burned my nostrils; it was a strange mixture of bleach and strong disinfectants mixed with pungent medicines—a combination likely to be found only in a hospital.

A voice droned on in the background. In one respect, it was familiar; yet in another, it wasn't familiar at all.

"She's still out," the voice was saying. "I'm waiting for the doctor to return. They have her on fluids…"

In an instant, my brain identified the voice and my eyes flew open with the horror-stricken knowledge that the one person who I decidedly didn't want to see me in such a state, was there looking over me. In a rush, I threw the covers off me, knocking the IV stand to the floor. At the same time, I felt a rip in my hand, and I realized I was attached to the very unit I'd just toppled.

"Whoa, there," came the voice as it neared me. "Calm down."

As Steve bent down to pick up the fallen apparatus, I realized there were two others in the room with us. Alex stood at the foot of the bed with an uncertain look on her face, and a nurse was rushing to Steve's aid.

Once the IV unit was back in place, the nurse inspected my hand, clucking as she did so. Her name badge identified her as Dot Cooper.

"You passed out," Alex said in answer to my unspoken question.

I tried to get up, but Nurse Cooper pushed me firmly back into the pillows.

"I haven't eaten today," I said sheepishly. "The heat just got to me."

Steve pulled a chair alongside the bed. "There wasn't any heat. Anyway, you've been out for a couple of hours."

I groaned in humiliation.

"You might have a concussion," Nurse Cooper piped in. "You need a lot more tests, young lady. You're not going anywhere."

I realized then that Alex was holding some of my clothes in her arms—a pair of jeans, an oversized sweatshirt, and a blue jean jacket. And the purse I'd recently acquired to replace the one I'd lost in the mall explosion hung from one shoulder while her own purse hung from the other.

"I'm fine," I said, managing to pull myself into a seated position. I straightened the thin cotton gown. "I just need something in my stomach."

Steve hesitated. I got the impression he was thinking through his response, and for some reason that worried me. "The most important thing right now is to find out the extent of your injuries. The Academy can wait. There's another class starting in the spring—"

"No!" My voice sounded desperate, and I loathed that. "Please don't drop me!"

"We're not dropping you. It's called 'recycling'. You'd go to the top of the list, and you'd be in the very next class."

"*Please* let me finish this one."

Steve leaned toward me and gazed at me with piercing and troubled eyes. His dark brows were knit together and his jaw was squared. For the first time, I noticed a slight indentation in his chin that made me think of Cary Grant.

"You're my responsibility. And if you're injured," he was saying, "and I allow you to return to the Academy, and something happens to you, my career could be in jeopardy. And I'm not willing to take that chance, not for you or for anybody else."

I leaned back into the pillows and exhaled sharply. I felt angry tears stinging the corners of my eyes. "I'm not that sick," I said. "If I was really that bad off, I wouldn't have made it this far."

Alex appeared uncomfortable, as if she were overhearing something she shouldn't be privy to, and I realized she was probably there for propriety's sake. Maybe that was a sign of a good agent: covering all the bases and covering his backside, too.

"Take a few days to rest," he said. "Let's see what the doctor has to say. And if he feels you can go back, then I'll work with you to catch you up on everything you've missed."

"Thank you!" I exclaimed, grabbing his hand with both of mine. "You won't regret this."

He cleared his throat and extricated his hand from my grasp. I definitely detected the color in his cheeks rising.

"I haven't done anything yet," he said. "We'll just wait and see what happens." He picked up his jacket from the back of the chair and cleared his throat. "Get some rest now. We'll talk later."

Alex made her way to the side of the bed. "I'm just going to leave these things here," she said, placing my clothes on the bed stand. "Call me if you need anything."

She turned to go, and then stopped. "Oh, I almost forgot," she said, pulling my purse from her shoulder and handing it to me.

"Thanks," I murmured as they left.

With a slight nod, Steve was gone and Alex was slipping away, closing the door softly behind her. The purse dangled from my hand for a moment before sliding away from me and onto the floor.

18

I remember a storm that swept through Sunnyside several years ago. I was sitting in 11th grade English class when the school closed early. When I got to the front doors where the buses were waiting to take us home, the sky was already a mottled gray, the winds had picked up, and the rains had begun in earnest. By the time we got within a mile of my house, electricity had gone out and the skies were nearly black, although it was only two o'clock in the afternoon.

The bus driver attempted to navigate the one lane gravel road to my house, but the creek had risen dangerously fast and was washing over the road as though a dam had burst. Fearful of being swept away, the driver backed out to the main road.

Helpless, I had no choice but to remain in the bus while we attempted to drive the other students home. Out of twenty students, twelve of us were stranded.

That afternoon was one of the most devastating days I'd ever experienced. The rain was coming in sheets at a sideways angle that bent the trees as though they were bowing to a northeasterly God, visible only when they brushed the bus windows on their way to the ground.

Under the direction of the bus driver, we all remained on the floor of the bus, waiting out the storm, attempting to shield ourselves from the potential of breaking glass, thankful we were at least dry but fearful of what we might see when the storm lifted.

I could smell the bodies around me as we huddled together, cramped between the rigid rows of seats. We were sweltering under heavy jackets and scarves, even as the temperature outside dropped, everyone afraid of removing even the tiniest piece of clothing in the event we'd have to suddenly buck and run.

I heard a noise and I realized I was hovering in that limbo between sleep and wakefulness, with one foot in the bus and the other foot securely tucked under a hospital sheet.

I felt myself drifting back into the darkness of the bus, the same blackness I experienced when the bomb exploded. And now, as I tossed and turned in the quiet of the night, I felt the same foreboding—

Nurse Cooper had given me pain medication earlier in the evening, even though I'd tried to tell her I wasn't in any pain. Now I wondered if it was giving me nightmares. Even in my sleepy state, I could feel the pillowcase under my head, drenched in cold sweat.

I slept fitfully, moving in and out of the bus in my dreams, and then moving in and out of the explosion.

I saw him again. His eyes stared straight into my soul as he lifted his hands in prayer. Those eyes that were gunmetal black, a black so deep they almost appeared otherworldly.

And then I tensed in anticipation of the explosion, the explosion that now didn't come. I was hanging in limbo, feeling the terror. Like it had in the mall that day, I felt the scream freeze on my lips. And again, I felt the blackness closing in around me and the suffocating dust from the debris piling on top of me.

I gasped for air. My throat was parched and tensed as if I was choking.

I tried to turn but the pillow felt glued to my head, the cold, damp cotton pushing against my nose, closing the nostrils. I tried to inhale through my mouth, but something was pushing on me, preventing me from breathing. I tried to open my eyes, but I was met with the same blackness and the same weight bearing down on me.

I struggled to awaken, to escape this feeling of limbo, of being unable to move in my dream. I could still smell the stench of perspiring bodies, now mixed with the pungent smell of wet leather, and something else… a food of some type. Strong spices…

With a gasp, I awakened. My entire body was tensed in terror. Another pillow lay across my face, and something— someone—was bearing down on me, trying to smother me.

I pushed with every muscle in my body; I tried twisting my body from side to side while struggling desperately to inhale another mouthful of air. I grabbed his neck with both my hands, frantically trying to choke him.

I could feel the tape securing the IV needle ripping away from the hairs on the back of my hand. Afraid to let go of his neck to buzz the nurse, I continued to struggle against him even as I felt myself losing my grasp on consciousness. In another moment, I would succumb to the darkness.

I couldn't let that happen.

In one final, frantic effort, I grabbed the needle from my hand and ripped it out, plunging it with all my might into my attacker. He screamed and cursed in a foreign language even as one hand left the pillow, and I seized the moment to sling the pillow away from me.

He was back, this time with both hands covering my mouth and nose, his ebony eyes staring back at me through the semi-darkness—those eyes that I will never forget, the eyes from the mall, the eyes that stared at me even as the hands were raised in prayer.

Feverishly, I reached out beside the bed for anything I could use to defend myself. My fingers caught the strap to my purse, and I hauled it with everything I had against the side of his head. He fell off of me, his fingers loosened once again. I slung my body to the side, away from him, and screamed for help.

His eyes were wide and glazed, his cheeks flush, his brows knit together into one long, heavy black line.

I grabbed the IV stand as if it were a baseball bat and swung it at his head. I heard a crack as the metal hit bone.

When he hit the floor, I thought I'd killed him, but then I heard his groans. His hand grasped the bed sheet to haul himself up.

I fled.

I raced past the vacant nurse's station and down an empty hallway, the sound of my heartbeat competing with the noise the man made behind me. I looked over my shoulder as I ran and saw him lumbering out of my room. I darted from one hallway to the next, frantically putting distance between me and the man who wanted me dead.

19

I stood in the stairwell next to the door with my back against the wall, shivering from the cold that penetrated my thin cotton gown. Slowly, I peered sideways through the tiny window. The lobby was as quiet as a tomb, the spotless tiles and short carpet marking a great expanse of empty space that would be teeming with activity within a few short hours.

An oblong Information Desk near the center of the room was manned only by a single young man with a mop of tousled, sandy blond hair, made all the more unkempt by the fingers he kept running through it. As the minutes ticked on, his head bobbed forward in reluctant sleep, his chin finally coming to rest against his chest.

A clock above the door ticked away the minutes, the hand methodically moving like nothing was amiss, as if I hadn't come dangerously close to dying at the hands of a terrorist inside this very building.

As I stood there weighing my options, the bell on the elevator sounded and the young man's head jerked upwards as the doors opened. A man clad in a light blue jumpsuit backed out, pulling a mop bucket behind him. After a word in greeting, the janitor turned his attention to the tiled floor.

This would complicate things.

I'd already been on a circuitous route through the hospital corridors, spending little time on each floor lest my assailant should appear and burst into hot pursuit.

At one point, I thought he had me—he'd come into the stairwell just as I was ascending. I saw the top of his head, his dark hair unkempt, as he peered over the banister onto the steps below. I quickly ducked back into the shadows. I wondered what I would do if he began climbing the stairs toward me, but after an agonizing moment, the door closed and I listened to his footsteps moving away, down the corridor.

I considered tripping the fire alarm, which could flood the hallways with hospital personnel to cover my departure, but I thought better of it. Not knowing if a real fire was in progress, they might force the patients to vacate the building. Just a few seconds of imagining that scene and I decided I didn't want to risk another's injury just to save my own hide.

I thought of screaming for help as I ran through the halls, and abandoned that idea as well, partly because I would be announcing to my assailant my exact location, and partly because it could put another in the line of fire.

He wanted *me*. I was the one who had seen him, who had looked into his eyes, who had told a reporter I would never forget his face as long as I lived. Me and my big mouth. I was the one who could identify him, and I was the one he wanted.

I surveyed the distance to the outside doors. Twenty-five feet, maybe. Perhaps a little more. The janitor was moving away from me, toward another hallway. As he moved out of sight, the young man's head jerked upwards but it dropped down again a few seconds later.

While I stood there thinking, the automatic doors opened. A gust of wind buffeted a man already hunched down inside a heavy wool coat as he made his way to the desk.

He spoke to the young man, who was shifting in his chair and trying to look alert. Then he turned and headed straight for the stairwell.

I ducked back, frantic.

I hurried toward the basement level, hoping the man would take the stairs upwards and away from me.

With long strides, he cleared the lobby in five seconds flat. I hadn't made it to the basement landing before he'd reached the stairwell. With one hand nervously pulling the two sides of my hospital gown tight across my backside, I tried to duck down, out of sight.

"Sheila?"

The voice was familiar.

"Sheila?" he said again. "What are you doing here?"

I looked up. I'm sure my face looked like a child's with her hand caught in the cookie jar.

"Steve?" I breathed.

"What are you doing?" he asked, moving toward me.

I placed my finger to my lips. "Quiet," I whispered.

He stepped closer. His eyes searched mine for an explanation.

"Give me your coat," I whispered. "And get me out of here."

20

I wrapped my hands around the comforting warmth of the coffee cup, dipping my face close enough to the rising steam to thaw my nose from the cold. A wintry mix of sleet and freezing rain had moved in from the Midwest overnight, causing the temperatures to plummet. Even so, my head throbbed and sweat popped out across my forehead. I realized now more than ever the heat I felt yesterday prior to fainting had been due to fever and not the weather at all.

Steve and I were seated at the Dunkin' Donuts on Route 1, not far from the main entrance to Quantico. Through the corner of my eye, I could feel his attention riveted on me as I sat snugly wrapped inside his heavy coat. I noted guiltily that he was shivering, his uncharacteristically casual red and black flannel shirt no match for the cold.

I'd just finished telling him everything that had happened in the hospital room, in between bites of a chocolate éclair and a chocolate cream-filled donut. I'd learned that in the best of times and the worst of times, chocolate was a necessary companion.

"You're still bleeding," he said, dipping a napkin into a half-full glass of ice water. I was quiet as he cleaned the wound where I'd torn the needle loose from my hand. It looked nasty, and I was sure to have a good bruise by which to remember my escapades, but at least it didn't appear to require stitches.

"What were you doing at the hospital?" I asked.

He shrugged. It was a moment before he answered. "Couldn't sleep," he said. "Thought I'd look in on you."

"At two in the morning?"

"As a class counselor, I'm somewhat responsible for you," he muttered, his face hidden as he leaned over my hand. "Besides, I said I couldn't sleep."

I was silent for a minute while he cleaned my hand. Finally, I asked, "How do you think he found me?"

"It wouldn't take a rocket scientist to figure that one out," he said, tossing the bloodied napkin onto the counter. "You were on the news again last night. Remember the camera crew taking a tour? They got a tour, alright. A tour of you falling face first onto the asphalt."

I groaned. "They didn't show that on the news, did they?"

He laughed. "You should have seen your eyes rolling back in your head. They got a close-up of that."

"Wonderful. Just wonderful." I took another sip of coffee and tried to hide my humiliation. "With all the news they've got to choose from…"

"Actually, it *was* news. They showed the clip again of your interview right after the mall explosion. They followed up with the PR staff at the hospital. So you were a victim of the biggest story to hit these parts in quite awhile. Add to that, you're an FBI Agent…" his voice trailed off.

When he continued, I felt the blood drain out of my face.

"I have to notify headquarters," he said. "They need to know someone tried to kill you."

"No," I said with so much conviction I even startled myself.

He looked up, his lips pursed in a heavy frown. "Not that it's going to change my plans, but why not?"

I hesitated. I really didn't know why I didn't want to report it. I just had a gut feeling that the fewer people who knew about this, the better off I'd be.

"There's a killer out there," Steve said. "A terrorist who wants you dead. It's up to us to stop him." He stood up and tossed some change on the counter. "We'd better get out of here. We're wasting time."

21

Only a few hours had passed since we'd left Dunkin' Donuts, but it felt like a lifetime. Now I sat watching the light filtering through the open blinds in my dorm room, casting everything it touched in muted shadows.

My gym bag was packed at the foot of my bed, although my plane to Nashville wouldn't depart for several hours.

The fact was that I was supposed to be in bed resting and recuperating. I'd tried sleeping but the light of day appeared to jeer at me, taunt me as though I was being purposefully and utterly lazy, something that went completely against my grain. It was difficult enough to be separated from my classmates, who I knew were in the midst of learning important investigative techniques—techniques that I would be expected to know as well. And then to be forced to stay in bed when I didn't have a life-threatening illness was just too much for me.

So I reasoned I could recuperate just as quickly sitting up. Then I deduced that there was no difference between sitting in front of my computer and sitting up in bed.

So here I'd sat for the past couple of hours, trying to get over my frustration at being room-bound by examining

the pictures I'd culled from the box Aunt Jo had given me.
I tried not to focus on the clock ticking the minutes away
all too slowly, causing the morning to drag on forever.

Eventually, someone would be here to drive me to the
airport, where I'd catch a flight to Nashville. John Davidson,
Phil Pippin and Steve had conferred early this morning and
decided the best course of action would be to remove me
from the immediate area, and get me back into a hospital.
I'd argued futilely that I should be admitted to the hospital
at Quantico, but they'd nixed that idea due to the flu
outbreak that was running through the base.

They wanted me close to family or loved ones, though
I wasn't quite sure why. I actually would have preferred to
go right down the road to Richmond, Virginia, where I
could be close to Margaret and the Reeds. But the flu was
having its effect on hospitals in Richmond as well, so off
to Nashville I would go.

Once I reached Tennessee, I would be met by an agent
from the local field office and be checked into Vanderbilt,
where supposedly my medical records were, at this very
moment, being transferred. I expected to be gone for a
few days; a week at most. Then I'd be back in the Academy,
where I'd make up the tests I'd missed, and hopefully fall
right back into the routine. I was determined to graduate
with my class. I wasn't going to let a little thing like a bomb
and an attempt on my life prevent me from realizing my
goal of becoming a full-fledged FBI Special Agent.

I finished scanning and enlarging a dozen pictures from
Aunt Jo's box and now I brought them up on my computer
monitor. Each one taken separately could be easily mistaken
for a random shot. Put together, I knew they would fit like
pieces of a puzzle.

I hunched forward, studying each picture and comparing
it to the others, zooming in on several. They were a bit
hazy when I enlarged them, but there was definitely a woman

in the background. It was difficult making out her features, because she was wearing a Middle Eastern hijab. In most of the pictures, she hung back from the man, and if I hadn't detected her again and again, I might have thought she was simply another shopper or bystander.

In all but one of the photographs, she held the material across her face, shielding everything from view except her downcast eyes. But in one picture, she was reaching for some cigarettes that appeared to be sliding off the cart, and the fabric had slipped from her face.

My heart was beating wildly as I enlarged that photo and zoomed in on her facial features. Warm brown eyes, the color of molasses, under long, curled black lashes. Flawless skin, the nose and cheeks plump, the lips full.

"What are you doing?"

I jumped and whirled around.

"You know you're supposed to be in bed," Alex admonished as she breezed into the room.

It occurred to me that she'd never finished confiding in me before I fainted. Perhaps it was just as well. I didn't want to seem self-centered, but the conversation I'd overheard between Alex and Ricky remained fresh in my mind, and I wasn't exactly keen on getting close to someone who was afraid her brother would ruin her FBI career. I was afraid that just the knowledge of what her brother might be involved in was enough to ruin mine.

"I can rest better over here," I said, turning back around.

"What have you got there?" she asked, peering over my shoulder.

I sent the enlarged photo to the printer. "Pictures my mom took shortly before she died."

"Hhmmm. Was your mother foreign born?"

"Nope. Heinz 57 American. Why do you ask?"

She shrugged. "I didn't know if this was a relative or something."

"No, it isn't," I said, watching the stranger's eyes take shape in the output tray. "The thing is, Mom took all these pictures… And I can't imagine why she would have done it."

"Was she a cop?"

"Not even close. An accountant. She kept the books for the family farm."

"Interesting," Alex said, leaning even closer to the monitor. "Maybe she was testing a new camera or something?"

I turned over one of the pictures and showed her the notation. "What could this mean, 'the beginning of the trail'?" I asked.

"Sounds like a cop hot on a case."

"But Mom—"

"You told me… But would that prevent her from investigating something on her own?"

I studied the picture as it popped out of the printer, the ink still damp. "Who could she have been watching? And why?"

Alex was silent but I felt her unspoken words hanging in the air: *we might never know.* I felt a cold chill move through me.

"Anyway," I said, saving the pictures and exiting the program, "what are you doing out of class?"

"Steve sent me to get you," she answered. "There's a car waiting downstairs for you."

"It's that time already?" I glanced at my watch. Somehow, the morning had slipped past me and I hadn't noticed; I was so engrossed in the photographs. I nodded toward my bag at the end of a perfectly made bed. "I'm ready."

"I'll carry it down for you."

I shut down the laptop and began unplugging the cables and packing it up.

"Remember to keep me up to date on what you're studying?" I asked.

"No problem."

Before I could get to the gym bag, she'd grabbed it and was heading for the door despite my protests. I snatched my laptop case and hurried after her. I hesitated briefly at the door as I turned around to close it. I had a sinking feeling I would never see this room again.

I tried to shake the negative thoughts out of my mind as we made our way downstairs. I could hear Alex's voice but it was my mother's face I was seeing in front of me.

Mom wasn't the nosy type. She wasn't a member of the local quilting or crafts groups, because she said they spent too much of their time talking about other people's business. And she hated that.

So what would make her follow people? To see what they were up to?

And where did this trail lead?

I wondered if she herself knew where it ended, or if her untimely death had stopped her short. I inhaled sharply. In that moment, I realized I had to retrace Mom's footsteps, to find out what she was doing before her death, and follow the path to its end—wherever that would lead me.

"Did you say something?" Alex asked.

"Not a word," I answered as we marched out the door. As we made our way to the back of the car, the front door opened and Steve stepped out.

"Your chauffeur," he said with more than a bit of sarcasm.

I caught a glimpse of Alex's face as she handed him my belongings to load into the trunk. She glanced up at me, barely concealing a sly smile.

Somewhere in between our exit from the building and settling into the front seat, Alex disappeared and soon Quantico could be seen through the rear-view mirror.

As he steered the car onto the entrance ramp to I-95 heading north, I could see the traffic southbound was bumper-to-bumper, stop-and-go. In contrast, we moved steadily at ten miles above the posted speed limit.

We rode along in silence for awhile. I studied the horizon where churning black clouds were forming, and hoped they didn't interfere with a prompt departure. I shivered, and without a word, Steve turned up the heat.

I watched cars of every description speed past us, only to be forced to slow within seconds due to the heavy traffic. I wondered where they were all headed in such a hurry.

"Class is out now for the weekend," he said, breaking the silence. "And Monday is a holiday."

I hadn't even realized it was Friday. "What holiday?"

"Veteran's Day. No classes."

"Interesting. I'll lose less time than I thought."

He half-nodded as he sped through the Springfield interchange as if he knew it like the back of his hand.

"I'm kind of surprised with the Academy," I said.

"How so?"

"I guess I expected something more like boot camp."

He chuckled. "We hire professionals. Before you can get into the Academy, you must have at least a college degree and two years' work experience. And we hire only the cream of the crop. We're not going to treat you like you've been drafted into the infantry."

I studied his profile. He had a Roman nose and his jaw was firm and squared. As my eyes scrolled upward, a short lock of dappled brown hair fell across his forehead, but he acted as though he hadn't noticed. His eyes were narrowed and focused on the road.

"How long have you been with the Bureau?" I asked.

"Eight years."

"Always been assigned to Quantico?"

He shook his head. "My first assignment was in Greenville, Mississippi."

"That must have been interesting."

He glanced sideways at me. "You have no idea."

I waited for him to say more, but he didn't. After a moment of silence, I said, "So you came to the Academy from the Greenville office?"

"From Greenville, I went to the Cleveland, Ohio field office."

"So in eight years, you've moved from attending the Academy, to Mississippi, to Ohio, and now you're back at the Academy teaching. All that moving must be hard on your family."

He looked at me again and I wondered if I'd become too personal. "What makes you think I have a family?" he asked.

I dropped my eyes to my lap and shrugged. "You don't?"

He hesitated before answering. "Not yet."

I tried to appear interested in the landscape flying past us—apartment buildings and businesses with names like *Landmark* and *Universal Computer Technologies* that were undoubtedly filled with people who might be watching our car flash past at this very moment.

We turned off I-95 and headed toward Reagan National Airport.

"Sheila," he said abruptly, "Are you seeing anyone?"

I paused. "Why do you ask?" I said, thinking this was a heck of a place for a pickup line.

"Just needed to know if we should notify anyone that you're headed back to Nashville."

I thought of the emergency notification card I'd completed on my first day at the Academy, and the extensive background investigation I knew they performed on me. I was sure Steve knew more about me than I knew about myself. Then I heard myself saying, "I'll call my aunt before we board."

He pulled into long-term parking. There was a quiet moment as he retrieved his parking pass from the electronic gate. Then he pulled into a parking spot and turned off the engine.

"You don't have to escort me to the terminal," I said. "You really could have dropped me off in front..."

"Ah, but I'm going someplace, too," he said, hopping out of the car.

I could feel my cheeks turning the color of flames. I stepped out and joined him at the trunk. I'd been so preoccupied; I hadn't even noticed his suitcase beside my laptop case and gym bag. Of course; it made perfect sense that he would take me to the airport if he was headed here already.

He grabbed the bags like they were light as a feather while I slung my laptop case over my shoulder.

We were almost to the terminal when I got the nerve to ask, "Where you headed?"

"Nashville."

22

It was Saturday morning, a mere two weeks since I'd started the Academy, but it felt like a lifetime. I stood at the top of a hill overlooking Neelley Valley, just a short walk from Aunt Jo's house at Sunnyside.

Since my parents' deaths, I'd managed to avoid returning to the house where I grew up. I'd focused instead on my studies and career when in reality, the answers to my future lay in my past.

When I was younger, this was all farmland that had been in our family for generations. I broke the chain, much to Aunt Jo's dismay, when my parents died.

I knew then, and I still know, that I am not a tobacco farmer. I sold the land after my parents' deaths because I didn't have a clue what to do with it or how to manage it, and I simply wasn't inclined to learn. Besides, with all that had happened, I was ready for a new beginning.

The neighboring farm was owned by the Beards, and they immediately expressed interest in buying the land. So it was sold, lock, stock and barrel: the house, the farm, and everything in it and on it, except a few photograph albums and mementos Aunt Jo and I removed before settlement.

I never thought I'd be back.

Yet here I was, standing at the top of the hill and looking down upon houses that had cropped up on fertile ground, the rows of tobacco leaves replaced by children's play sets and picket fences, concrete driveways and vinyl clad homes.

Old houses I remember from my youth and my father had remembered from his were long gone, torn down by developers. Every now and then, an old church steeple or cemetery with twisted headstones covered in moss would crop up, interrupting the modern landscape, but I knew all the way to my soul that it had changed forever.

I knew when I sold the property that the Beards didn't need or necessarily even want my old home. They acquired it because it came with the land as a package deal. I hadn't questioned their use of the land, naively believing they wanted it in order to double their tobacco yield.

I walked toward the house where I once lived, the dirt and gravel replaced by asphalt with stark yellow and white lines. In my childhood, it had been an adventure going from my house to Aunt Jo's; a trek along trails surrounded by wild hydrangeas and a profusion of white flowers and buttercups that invaded everything in sight. Now it was a short walk on a blacktopped road, broken every now and again by a car rolling past.

I reached the driveway to my old home, and stepped off the pavement and into dormant winter undergrowth that covered what was once a gravel road.

A rusted chain swung from one side of the drive to the other, with a weathered sign in the middle with the faded proclamation "No Trespassing, No Hunting".

My eyes scanned the surrounding terrain; the native honeysuckle I loved had been replaced by invasive wild grape and poison ivy. In the haunting, barren landscape, the vines wrapped themselves around everything in their path like octopus tentacles. And just like the sea creatures from badly made movies, I knew they would eventually kill anything they latched onto.

I made my way around the chain, my feet sinking into soft dirt, hidden from view by withered weeds that once were waist-high but now were bowed under the winter sun. I found my way to the center of my driveway only through a quick analysis of the chain's location.

I stopped and looked back once, almost wishing someone were behind me or a car would pass by to remind me I was not that far from civilization. Somewhere in the distance I heard a motor running, but even that faded quickly, leaving only the rustling of hollow winter vines and the scratching of naked limbs caught in the breeze.

It would be another hour before Steve was to pick me up at Aunt Jo's house and take me to Vanderbilt. He claimed to be visiting friends in Nashville, but I had a deep suspicion he had checked into a hotel and spent the night alone, though I also suspected he would never admit to it...

The drive twisted and turned, seeming much longer than it ever had when I'd lived there, and I eventually lost sight of the road behind me.

I could see the roof before I saw the house itself, the gabled windows staring out blankly, the curtains stilled, the paint chipping, the shingles misshapen as if ruffled by an angry wind. I was caught between relief that it was still standing, that it hadn't yet been torn down to make room for another tract of houses, and despair at its unkempt and ragged appearance.

My head pounded in my temples and for a moment I thought how foolish it had been of me to disappear from Aunt Jo's house and wander out here by myself, where it appeared as though no one had ventured since my parents' deaths. I stared at the brick, now covered in a filmy mold, the front door that had always appeared so inviting now hidden in shade, the bright yellow door now faded to dirt brown.

My instinct begged me to turn around, to go back and never return. And even as it cried out for me to stop, I took a step forward, knowing I could not go back until I had confronted the ghosts within.

23

I really didn't expect to find the front door unlocked but I checked it anyway.

As I followed the wrap-around porch, I discovered the curtains on the windows were parted, as they were on that last day when I turned the keys over to the Beards, but they were filthy now and hung unnaturally, the panes dingy from two years of neglect. It was too dark inside to make out each room's contents, although incredulously, it appeared as though nothing had changed since I'd last seen it.

I reached the back of the house, where wide steps faced the kitchen door and led into the back yard. There was a tear in the screen door, just where the hook latched. I felt a lump form in my throat. Mom would never have allowed a tear in the screen, not for a minute. She was always meticulous about how she kept her house. I reached inside to unlock it, but the hook was already dangling.

I opened the door and tried the doorknob. It was locked. I let the screen door close with a bang, half expecting Mom to holler at me not to let the door slam.

When I was younger, Mom worried that I'd lose my key to the house, so we'd devised a plan together to hide it, although when I grew older I suspected she had really concocted the plan herself and led me along into thinking it was my idea. Now I walked down the steps in the back of the house, and lifted a two foot section of lattice work where it bordered the porch. I knelt to the ground, rolled onto my back, and pulled myself underneath the porch. There, against one of the floor joists, was the little wooden box Dad had fashioned. I slipped the hook from the lid and reached inside. The key was still there, as if I was ten years old and only a day had passed since I'd used it last.

I slid back out and made my way to the door. I opened the screen door, and slid the key in the lock. It turned stiffly. Hesitantly, I pushed open the door.

I debated whether to tuck the key into my sweats or return it to the box under the porch. Habit told me to return it. Logic told me there wasn't any point to it. The adage that old habits die hard won out and I returned the key to its rightful place, carefully covering the entrance with the lattice work.

Then I returned to the kitchen door and, with my heart in my throat, I entered the house.

The air was stale and dusty, and I coughed as it penetrated my nostrils and throat. The room was damp, the wallpaper spotted with mold. Dead plants lined the kitchen windowsill and covered the tops of the cabinets.

The open cabinets still stocked plates and cups and glasses, exactly where Mom or Dad had stacked them, only now they were covered in thick blankets of dust.

For some strange reason, I walked straight to the refrigerator and opened the door. The stench caused my stomach to churn. All of the food that had stocked the fridge when my parents died was still there, some two years later, now spoiled and rotted. Even a pitcher of iced tea was sitting in the center of the shelf; after all the time that had passed, there was a layer of sludge at the bottom of it.

I fought the nausea that threatened to overtake me and closed the door.

I knew when I sold the Beards our land that they hadn't been interested in the house. After all, they had their own home just over the next hill, and it was bigger and newer than this one. But I had assumed they would rent it out or parcel the land and sell it off and someone would be living in it now, enjoying its homey feel just as I did while growing up.

I never expected it would be sealed and abandoned like a forgotten tomb.

I wandered from one room to the next, noting the den sofa where I spent so many hours studying, the recliner where Dad would take a nap every evening during the news, the coat rack in the laundry room where muddy boots and rain slickers would be kept, a puzzle half assembled on the dining room table, the remaining pieces waiting for hands that would never return them to their rightful place...

I threaded my way through the downstairs and then haltingly climbed to the second floor. The boards creaked and moaned under my feet as though being awakened from a deep slumber.

The bedrooms were just as I left them two years ago: mine cleaned out, the closet bare except for a few wire hangers; Mom's sewing room still laid out, with a half-finished pair of curtains draped across the back of the seat; Dad's study still filled with books, one opened and face-down on the desk as though he would return shortly and pick it up again.

I entered their bedroom last.

It was here that they'd been found, dead of carbon monoxide poisoning. Aunt Jo found them on an especially cold Sunday morning. I'd been attending Vanderbilt at the time, and had hurried home after receiving the news.

It had all been a blur, the first few days spent in shock while friends and relatives were notified, people I knew and many that I didn't, milling around at the funeral home and during the graveside ceremony, and gathering at Aunt Jo's house afterward to offer further condolences. After a few days spent taking care of the estate, meeting with lawyers and accountants and bankers, I'd returned to school, where the full impact of their passing finally caught up to me. In the months that followed, I experienced a myriad of emotions from depression to anger, and finally to a numbness that settled into my bones.

I sat on their bed for awhile, feeling the warmth of their love and the emptiness in my life, until I shook myself back to reality. I returned to the hall and paused for one last glance.

A glass sat on the nightstand. I thought of the pitcher of iced tea downstairs. For some reason, the glass seemed to beckon to me and I returned and picked it up.

Inside, there was a layer of the same sludge I'd seen in the pitcher. This time, I held it against the light from the window. It was so thick that it looked like molasses, but I knew it couldn't be. I held it to my nose and sniffed. I hesitated and then I sniffed again.

It smelled faintly of tobacco.

That was odd. Though my parents owned a tobacco farm, neither were smokers. And the odor wasn't prevalent in the rest of the house.

I wandered to the other side of the bed, where another glass sat next to my father's side. Instead of a consistent sludge, there were only flecks. I was tempted to reach inside and feel them but I didn't. I knew one thing for certain: this wasn't tea.

I set both glasses down on the nightstand. I would retrieve them before I left. Perhaps with Steve's help, I would find somebody to run some tests on it.

With one more glance behind me, I returned to the hallway.

At the end of the hall was a door leading to the attic. I approached it slowly and turned the glass knob. It opened with a groan. I left the door ajar and stepped into the musty stairwell.

The attic could easily have been converted into another bedroom, with its sloping roofline and gabled windows. It had been used instead for storage of everything from old clothes to furniture to Christmas decorations. I walked to the front of the expansive room and glanced out the grimy window.

I could see the drive curling through the woods, the lawn rising wild and unkempt as it met the tree line and stretched toward the house. I could even see the chain from here, stretched across the entrance of the drive, and the asphalt road that lay beyond.

I turned and surveyed the items stored in the attic, remembering days gone by when I climbed those stairs and entertained myself for hours, dressing in my great-grandmother's clothes from the roaring twenties, covering my neck in strands of pearls, wearing high heeled shoes that swallowed my feet.

And when I became a teenager, how I'd sit in the window seat and read for hours, perfectly content with *The Secret Garden* or *Gone With the Wind* or a Daphne du Maurier classic.

My eyes came to rest on a piece of paneling. I smiled as I bent down and ran my fingers along the groove.

Dad had fashioned this piece of paneling when I was a little girl. Between the paneling and the stairs, Mom hid my birthday and Christmas presents, and she never suspected that I'd known about the hiding place all along. I would debate myself for hours, whether to peek and spoil any surprises, or try to guess what was behind the paneling. In the end, the peeks always won out. And Mom and Dad were never the wiser.

I pulled the paneling away from the studs. It was dark inside, and I thought I heard something scurrying. Field mouse, probably. I poked my upper body inside, and felt around until I located the flashlight Mom had always kept there. I held my breath while I turned it on. The battery was weak, the light yellowed, but it still worked.

The area was smaller than I remembered it. It was empty except for a few rolls of wrapping paper. I started to retreat when I caught a glimpse of a box pushed against the wall.

I climbed inside and clutched the box. It was small, not much larger than a shoebox. I tried to steady the flashlight on the lid while I opened it.

There was a single key inside and a folded sheet of paper.

I held the paper to the light as I unfolded it.

"Dear Sheila," it began in my mother's precise, tiny handwriting, *"I knew if anything ever happened to me, you would find this. Yes, I've always known you were aware of my little hiding place… You could never fool me.*

"Remember the place where Old Man Fuddy worked? The address was 127… You'll need this key. There you'll find evidence. Take it to the police, my darling daughter.

"And remember that I am never really gone. I'll always be with you. I'll always watch over you.

"God bless you, Sheila."

It was signed, *"Love forever, Mom"*

I leaned back and wiped the tears from my eyes. God, how I missed her. I pressed the letter to my breast, feeling Mom's presence, smelling her perfume on the writing paper, almost hearing the sound of her voice.

I don't know how long I remained there talking to her as though she were still alive, before I returned to the words in her letter.

There was no Old Man Fuddy. There was a guard at the bank in Columbia who never smiled, although each time Mom and I went there, we always greeted him warmly. We came to call him an "old fuddy-duddy". Why would she mention him in a note like this?

I looked at it again, the number 127 followed by the ellipse staring at me. There was no street mentioned, because there was no street. It was a bank deposit box, number 127.

Whatever she had been investigating was significant enough for her to place the evidence she'd gathered in a bank deposit box, where she hoped I'd find it if anything happened to her… Little did she know that a faulty gas heater would end her life prematurely. Or that it would take her only daughter two years to work up the nerve to come back here.

As I slipped the key into my sweats, I heard the sound of wood splintering downstairs. Someone was breaking down the front door. And then the light from the flashlight flickered once and died.

24

There are times in a person's life when the only appropriate thing to do is tear down the stairs with a sword drawn, like Melanie in *Gone With the Wind*, or better yet, stand on the stairwell looking sultry like Scarlett until the bad guy gets close enough to get his face blown away.

Then there are times like these, where the only weapons available are the stiletto heels on Mom's old shoes, and try as I might, I can't picture myself rushing the bad guys with two shoes drawn.

I rushed to the window at the front of the house, but I could see nothing below except the roofline that jutted out above the front porch. In the distance, a storm appeared to be brewing from the northwest; a vast army of clouds rolled and tumbled, fat with a cold winter rain, as they advanced upon me. Through the trees, I spotted a dark sedan stopped about midway down the remnants of the driveway. I could barely make out a man standing beside the car, a puff of smoke wafting upwards from his cigarette. When he abruptly looked up at the house, I ducked to the side.

I heard two voices below me; they were speaking in a language I couldn't quite place. The windowpanes shook as they broke through the front door. A run-of-the-mill burglar would have gone to the rear of the house where he would have been less likely to be spotted, attempting a more subtle form of entry, perhaps through a window. It was obvious these people didn't care—or they were in an awful hurry.

I never went anywhere without my cell phone, something I'd learned this past summer when I found myself in dire need of assistance. Now I pulled it out of my sweatpants pocket and with shaking fingers, dialed 911.

Only seconds must have passed before I was connected to the Maury County Sheriff's Office, but it felt like an eternity. I reported a break-in and rattled off the address as though I still lived here. By the time I'd gotten the address out of my mouth, the shaking stopped and I could hear voices directly below me. They were inside.

The Sheriff's office employed fewer than a hundred deputies, less than half of them at work at any given time. Maury County was stretched out across 613 square miles. My mouth was as dry as cotton as I realized it could take them some time to reach me.

The dispatcher was talking on the other end of the line, but I barely heard her. My attention was focused on the movements below. It was as if dresser drawers were being tossed about and furniture moved, as though they were searching for something.

I listened as one pair of footsteps climbed to the second floor and made their way to the far end of the hall. In my mind's eye, I pictured this faceless intruder with the rapid-fire speech stealthily moving from one room to the next, opening every door, every drawer, and violating every inch of my parents' home. It was hard not to panic as I listened to doors banging, furniture legs scratching the hardwood floors as they were unceremoniously moved, and glass crashing as if anything in his way was being tossed aside.

Now the second man was ascending the stairs, calling out to the first. As I stood there listening, it occurred to me that the dispatcher was still talking to me, trying to get me to respond, when I heard a heavy boot on the bottom step to the attic.

Panicked, I switched off the cell phone, afraid they would hear the dispatcher's voice coming through the speaker. My eyes panned the room for a place to hide. Even if I dove underneath a pile of clothes or behind a bank of boxes, it wouldn't matter. They were going through everything in the house, and no matter where I hid, they would find me. No place was safe.

I peered across the room at the rear window. The window lock must have had twenty coats of paint on it, ensuring it would remain shut for eternity. Even if I managed to open it, I'd have to get there first—which meant running past the top of the stairs, directly in front of them.

The front window was no better. The man in the driveway would see me. The odds were against me.

The steps creaked as they ascended, the voices simultaneously growing nearer even as I began to lose the sound of their voices in a thick mental fog.

A shadow fell across the floor and grew steadily larger until it seemed eight feet tall. Then as if a rocket was propelling me, I dove into Mom's hiding place under the stairs. Just before I slid the paneling across the opening, I spotted the tip of a black boot.

It was pitch black inside the cubbyhole. I was crammed inside with my neck bent against the underside of the steps, my legs and arms feeling like pretzels in the confined space. I could feel the weight of the men as they paused directly above me.

Their talking stopped abruptly. My heart was pounding so loudly that I was certain they could hear me. I closed my eyes and tried to will my heart to beat silently. I held my breath for as long as I dared, afraid when I began breathing again that the exhale would give me away.

One of them spoke softly, the sentence forming a question.

Something rustled behind me, and fur brushed my ankle. If it bit me, I would die right there from pure mortification. It was almost as if they heard it, too, and were cocking their heads to listen.

Then a heavy pair of boots entered the attic and stopped on the other side of the paneling, not six inches from me.

My eyes were adjusting to the darkness now. A pinpoint of light was a few feet from where I crouched. I realized as I focused on it, a hole had been eaten in the drywall.

The other man spoke in a hushed tone.

My muscles were so cramped and tense that I felt like a coiled spring.

I felt the creature now, crawling under my body. As it neared my left hand, I flexed my fingers in a sudden, rapid motion. Caught by surprise, it fairly flew across the floor. I caught a glimpse of a fat gray mouse as it scurried through the cubbyhole.

I heard a shout, and then a thick boot slammed down on the unfinished attic floor. The sound was followed by laughter, but even that resonated of raw evil.

Surely I would hear the sirens of the Sheriff's cars any moment, and these men would flee. But as I waited to be rescued, the seconds ticked past so slowly that it was sickening.

I listened as the second man crossed to the front window, his steps lighter than they had been just moments before, as though even while he walked he was listening intently. The footsteps paused near the window.

In my mind's eye, I pictured the third man down below, standing sentry, perhaps waving to him to indicate the coast was clear—or motioning to him to hurry up.

And almost in response, there was a flurry of activity. Something was thrown against the paneling, startling me so that I almost gasped aloud. I heard all matter of things being bandied about—clothing, bric-a-bracs, memories from a lifetime that seemed in one respect to be so long ago and another, to have been only yesterday.

I fought the anger welling up inside me. It took every ounce of restraint to remain still and listen to them destroy everything they touched.

I realized I held the key so tightly in the palm of my right hand that it was cutting into my palm.

The footsteps died away, moving back down the stairs to the second floor, and then to the first, seeming to pick up speed as they progressed. I crouched in the cubbyhole, too afraid to move, wondering if I'd be able to hear the car crunching back along the gravel drive to leave me here alone again.

Somehow, I managed to slide the key under my sweatshirt and inside my bra.

Just as I was beginning to breathe a little easier and contemplated climbing out of my hiding place, the voices were back. Then I heard a distinct sound that caused my whole body to recoil in terror. As they made their way back upstairs, I knew the sound of liquid splashing onto the floor could only mean one thing. As if confirming my wildest fears, the stench of gasoline tickled my nostrils. I realized they were going to burn the house down—and me with it.

25

I was listening to the gurgling sound made by the gasoline pouring out of the can, my heart in my throat. In my mind's eye, I could see them moving about the room, saturating everything in their path. I knew I'd have no choice but to come out of my hiding place and attack these intruders before the house went up in flames.

I had my hand on the paneling, ready to push it aside, when I heard the wailing of a distant siren. The pouring abruptly stopped. I hesitated, my hand still poised to push my way out of here, my heart thumping wildly. Hurried footsteps crossed the attic and seemed to stop at the front window. Then they were rushing down the stairs, two excited voices wafting upwards to where I crouched hidden in the darkness.

The siren grew closer; I knew the Sheriff was closing in. And not with one car, but with two, and from the sound of things, they were approaching fast.

The reek of gasoline was penetrating the air, burning my lungs and threatening to overcome me. I didn't know where the intruders were now, but I had to take a chance. I pushed the paneling out of the way. As I crawled out, my shoe slipped and I glanced down to see a stream of gasoline spreading across the floor.

I pulled my sweatshirt over my mouth and nose to protect me from the biting stench. I dashed to the front window and peered outside.

The man I'd seen earlier was crouched at the front of the car, his back to me as he watched the cruisers careen into the driveway and stop just yards from the sedan.

The deputies sat in their cruisers for several long moments. I wondered why they didn't simply jump out and rush him. At the same time, I heard footsteps racing through the house, and I knew the others were headed for the back door and the thick woods beyond the back of the house. I had to warn the Sheriff.

No longer afraid the intruders would hear me, I pounded on the window and tried to open it, but it was wedged shut under thick coats of ancient paint and warped framing.

They emerged from their cruisers at exactly the same moment. Four of them, each with a hand on their weapons, all of them watching the man behind the vehicle.

I heard one of them shout, but I couldn't make out the words. From the looks of things, I surmised that he was ordering the man to come out with his hands up.

They crept closer, their movements so stealthy that they didn't appear to be moving. One moment they were a distance away, and the next, they had closed in around him: two of them in front of him—one to his left and one to his right—and two more fanning out to each side.

One of the deputies continued to shout at him, but the man remained crouched, obviously using the vehicle as a shield. In another moment, the two deputies moving to his sides would have an unobstructed view.

I heard the back door slam, and in a flash, I realized while the deputies were busy apprehending the man in the driveway, no one was pursuing the other two that were fleeing. It was up to me.

Just as I started to turn about and rush to the stairs, the man rose to his full height from behind the vehicle with a weapon brandished.

As if in slow motion, he pointed it at the deputy closest to him.

The response was immediate. All four deputies drew their weapons and in a volley of gunfire, the man stumbled backwards before dropping to his knees. Almost in unison, huge splotches appeared on the back of his shirt, turning it crimson. The weapon slipped from his hand. Then his torso bent backwards and hit the ground. He jerked once and then was still.

The stench of smoke wafted upwards to my nose and for a moment, I thought I smelled the acrid aftereffects of the gunfire. Then I heard a cackling sound just beneath my feet.

The room became a blur as I fled, my shoes slipping on the wet surface and propelling me forward. As I reached the top of the stairs, a movement caught my eye and I turned and glanced out the back window just as the two men reached the edge of the woods. One stopped and turned back to the house. His head jerked upwards and I found myself staring into his face. Then he turned abruptly and was swallowed up in the thick underbrush beyond the house.

I rushed down the stairs and bolted for the back of the house, hurtling myself through the kitchen door onto the back porch. Then I was down the steps and across the yard. I heard shouting from the direction of the cruisers as I reached the garden hose by the garage, but I didn't stop. I grabbed the end and sprinted toward the front of the house, screaming for them to help me.

It wasn't until I'd reached the house that I realized I had no water. Though we had a well, the pump wouldn't work without electricity. It vaguely registered that the deputies were behind me, radioing in their position and calling for fire trucks and an ambulance. The seconds passed in agony as I stood helplessly by.

Somewhere in the distance, I heard sirens screaming, their progress excruciatingly slow. I heard the deputies ordering me away from the house, but I paid no attention.

Then I felt strong hands fiercely pulling me away. The fire trucks were there now, but with a sinking heart I realized we had no fire hydrant—we were too far into the country. They'd have to drain the creek and hope it was enough to save the house.

26

It was impossible to control my exasperation. "I've already told you," I said, "I don't need to go to the hospital. I'm fine."

I pushed the paramedic away and sat up on the edge of the stretcher. I was in the back of the ambulance, and if the medic would just move from my line of view, I could see what was left of my girlhood home. I'd already wasted precious time debating my physical state.

"What's going on here?"

"Steve, thank God you're here," I said. "Maybe you can convince this man to let me go."

"What happened?" he asked.

"We're trying to take her to the hospital," the paramedic said, "and she's giving us a hard time."

"Can I speak to her alone for a moment?" Steve said with a calmness that immediately roused my curiosity.

The paramedic shrugged, climbed out of the ambulance, and sauntered off, shaking his head.

Steve climbed into the ambulance even as I started to climb out.

"You just hold your horses there," he said. "You'd better fill me in on what happened here."

"This was the home I grew up in," I said, motioning toward the house. My eyes caressed the structure and drifted upwards. The walls and the roof were still intact. From the looks of the outside, the house did not appear to have extensive damage. Perhaps the Sheriff had shown up before the men had a chance to fully ignite the gasoline.

I glanced at the attic window where I'd stood just moments before. "I stopped by—trip down memory lane, I guess—and three men showed up."

He gestured toward the driveway, where enough deputies were gathered to have captured an entire Army. "That man over there was one of them?"

I leaned forward and peered outside, although I knew exactly who he was referring to. He was still in the same posture as when he'd fallen. Two uniformed women were taking pictures from every angle, their faces immobile as though they were staring at a chunk of cheese. I wondered when rigor mortis set in, if they would have to break his legs to straighten them out. He'd been on his knees with his torso bent backward, the top of his head touching the ground, for so long now, that I could picture them sitting him up in the ambulance when they transported him to the morgue.

"Yes. He was the lookout."

"I'd say he didn't do too good of a job, wouldn't you?" he said.

"It was suicide," I said quietly.

"You're kidding me, right? The guy's riddled with bullets."

"That's not the kind of suicide I meant," I said, looking into his eyes. "It's called 'suicide by cop'. You've heard of that, haven't you?"

"Of course I have. But why—?"

"He pulled a weapon on one of the deputies. There were four of them, and he was alone. As soon as he drew the weapon, he had to have known they'd open up on him."

"You said there were three men. Where are the others?"

"They ran out the back door."

"They get away?"

I nodded. "One of them saw me."

"You're lucky you got out."

"I wouldn't have had a chance, if they'd set the attic on fire. They must have panicked when the cops showed up…"

"Did you recognize them?"

I shook my head.

"Are you sure you're telling me the whole story?"

"What do you mean?"

He stared at me. "You were at the mall when it was bombed. Someone tried to kill you at the hospital. We travel halfway across the country—"

"—Tennessee's really not halfway—"

"—and somebody tries to burn you alive." He let out an exasperated sigh. "And you don't think I'm smart enough to connect the dots?"

"You don't think this is all related, do you?" I said, my voice barely above a whisper.

"Well, I'll put it this way. If it isn't, you sure do make a lot of enemies."

We both fell silent.

"You don't think the mall was bombed because someone was trying to kill me, do you?"

I thought I heard a gasp, and I looked up. His eyes were wide; I realized he hadn't thought of that possibility. Now he steepled his hands and peered at me thoughtfully. "Who would want to kill you? And why?"

I felt the key brush against my skin, the cold metal causing me to shiver. "It's my mother," I said suddenly.

"I thought your mother was…" his voice trailed off.

"Just before the men showed up, I found a letter and a key she'd left for me. She was onto something—or someone—before she died. And she left the evidence for me in case anything happened to her."

"What did the letter say?"

I realized I didn't have it with me, and I glanced again at the attic window. Was it still there?

"She left evidence in a safe deposit box at the bank, just in case anything ever happened to her."

"How did she die?"

It felt irreverent to speak of her death in so detached a manner. "Carbon monoxide poisoning," I said. "They found them in their bedroom."

"Here?"

I nodded.

There was a long moment of silence. The paramedic began approaching the ambulance, but Steve waved him off.

"Was the death ruled an accident?"

"Yes," I said, my voice sounding blunt and flat. "But," I added suddenly, "I found glasses beside their bed, glasses of—I think—iced tea. But there's something else in the glasses. What if they'd been poisoned?"

"Aren't you jumping to wild conclusions here?"

"I have to get to the bank and find out what's in that safe deposit box. It might have clues to their death."

"But it's Saturday."

I glanced at my watch. Adrenaline coursed through me and I jumped out of the ambulance before he could stop me. "The bank closes at noon. We have less than half an hour. Where's your car?"

27

We were in downtown Columbia, just a few miles from Neelley Valley. I could barely see the bank building; the red bricks turned gray and mottled under the torrent of rain as we pulled into a parking space. The skies had opened up with a vengeance, and I had an ominous feeling that I just couldn't shake. As we leapt from the rental car, a bolt of lightning flashed overhead, followed instantaneously by an evil thunder that shook the very ground under our feet.

I was at the door with my hand on the door handle when Old Man Fuddy flipped the deadbolt.

I gaped at him through the glass. He had thinning black hair that looked as though he might have dyed it with shoe polish and eyebrows as white and bushy as two cumulus clouds on a summer day, beneath which cold gray eyes glared back at me with an angry glee. His thin, flesh-colored lips were held in a Cheshire grin, and his thin chest was thrust forward as if to give him added stature.

He pointed to his watch, the smile still affixed as if it were chiseled on.

Then I felt Steve push me out of the way as he slapped his FBI credentials against the glass. "FBI," he shouted. "Official business! Open this door *now!*"

The gleam in Old Man Fuddy's eyes turned to concern as he fumbled with the lock.

Out of the corner of my eye, I saw an elderly woman crossing the marbled floor at such a rapid pace that her fine, straight silver hair appeared to be riding a wave behind her. She propelled her overweight body forward in an elaborate waddle that spoke of years of physical neglect and inactivity. She was saying something to Old Man Fuddy, her words lost in the rain swirling around us, as she brushed past him.

"Sheila Carpenter, what do you think you're doing?" she gasped.

I almost fell inside with Steve close on my heels.

"Mrs. Birch, it's an emergency," I managed to announce. I held up the key. "I have to open a safe deposit box."

Mrs. Birch's eyebrows, normally meticulously drawn into two straight little lines, were knit together into a pyramid.

"Please," I said. "I just found out my mother left something for me. I have to get it."

The mention of my mother had the desired effect. She straightened to her full height and wrapped her arm around my shoulder, leading me away from the door.

I stole a quick glance at Steve. He was following us, staying a discrete two feet behind us as we put distance between us and Old Man Fuddy, who was relocking the door.

We reached a steel gate, beyond which the safe deposit box rested alongside dozens of others. Mrs. Birch fingered a five-inch diameter key ring that descended from a matronly belt. She immediately found the exact key. Deftly, she slipped it into the lock and a moment later, the door slid open.

We stepped inside. My heart was pounding in my temples as I watched her open a file cabinet and rifle through it. A moment later, she pulled an index card out and laid it on top of the cabinet, her eyebrows knit together even fiercer than before.

"We have a small problem…" she began, her voice fading as she spoke.

I peered over her shoulder. The index card was filled with entries—dates beside my mother's signature, the small letters formed in a brisk, simple manner devoid of flourishes. The last day she'd been here was just two days before her death. I found myself swallowing hard.

"A problem?" I parroted. My heart was already sinking. I knew what her next words would be before she opened her mouth.

"Your name is not on the signature card," she said, almost apologetically.

"But Mrs. Birch," I pleaded, "You know my mother is gone. And you've known me all my life. You know I wouldn't ask you to do this if it weren't important."

"I know," she said, her lashes fluttering downward, avoiding my gaze, "but rules are rules."

"But—what do I do?"

"Petition the court," she murmured apologetically.

"That could take weeks—"

An arm was suddenly thrust in front of us. All eyes focused on the outstretched hand, yielding a black leather identification case with a gold badge.

"FBI Special Agent Steven Moran," he said solemnly. "This is official business."

I stared at Mrs. Birch, who was staring at the badge.

"It's true," I said, my mouth dry.

I saw a myriad of emotions cross her face, as though every bit of bank training she had was racing through her mind. I hoped she didn't demand a search warrant. Watching her eyebrows twitch and her mouth pucker, I knew she was trying to grasp onto any bit of knowledge that might help her.

"It's my mother's safe deposit box," I said quietly. "I'm the only heir to the estate. And what is contained in that box is wanted by the FBI."

Mrs. Birch reached for a pen with a shaking hand. "Sign here," she said curtly.

Less than two minutes later, Steve and I stood in a tiny, partially enclosed alcove. We were both staring at a steel gray container the size of a breadbox that Mrs. Birch had just set on the table before discreetly leaving us alone.

"Would you like some privacy?" he asked, his voice low, his mouth just inches from my ear.

"No," I heard myself saying as I opened the top.

28

We sat in the living room at Aunt Jo's house. I glanced at Steve, now perched on the edge of the faded sofa, from my armchair a few feet away. He was filling a plate from an old-fashioned Lazy Susan in the center of the coffee table, heaped with stout homemade biscuits and fig preserves. In an apparent attempt to appear modern, Aunt Jo had added cheese cubes around the periphery of the plates. I'd popped one in my mouth just a moment earlier; it tasted suspiciously like Velveeta.

I knew without looking that Steve was using the same yellow china with the flower pattern that my aunt had owned ever since my earliest memories and the jam knife was real silver and needed polishing, as it probably had for the past hundred years. I knew eventually he would find the anomaly between the treasured if worn antiques and the tiny house Aunt Jo lived in.

Somewhere in the back of my mind, it registered that the refrigerator door was opening and closing and Aunt Jo was whistling the tune from The Andy Griffith Show. And I knew without thinking that she would appear in the doorway with a silver tray desperately in need of polishing, upon which two glasses would sit on either side of a glass pitcher filled with freshly squeezed orange juice.

Even with all this activity around me, I felt oddly detached from it all. In the palm of my hand was the only item we'd found in the safe deposit box: my mother's cell phone. Fortunately, it used the same type of battery as my own, so I'd made the swap almost immediately. I'd already begun to study the contents.

Now I knew how my mother had been able to take all the pictures at the warehouse store: they'd been snapped with the cell phone, possibly while she appeared to be carrying on a conversation, and while no one was the wiser, the thumbnails of the prints I'd seen at the Academy were being stored neatly in the phone. From all appearances, my mother had just begun using it one month before her death.

"Find anything interesting?" Steve asked between bites of biscuit.

"Lots," I muttered. When I glanced up, I caught a thinly veiled look of disappointment in his eyes. Obviously, he was expecting a response with more meat in it.

"This shows a bit of travel," I said.

"Oh?"

"It appears that right before my mother died, she traveled to two places—Chesterfield, Virginia and Lumberton, North Carolina."

"Business or pleasure?"

I shrugged. "Wish I knew." I hesitated. "I don't think it was either one."

"What do you mean? What else is there?"

"The thing is, we don't have family in either state. And as far as I know, Mom didn't have any friends there, either…" I could feel my voice fading. I hated to appear uncertain but here I was, my voice wavering just above a whisper. I pulled my legs off the edge of the chair and sat up straight.

"Then it would have been business," Steve said.

"Aunt Jo said Mom had attended a tobacco grower's association meeting in Richmond shortly before she died. Chesterfield is the county bordering on Richmond. Other than that, there was no need to travel anywhere. They ran their business right here." I took a deep breath. My words began tumbling out. "My parents rarely traveled, hardly ever went on a vacation, rarely even visited relatives or friends who were more than an hour's drive away. They were homebodies in every sense of the word."

"So what were they doing?"

"What was *she* doing?" I corrected. "I don't know if Dad was with her." I thumbed through the calendar. My stomach growled and I peeked across the room at Steve. He didn't appear to have heard it. And from the looks of things, he'd never had homemade biscuits and preserves before and was trying to catch up.

"She went to one of those wholesale stores," I said, holding up the phone so he could see for himself.

Steve stopped eating long enough to study the pictures. "Smuggling," he said at long last, the word hanging in the air like a thick fog.

"Yes. We've had this conversation before," I said, trying not to sound too flippant.

I stared at the picture on the tiny screen. The dark skin and narrowed eyes seemed to morph into the face of the female terrorist in *The Washington Post*, and then just as quickly turned into the face of the man I'd seen in the food court. A myriad of emotions passed through me: how happy Margaret and I were that day, how quickly things changed, how she'd come out of her coma, and how my head ached.

"So," I said, "assuming this is a trail, where do we begin? On the last day she used this, or sometime before?"

Steve stopped chewing and glared at me. "You must have forgotten you're overdue at the hospital."

"Are you a Yankee?"

I hadn't noticed that Aunt Jo had appeared in the doorway and from the look on Steve's face, he hadn't noticed, either.

"Excuse me?" he asked.

Aunt Jo strolled into the room with a tray, which she set on the coffee table. She stood tall and placed her hands on her hips. "I want to know if my niece is dating a Yankee."

I could see Steve's eyes darting a bit. I thought of rescuing him but I have to admit, I was having too much fun watching him squirm. It was clear that Aunt Jo was going to stand firm until she received a satisfactory answer.

Finally, both of us spoke at the same time.

"Aunt Jo, we're not dating—" I began.

"No, ma'am, I'm not a Yankee," Steve said.

"Where are your people from, young man?"

"Aunt Jo—" I said, trying hard not to laugh.

"Texas."

"They are?" I looked at Steve in surprise. Somehow, I wouldn't have suspected that. But now I could kind of picture him on a horse. Yes, he could be cowboy material. Maybe even wear a hat. Maybe not.

"What are your intentions with my niece?"

"That's enough," I said, rising.

"Are you married?"

"No, ma'am."

"Ever been married?"

"No, ma'am."

"No?" I said, turning to Steve.

"What's wrong with you then?" Aunt Jo demanded.

"That is *really* enough," I said.

"Ma'am?"

"You're a fine lookin' young man, Confederate stock, good job even if it is with the government, and you don't have a wife? Why not?"

Steve turned ten shades of red.

"That is *really enough*," I said, pulling Aunt Jo away from Steve.

She shook her head and muttered something under her breath as she retreated to the kitchen. I steeled myself for round two.

"I'm sorry," I whispered to Steve. "She doesn't get out much."

He half-nodded and didn't respond. I noticed it took some time for the color in his face to return to normal.

I skimmed through Mom's activities on the cell phone calendar. I could feel Steve coming to his feet. A moment later a hand was thrust toward me.

"Let me see it," he said.

I pulled away. "No."

"Don't act silly—"

I abruptly stood up. "We're late to the hospital," I said. "And I need some rest. Are you going to take me, or do I have to call a cab?"

Aunt Jo's voice floated out from the kitchen. "Why are you going off to some hospital when I can take better care of you here?"

Steve stepped to the door. "I'm sorry, ma'am, it's just something she has to do."

"Well, I don't see no broken bones," Aunt Jo said. "And she's not unconscious. It's a waste of time and money, if you ask me."

I slid past Steve and gave her a quick hug. "Don't worry, Aunt Jo, I won't be there for long. I promise."

He grabbed a biscuit and headed for the front door. We'd almost made it through when he stopped, stepped back inside, and grabbed another one. Then he ushered me through amid Aunt Jo's good-byes, and as he waved and I blew her a kiss, I slid the phone deep into my pants pocket.

29

The clock on the hospital room wall ticked past two o'clock in the afternoon. I barely noticed the time passing, so intent was I in rummaging through my mother's calendar in her cell phone, mulling over her travels in the days before her death. Less than a week before that fateful day, she checked into The Triple R, a resort or motel a few miles outside Lumberton, North Carolina. While she was there, she apparently made several visits in and around town. I had no idea what the purpose of her trip was, but I felt sure it had nothing to do with the family farm, and it wasn't a vacation.

And I had to go there.

I swallowed hard, my eyes shifting toward the door. Outside my hospital room was Officer Pearce Buchanon from the Metropolitan Nashville Police Department, who was assigned to protect me. He'd arrived soon after I was checked in. He seemed nice enough as we made small talk about his two small children and their new puppy, and I couldn't help but wish they'd picked someone without a family. Someone who wouldn't be sorely missed if things went sour.

Steve stayed only a short while before announcing that he was going back to the house to retrieve the iced tea glasses and the pitcher. He would then be en route to the local field office to get it submitted for testing.

Mom's phone service had been disconnected after her death, so I pulled out my own cell phone and logged onto the Internet. Lumberton was 572 miles from where I now sat huddled under a hospital sheet, roughly nine hours of drive time one-way. That would never work. I needed to get there promptly, check things out, and get back right away.

I ran a quick Internet search on North Carolina airports. Several airlines actually ran non-stop flights to Charlotte, which was about a three-hour drive from Lumberton, but that would have to do. The next flight was at four thirty.

I glimpsed at my watch. That was barely two hours from now. Assuming I could make it past Officer Buchanon, the airport was about twenty minutes away. That is, if I was lucky enough to grab a cab without too much difficulty.

I pushed the sheet off me and made my way to the window. Below was a parking lot which appeared to be for employees, judging from the proliferation of white shirts coming and going. I absent-mindedly watched a taxi meander through the streets in the distance.

I grabbed my jogging suit and quickly dressed.

The taxi had made slow progress. I watched it come to a stop some distance from the hospital, in a line of traffic that seemed to appear from nowhere.

I felt my breath catch in my throat. *A taxi.*

In the blink of an eye, I'd gauged the distance between the building and the vehicle.

My cell phone remained in my hand, still logged onto the Internet, the cursor blinking at me as if to say, *what now?*

I swallowed hard, and clicked into Reservations.

30

It was after ten o'clock when I pulled into the darkened parking lot of The Triple R.

I'd flown from Nashville to Charlotte, rented a car, and driven roughly ninety miles toward Lumberton, located less than twenty miles north of the North Carolina-South Carolina border.

The resort was approximately twenty miles west of town, off Interstate 74. Once off the main road, I took increasingly more rural roadways that led me deeper into the blackness of night.

The sky was dark and foreboding, a mere sliver of a moon appearing infrequently through thickening clouds. I drove past thickets of pine trees, their evergreen needles resembling craggy fingers pointing downward in the glare of my headlights; then the pines gave way to cedars with contorted trunks that billowed out as they reached the ground. The flatlands were replaced with spongy wetlands marked by floating sedge, the cedars continuing to rise out of the blackened waters, their branches naked against the sky.

I crossed a number of tiny bridges, some proclaiming the names of swamps over which I passed, until I located a rusted sign hanging by one corner, swaying in a haunting wind. I tried to peer down the dirt road, but it curved and became narrower, effectively hiding The Triple R from view. As I turned onto the dirt road, the headlights shone through several holes in the sign that made it appear as though it had been used for target practice.

The road became barely more than two ruts that ran parallel through a series of swamps and marshes. At the end was a dilapidated, darkened set of wooden buildings arranged in the shape of an inverted "V" overlooking murky waters. The two sides were one story while the center of the "V" was two stories. And in the middle was a decaying sign announcing *The Robeson Repose and Resort*, beneath which read *The Triple R Hunt Club*.

A movement caught my eye and I looked upwards to dozens of bats circling overhead. Obviously the building was deserted; a giant tree lay across one section of the roof, partially caving in a window.

As I drove slowly through what was once a parking lot, the headlights caught snippets of foxfire along the borders of the swamp, their luminescence the only color in a darkening pit.

I couldn't imagine what my mother could have been doing here.

I reached the edge of the marsh. I put the car in reverse and had started to turn around when I glimpsed a light in my peripheral vision. I jerked to the left as I heard a car door slam.

A figure stood beside a car about 50 feet from where I sat. I could only see the silhouette of the vehicle and a lone figure that stood completely still beside it. I was being watched.

My first impulse was to floor it and get out of here. In my mind's eye, I imagined careening back down the rutted road, sliding out of control and plummeting into the swamps, which would probably swallow me up.

And no one knew where I was.

The figure moved toward me.

I sat there with the car idling, the headlights casting a yellowish glow around the front of the car, my foot pressing the brake so hard my leg began to ache.

The figure slowly approached. I glanced about but didn't see anyone else.

As the figure grew closer, the headlights caught the profile. I gasped as I saw a shock of auburn hair cascading down the shoulders onto a crisp navy trench coat. It was a woman.

I rolled down my window. "Hello!" I managed to call out.

She cocked her head as she neared. "Can I help you?" she said in an incredulous voice.

"I'm afraid I'm lost," I answered sheepishly. "I was looking for The Triple R—"

"This is it," she answered in that same disbelieving voice, "or *was* it." Funny, she didn't seem to fit here. Her speech was clipped, as though she was from a northern state; her coat was tailored and smart-looking. Her hands were shoved deep into thin coat pockets as she drew closer, her eyes wide and searching. I could see her glancing to the seat beside me and trying to peer into the back seat.

"There must be some mistake," I said. "You see, my parents stayed there on their anniversary and they just raved about how wonderful it was—"

"They didn't stay here."

She was so close to me now that I could smell her lavender-scented perfume. She appeared to be around my age, which made me a bit more courageous than I should have been. And a whole lot more curious.

"So," I said, "do you have any vacancies tonight?"

She stopped peering into the car and gaped at me. "You'd be better off finding a hotel room in town."

I slipped the car into park. "Are you sure?" I said in my best naïve-blond look. "I'm not from around here, and I'm *so* tired."

She didn't seem to be buying it. "Trust me, you'd get more rest someplace else." She removed her hand from her pocket and waved it. Her nails were neatly manicured, her hands petite. "Just follow this road until it ends. Turn right, and follow that road until it ends. Turn right again, and you'll see a sign—"

"Please," I begged. "Just let me get a few hours' sleep here tonight."

She stared at me with the kind of look I'd expect to get if I was a kook. Come to think of it, maybe I was.

"This place isn't for the faint of heart," she said after a pause.

I wanted to ask her how she came to be here, but I didn't. I only assumed she worked here, but she didn't make any effort to correct me. I also knew that I'd rather sleep in the car than this God-forsaken place, but I was trying desperately to keep her engaged in conversation long enough to get some idea what was going on.

She exhaled audibly as though exasperated. "Park over there."

I swallowed and followed her instruction, pulling into the deep shadows between the center structure and one side. As I shut the car off, I turned to see her waiting patiently for me at the edge of the building, her figure now just a ghostly outline.

I climbed out and slammed the door shut. The sound echoed in the darkness. Somewhere in the distance I heard the hoot of an owl.

As I approached her, she said, "Better get your suitcase."

I nodded, wondering if this was some sort of test as I returned to the car. Leaving my laptop case in the trunk, I grabbed my gym bag.

I followed her around the building to a door in back. As she eased it open, I almost gasped.

The room was swathed in a blue light emanating from a television set against one wall and a computer screen against the opposite wall. There were two desks and a half a dozen chairs. There wasn't an empty spot on either desk; they were both piled high with computer printouts. In fact, there were printouts in all but two of the chairs, and in stacks around the walls.

I closed the door. There were three deadbolts installed on the door.

She was at one of the desks, rummaging through the top drawer.

Now that we had more light, I could study her profile. She was Scottish or Irish, no doubt about it. Her hair was a cascade of copper curls that reached almost midway down her back. I caught a glimpse of her eyes; they were light, either blue or green—it was impossible to tell in this light— beneath thick lashes.

The room was musty-smelling and dank; mold was growing along one wall. As she placed items from the drawer onto the desk, small clouds of dust rose into the air. I wondered when anyone last stayed at this so-called resort, and for the umpteenth time, I contemplated what attraction it had held for my mother.

Finally, the young woman retrieved a key on a large plastic ring and held it out to me.

"Room 6," she said curtly. "It's at the far end of the building, on the corner."

I nodded and made my way to the door. Once I'd opened it, I hesitated. I peered into the pitch blackness, trying to focus. I couldn't even see the end of the building.

I debated whether I would be successful in engaging in a bit of chit-chat with her. My curiosity was growing by the second.

"You're sure you want to stay here?" she asked. It surprised me how close she was. She'd walked up behind me with the softness of a cat.

I turned. Her brows were knit together and if I didn't know better, I'd say she looked genuinely concerned.

"You'd be much better off in town," she said in a soft voice.

"I won't be here long," I said, my voice sounding stronger than I felt. "I just need a place to lay my head for a couple of hours. Besides, you're here, right? How dangerous could it be?"

Her head jerked and a veil seemed to cover her face, making her expression perfectly immobile. So much for chit-chat.

I stepped through the door and abruptly stopped.

"What is it?" she hissed. Her hand jerked instantly to her coat and disappeared in the depths of the pocket. For the first time, I noticed an outline that looked like a gun barrel. No wonder she'd had her hands in her pockets as she'd approached me.

"Nothing," I said. "I just remembered—I haven't paid you."

I looked her directly in the eyes, trying to keep an eye on her pocket with my peripheral vision.

"Pay when you leave," she said. She pushed past me into the night. "Just go to the end of this building. Your room is the last one. Your car will be safe where you parked it."

I took a couple of steps before half-turning. She was peering into the darkness, away from me, toward the road I'd driven in on. Her head was cocked as if she were listening.

"You'd do well to lock your door," she called after me, "and stay inside until morning. There's no phone in the room, and I'll be leaving shortly. There won't be anyone around if you need help."

Before I could answer, she disappeared inside the building. In the stillness of the night, I heard the bolts locking her inside.

Every instinct told me to leave now, while I still could. To just march right back to the rental car, get in, and get out of here.

My grip tightened on the gym bag. I heard the sound of an animal howling in the distance, and I wondered if there were wolves in this part of the country. I involuntarily shivered.

Then I stepped out smartly, determined to get to my room as fast as my feet would carry me.

31

A stale, pungent odor reached my nostrils even before the door was closed. As I groped in the darkness for the light switch, I heard the scampering of tiny feet across the floor behind me. There was panic in the sound, as if they'd been startled by this human invader. I didn't know who was more unnerved—the mice or me.

As I groped for the light switch, something large, hairy and thick crawled across the back of my hand. I stifled a scream as I shook it off me, instinctively brushing down the front of my clothes lest it land somewhere else on my body. I reluctantly returned to the wall, found the switch, and flipped it.

A single bulb flickered on overhead, bringing wraithlike objects into shadowy view. There was a floor lamp turned a mottled moss green with mold, its shade infested with spiders that were now scurrying out of the light. Beside it was a three quarter bed under a layer of dust so thick that it left the bedspread pattern under it virtually indistinguishable. On the opposite side of the tiny room was a leather chair that may once have been black but was now the dappled brown of a pecan shell.

The carpet had been eaten through in several places, and from the looks of the droppings, I knew the sound of scampering feet I'd heard were rats, not mice.

I heard a car door slam and an engine start. I stepped to the window and pulled back the heavy, dank curtain. A green and brown lizard darted out from behind the material and stopped, its body clinging to the wall as if its toes were made of adhesive.

The sound of tires crunching over hard ground refocused my attention on the parking lot. The young woman was leaving, her car making the same grinding noise as she drove over the crumbling ground as one would make on a gravel drive.

My first instinct was to hurl open the door and race after her, begging her to wait so I could follow her out of this hellhole. But just as quickly as the thought raced through my brain, the taillights disappeared around the bend.

There was no doubt now that I was the only guest. Had it not been for the presence of the woman here, I would have concluded this place had long ago been abandoned.

The office, though, intrigued me. To have a functioning computer, working electricity and stacks of printouts in a place like this was just too juicy an opportunity to pass up. I wondered if she'd locked each of the deadbolts, and how difficult it would be to break in.

This room held no secrets of what my mother had been doing here. The answer was in that office. I was sure of it.

I'd started through the room when I heard the sound of tires crunching again. She couldn't be back this quickly. She would have had barely enough time to get down the drive to the main road.

I crossed the room to the window, flipped off the light and gently parted the curtain.

A white van was turning around in the parking lot in front of my window.

There appeared to be just one person inside. He rolled down his window and flicked a cigarette onto the ground and then lit another. Then he pointed the van toward the road. I heard the van shift into park.

He sat there calmly, as if waiting, the headlights casting an ethereal light into the swamps.

I thought of my car parked in the shadows. Could the woman have directed me to park it there precisely for this reason?

A few minutes passed. I spotted two beams of light rounding the bend, like tentacles reaching through the darkness.

In the cold damp air, my breath was beginning to fog the window. I stepped to the side to direct my breathing away from the glass, while still keeping a watchful eye on the approaching vehicle.

It was a black limousine. There was no license plate. It stopped a few yards from the van. Both vehicles kept their lights on.

After a moment, two men emerged from the car. They were spotlighted in the van's headlights. One wore a dark leather jacket above black pants. The other wore a heavier coat that reached almost to his knees; he brushed his long, dark hair away from his face. For a split second, I thought I recognized him.

My heart was pounding in my temples now, my breath coming fast and shallow. If they spotted me, there would be no escape. The woman's words came back to me now, both haunting and taunting me: *stay in your room until morning. There won't be anyone around if you need help.*

The man in the white van was approaching the two others, warily meeting in the middle where four headlights shone directly upon them. He gestured as though he was punctuating his speech, but they were too far away for me to hear even a murmur.

He reached in his pocket and handed one of the men something small, appearing at this distance to be no larger than a credit card. The man with the dark hair rubbed his fingers and thumb together as if requesting money.

Now the voices were getting louder. There was no mistaking the tension in the exchange.

I was afraid to continue standing there with the curtain agape, but terrified to close it lest the movement attract their attention. So I stood there, transfixed, my feet glued to the floor, no longer hearing the scurrying behind me or feeling the dampness on my neck.

Then the man with the dark hair and long jacket reached into his pocket and pulled out a gun, firing three shots point-blank into the other man's body. He crumpled to the ground in a widening pool of blood.

The two men left quickly but without the panic or sense of urgency one would expect after having killed a man. I waited until they were out of sight before cracking open the door.

32

I crouched next to the body, my fingers shaking as much from the tension as the cold night air. It was impossible not to stare into his unseeing eyes. They were spaced wide apart, the iris a deep, rich brown. His skin was blanched though I suspect it had once been swarthy; it appeared leathery and pockmarked, like someone who'd spent years toiling out of doors. His mouth was open, revealing yellowed, uneven teeth.

He was dead.

I patted his thin jean jacket and checked the pockets. Credit cards? I wondered as I removed my hand.

I leaned back on my haunches and stared at the contents of the pocket. It was filled with drivers' licenses. They were all of dark skinned people, all fairly similar in height, weight, skin, eye, and hair color. And they all appeared to be Spanish—Gomez, Campos, Rivera, Perez, Balderas, Fernandes, Estrada...

Estrada. My mother's maiden name.

I tossed the cards into my bag, my mind reeling. I searched his other pockets, and found about five hundred dollars in cash surrounded by a rubber band. I returned it to his pocket. He did not carry a wallet.

I realized I was crouched in front of the headlights and his van was still running. I shielded my eyes from the glare as I approached it. The driver's side door was still open. I leaned inside.

The back of the van was separated from the front seat, like a work truck carrying supplies. I checked the glove compartment and the sun visors but found nothing else— not even a vehicle registration.

I returned to my room, grabbed my bag and hurried to the rental car. I popped the trunk and tossed my bag inside. Then I rummaged through the trunk but the only things there were a spare tire and tire changing equipment. I grabbed the lug wrench. It would have to do.

I approached the door with more than a little trepidation… three deadbolts. They didn't make this easy for me. I stood on the outside and stared at the deadbolt locks. I had to assume the mysterious woman had keys to the deadbolts, and they were all locked.

That meant I had to try the other side of the door.

I tried to slip the flat edge of the lug wrench between the door and the jam near the hinges, but the fit was too tight. The rest of this place was falling apart, but the only room I needed to get into was built like a prison.

Wait a minute. I stepped back and surveyed the building. The end of the building farthest from the parking lot could not have been more than five feet away. I tried to remember what the office looked like inside—the mounds of paper, the television, computer, desks… Had there been any windows?

I rounded the corner.

This side, like the others, was covered in wood siding, the boards old and bent, some hanging loose from the nails. But there, not four feet away, was a window; it was small, perhaps no more than three feet tall by two feet wide—but large enough for me to crawl through.

I went to work with the lug wrench, yanking the flimsy screen off and tossing it in a bank of weeds behind me. Then I examined the window, took a couple of steps back, and swung the wrench like a baseball bat.

The wrench smashed through the thin glass, shattering it into a hundred pieces.

Once the glass stopped flying, I used the wrench against the sill to break off the remaining shards, then brushed them away with my jacket sleeve.

I grabbed the sill with both my hands and catapulted myself onto the ledge. A moment later, I was dropping down on the other side.

I was in.

33

I groped my way along an inside wall. I bumped into an object perhaps four feet tall; when I felt my way around it, I realized it was a stack of computer printouts. I tried to remember the way the room was laid out—where the light switch had been, the desks, the television, and the computer. I finally reached the door, my fingers searching for the light switch which should have been inches from the doorframe.

The single bulb overhead cast a yellowed glow over the area. There were two doors in the office on the opposite wall from the door leading outside. From the single open window came a blast of frigid night air that rustled the pages of the printouts and blew decades of dust about the room. I narrowed my eyes in an effort to protect them from the assaulting particles as I surveyed my surroundings. I didn't know what I was hunting for, so I didn't know where I would find it—or if I would recognize it once I did find it.

I tried to think like my mother as I rummaged through desk drawers. What would she have been searching for? I glanced through yellowed pieces of paper with faded penciled notes, rifled through a prehistoric monstrosity resembling a Rolodex, and groped my way through ancient hanging folders filled with decaying maintenance records, accounting, and time sheets. My fingers stopped and hung tentatively over the accounting files before I yanked them out and slung them onto the desk. That would be the one thing my mother would have honed in on, and perhaps the reason she'd been here.

I went through the other desk, past personnel records and purchasing receipts. I was shivering from the cold, the adrenaline that caused my blood to heat now waning, the open window allowing the moist, clammy air to sink right through my bones. The pages atop the computer printouts opened and swayed as though they were alive.

The bulb overhead flickered, causing the shadows to jump and come alive. I held my breath, hoping I wouldn't lose electrical power. Though I had to admit it was downright curious how the office could have live electricity, considering the condition of everything else around here.

I was wasting time. I knew the man in the parking lot would not be a threat, unless his spirit decided to pay me a call. I shuddered involuntarily. That was the last thing I needed to think about in a place like this.

No, it was the people still alive I needed to be concerned about. Would the two men who murdered him return? I didn't think so; they didn't seem disturbed at all about leaving his body lying in the middle of the parking lot. And how did the woman with the long auburn hair fit into all of this? Who was she?

I heard fluttering directly above me. I studied the ceiling, remembering there was another floor above this one. As the sound built to a crescendo, I realized there were bats just above my head. Like mice with wings, they would need the smallest of openings to penetrate this room and surround me.

I wiped the perspiration from my brow. It was crazy for me to feel so hot. I didn't hear any furnace, and I seriously doubted this establishment had a functional one.

The bulb overhead began to take on a life of its own. It morphed from a fading light fixture to a sunshine-yellow beacon staring at me, burning mercilessly into my eyes.

It was just like the run, right before I passed out.

I sat down shakily, causing a puff of thick dust to rise into the air, choking the oxygen. I couldn't pass out now. If I were laying here unconscious and they returned, God only knew what would happen to me. The refrain *no one knows where I am* kept beating through my skull like a conga drum.

The mounds of computer printouts appeared daunting—each one at least four feet high and piled in every corner of the room. Then my eyes fell on a wide dot matrix printer, so large it appeared to be something out of the 1970's. A stream of computer paper, brown-edged with age, was loaded into it as if waiting for the command to print. I stood and in two full steps I was there, peering over it. A solid coat of dust covered most of the printer, but the keys were clear. Of course.

I whirled around. The computer.

I held my breath and turned it on.

The computer groaned and whirred to life. Above me, the sound of batwings intensified, and I wondered if they heard the noise and if it somehow irritated them. It took forever to boot.

I pulled up a chair and went to work.

But again, it was like the information inside the desk drawers: I didn't know what I was searching for, so I didn't know if I'd found it. I located an accounting system filled with receipts for nights' lodgings, payroll, expenses... There had even been a restaurant here at one time, and a meeting room that accommodated ninety people. I saw the buildings again in my mind's eye; had the restaurant and meeting room been destroyed, or was there yet another building I hadn't seen in the darkness?

I scoured the files for anything that might be helpful. A drop of perspiration landed on the keyboard. As I reached my hand to my forehead, I heard the sound of a car door closing. Panicked, I raced to the door and unbolted it. Then I cracked it just enough to see my rental car, still sitting in the shadows where I'd left it.

I heard the crunch of tires, and I quickly turned off the office light and raced outside, staying to the shadows so I wouldn't be spotted. I was just in time to see the taillights of the van as it rounded the first bend.

I stood there, peering into the darkness, trying to see whether the body was still there. He was dead; I'd checked him myself. He couldn't have arisen, returned to his van, and taken off. It wasn't possible.

An owl hooted just beyond the building, startling me. My nerves were on edge, the adrenaline beginning to course through my veins again. I rushed back to the office, slammed the door shut, and bolted it before I remembered the unobstructed window just a few feet away.

I flipped the light on and raced to the desk, nervously rummaging through the drawers, spilling the contents onto the floor until I located a screwdriver. I was at the computer in a heartbeat. I slammed the monitor to the floor, and popped open the system unit before I thought to shut off the computer. A mound of dust flew from the back of the unit, and I coughed and pushed through the whirlwind.

I had the computer apart in two minutes flat, the hard drive detached and in the palm of my hand. This little baby was coming with me.

And then the doorknob turned.

34

I t was nearly imperceptible at first. The door knob turned so slowly in one direction that I almost thought I'd imagined it. But as I watched in rising horror, it rotated 180 degrees twice more. Whoever was standing on the opposite side of the door then pushed against it.

As dilapidated as this place was, I knew the door wouldn't hold anyone at bay for long, even if it did have three deadbolts on it. I felt the blood drain from my face and my fingertips went numb. The single, dim bulb overhead now felt like a headlight pointed in my direction.

Somehow I managed to come out of my trance long enough to slide the hard drive inside my sweatshirt. It was blazing hot against my skin.

My mind raced. Directly outside was my rental car. They couldn't have reached the door without seeing it. And as long as they remained there, they were cutting off my best means of escape. Without that car, I would be forced deeper into the building, wherever that led—or into the swamps on foot.

I needed a diversion. The sound of hundreds of bat wings fluttering simultaneously overhead reached my ears like natives beating out a message on drums.

I quickly scanned my surroundings. There were two doors opposite me, and I had no idea where they led. They could be closets for all I knew. My eyes came to rest on a double light switch beside one of the doors. If I guessed correctly, it meant one of them worked the light over my head and the other operated a light in a hallway or stairwell.

I no longer heard the doorknob rattling, which was even more nerve wracking, as I no longer knew the location of the person lurking outside.

My other means of escape was through the window; although it was around the building corner, it was within a few feet of the door. I could fall right out of the window into their arms.

In a fraction of a second, I'd crossed the room and flipped both light switches, plunging my room back into darkness. At the same time, the fluttering increased as if hundreds more bats were being added to the mix. I held my breath and threw open the door.

In an instant, a hundred bats surrounded me like flying rodents. Their wings were small and looked more like webbed hands than feathered bird wings. They had pointed faces, not at all like that of a bird's beak, but more like the nose of a rat. They looked like some prehistoric monstrosity, and they kept coming at me in the hundreds.

I stifled a scream and ducked my head, rushing up the ramshackle stairs. They moved out of my way as if anticipating my movements, but I felt several near my head, causing me to instinctively brush my hair with my fingers lest they become captured in the strands.

Above me, a gaping hole opened to the night sky. I caught the light of the moon overhead, its mere sliver serving me like a beacon from a lighthouse. I tried to remain focused on it, letting it guide me upwards past the onslaught of winged creatures, though I had no idea where I would end up once I reached the top.

As I raced upward, my right foot landed on a decaying step, the rotting wood collapsing under my weight and threatening to suck me downward. I grabbed onto the stair rail, the coarse wood splintering beneath my palm. Frantically, I grasped at the rail while heaving my right foot ever higher, trying to reach the top before the entire staircase buckled beneath me.

I threw myself onto the floor at the top of the stairs as they imploded in a thundering heap, sending a cloud of debris and dust upward into the night sky.

So much for the quiet escape technique.

But as the cloud dissipated and I surveyed the cavernous opening below me, I realized no one would be able to follow me.

I sat on what I hoped was a relatively safe section of flooring and assessed my situation. Great. So I was now stranded on the top floor of a building that should have been condemned and bulldozed, staring through a twenty foot gap in the roof, and surrounded by flying rats. Add to that, the fact that my right foot had been twisted and was now throbbing in pain, and I was pretty sure that my right palm had about a thousand splinters in it. But other than that, Mrs. Lincoln, the play was just peachy keen.

I stared upwards at shifting and roiling gray clouds that looked like thick cabbage soup. I rose and tentatively crossed the building; the boards, weather worn and slippery, creaking and moaning under my feet.

I stopped at a window encrusted with grime, and peered through a broken section to the ground below. Directly behind my rental car was a dark, late model, four-door sedan, possibly a Crown Victoria. I studied its location in proximity to my car, realizing with a sinking heart that it was blocking me from leaving.

As I watched below, a shadow appeared close to the building, inching its way toward the back of the structure.

From the size and shape, it had to be a man, but whether it was one of the two men I'd seen earlier, I couldn't tell. He certainly was driving a different vehicle now.

He paused at the corner for what seemed an eternity before spinning around it, the arm extended and the torso bent forward. He had a gun. And he was searching for me, the gun extended, no doubt ready to fire.

I moved to a hole in the crumbling wall and watched him inch his way along the back.

He found the window. The shadow was less clear now, and then it disappeared. He was inside.

Now was my chance. While he was calculating his next move, I would be making mine.

I rushed to the opposite side of the building and raised a window in a rotting wood frame. I climbed onto the sill. I'd just started to take a deep breath and prepare myself for the two-story jump when the wood gave way. I teetered backward, my arms flailing wildly inside the room. Then the wall collapsed under me. I felt my legs and then my torso sliding outward, into the abyss below.

I grasped frantically for anything that could break my fall. Just as I was preparing to kiss the pavement, my hand grabbed onto a piece of wood—the window sash. I hung there momentarily, debating whether it would hold long enough for me to pull myself back inside. Then with a sickening crack, it broke off in my hands, plunging me to the ground below.

My right foot hit the pavement first, my already injured ankle twisting further, followed quickly by both my knees. The impact knocked the wind out of me, and I threw my hands in front of me to belatedly soften my fall.

Instinctively, I exhaled but there was no air left inside me; my chest felt as though it was folding inward on itself. When my breath finally returned, I found myself gasping for it, involuntarily groaning as I wondered if I'd broken any bones.

I was contemplating crawling into the shadows where I could nurse my wounds for as long as possible when I heard a cracking sound as though someone had just stepped on a twig or branch and broken it.

I pushed myself against the wall and fumbled for a piece of the nail-impregnated window sill. It was in my hand in an instant, and I was poised and ready, both splinter-and-gravel-infested palms wrapped around it.

"Drop it!" the sound came from the darkness. My chest heaved even while I fought to calm myself.

I turned in the direction of the voice but saw only the shadows of ancient cypress bending in the night breeze, playing tricks on me as if an army of shadows were just beyond my reach, ready to assail me.

"Drop it, NOW!" came the voice again.

"You'll have to kill me first!" I shouted in what I hoped was my best imitation of Bonnie Parker.

There was a brief silence. I could hear the person moving, but I still could not see him.

"Sheila?"

The voice had changed now; it sounded incredulous.

"Steve?!"

35

I sat in the passenger seat of Steve's rental car in the middle of the parking lot. The high beams were focused on a puddle of blood that was soaking into the ground. At least now he couldn't deny my story, even though I was an eyewitness to a cold-blooded murder with no corpse. I took advantage of the time to use the overhead light to illuminate my palm while I dug out splinters.

While Steve appeared to be pondering my account of the night's events, I was wondering if there was an all-night drug store nearby. All I needed was some Epsom salts and warm water to get out the rest of these pesky things.

"So what were you doing here to begin with?" Steve asked after a long moment of silence. "This doesn't look like a hospital room to me."

I was glad to have my palm to attend to so I didn't have to look in his eyes. I'd done that already and regretted it pretty quickly. "I'm following my mother's footsteps, where she was in the days before she died."

I could see him nod out of the corner of my eye, but he didn't respond. I stole a sideways glance at him; he appeared to be biting the inside of his cheek.

"How did you find me?" I asked.

"I knew you had something up your sleeve when we left your aunt's house," he said. "So I told the cop at your door to give you a bit of room, and let me know if you left."

"That was smart thinking," I blurted out.

"Yeah. Well, it didn't take long, did it?" When I didn't answer, he continued, "I didn't think it would. So I sat in the parking lot, saw you get into the cab, and followed you to the airport."

"Why didn't you stop me there?"

"Because I was tailing you. If you were a good agent, you'd have seen me."

"So why did it take you so long to show up here?" I asked.

"Your flight was full. I had to wait for the next one out."

"If you were a good agent, you'd have been faster," I said.

"And if you were a good agent, you'd have kept your butt in the hospital."

There was a lengthy moment of silence. I thought of the three men standing right here, and how cold and calculating the murder was. I was glad Steve hadn't come barreling down the road at that moment. I shuddered instinctively, realizing for the first time how close I might have come to accidentally leading Steve right into an ambush.

"So," I continued, "You knew what airport I'd flown into, but how did you find me at this place? I can't believe it's in a tourist guide."

"That was trickier," he said. I thought I detected a wry smile. "When you rented your car, you asked for directions to Lumberton. But I didn't know exactly where you'd gone. So I had you traced through the GPS locator in your cell phone. And even then, it was tough finding a road back here."

I nodded and filed this tidbit of information. I never knew when it might be of use.

Steve flipped up the console between the two seats. Then he half-turned toward me, his back leaning against the driver side door. One lock of his dark brown hair fell across his forehead. "Give me one good reason why you shouldn't be kicked out of the Academy."

I swallowed. "Give me one good reason why I should be."

"I could give you ten good reasons," he said. The ire was back. "You've been just like a little ricochet lately."

"What's that supposed to mean?"

"You know what a ricochet is, don't you?"

"Of course I do," I said, "it's—"

"It's a projectile out of control," he barked. "And that's exactly what you are. You start off in one direction and then you ricochet in another direction, and just when I think I have your next movement figured out, you're rebounding out of control, all over the place."

"I'm just trying to follow my mother's—"

"I'm not prepared to lose my job over your shenanigans."

Well, that was totally unexpected. I leaned against the passenger door and tried to appear impassive. "How could you lose your job?"

"I'm responsible for you right now," he said. "Think about it: the night before you start the Academy, you're a victim of a suicide bomber. You're on TV telling the world that you'll never forget the bomber's face. Not the smartest move I've ever seen."

Before I could respond, he continued, "Then it turns out our number one witness—you, in case you're not following me—has a concussion and ends up in the hospital. So now you're on TV because you picked the very moment the media is filming to—"

"I'm your number one witness?"

"And then—oh, big surprise—the bomber is in your hospital room trying to kill you."

"But the news reports said it was a woman bomber; how did you know—?"

"But that's not enough for you. No, we arrange—at great trouble, I might add—to get you into a hospital close to your family. And I'm given the job of protecting you. But I can't even get you into a hospital room before you're almost burned alive. And now we have two more suspects who know your face. We're batting a thousand here, aren't we?"

My cheeks were burning now, and I longed to turn down the heater even though my fingers felt frozen solid.

"Oh, but I manage to reel you back in, get you checked into the hospital, assign an officer to guard your door. And the first chance you get, you give us all the slip and leave town. Now I find you hundreds of miles away at a deserted motel, and you're a witness to *another* murder?"

"It's not like I'm trying to—"

"You're a regular Calamity Jane."

His words hung in the air. I waited for him to continue his rant, but he fell silent. I couldn't tell whether he was waiting for me to respond, or if the moment I opened my mouth, he would jump back down my throat.

"I'm sorry," I said. "I didn't realize how all this must have looked."

He turned and stared out the front window.

"It's kind of like I'm working a case," I offered.

"You *are* the case."

I ignored his response and continued, "I have all these clues. And I'm just trying to put them all together. I know that my mother was onto something just days before her death. But I don't know what. And I have this feeling that she"—I swallowed—"that she was murdered."

When he turned back to look at me, his face appeared softer. "If you were abrasive or unintelligent or just plain rude, I could drop you from the Academy faster than you could say your name—with exactly the same set of facts I'm looking at right now. But the thing is, Sheila, you are FBI material. If—and this is a big IF—you can stop being a—"

"A ricochet," I interrupted.

He fell silent, and I didn't know whether to use this opening to plead my case, or just shut up. "If I'm a ricochet, it's because this case is one," I said.

"I'll let you in on a little secret," he said. "Agents don't go off on hunches by themselves. *There are rules.*" He paused and looked at me pointedly. "And if you can't follow the rules, then you can't be an agent."

"Are you asking me to give up trying to find out what happened to my parents?"

"No," he said firmly.

It was dark in the car and his face was in shadow, but I could feel his eyes focused on me.

"No?" I said hesitantly.

"I can see this means a lot to you," he said. "And I can understand that you think there's nothing more important than finding out how your parents really died."

I opened my mouth to speak, but he cut me off. "But, if you want to continue this, you're going to have to do that with my help. We're going to have to be a team. Do you know what that means?"

I nodded.

"It means *no secrets*," he continued. "It means telling me everything that you know; sharing with me everything you'd planned to do. It means not giving me the slip every chance you get. Do you understand?"

I nodded again.

"Say it."

"I understand."

"This is your last chance," he said, straightening up and leaning toward me so I could see his eyes. "You screw up one more time, and you're out of the Academy."

36

The Triple R was illuminated like the front lawn of the White House, the harsh spotlights unveiling an unpainted clapboard structure that had more shingles missing than were in place, and indeed, at least a third of the building didn't have any roof at all.

While the lights created almost a daytime atmosphere close to the building, it served to create shadows that jumped and swayed in the obscurity of the bogs, and I envisioned wetland animals moving to the safe periphery of the shadows, where they could watch us undetected.

The road's dead end that served as a parking lot was teeming with investigators and technicians. Steve had contacted the Senior Resident Agent of the field office in Fayetteville.

He'd arrived so quickly I wouldn't have thought it possible he could have driven over those circuitous roads in such a short time. His name was Derek Greville. He appeared to be in his early 40's. Judging from a neck, chest and shoulders that looked like David Banner popping out of his clothes into the Incredible Hulk, I thought it safe to say he was a serious weight trainer.

He'd listened attentively as I debriefed him. It turned out there apparently was a lot more to the swamps than meets the eye; at one time there had been quite a following who hunted deer, fox, rabbit, raccoon, squirrel, and even quail and various waterfowl. It was hard to believe, staring at the dilapidated condition of The Triple R now, that it had been a premier hunting lodge complete with taxidermist.

According to Derek, Hurricane Floyd had swept through Robeson County in September 1999. It came ashore during the wee hours of September 16, bringing with it rains that began swelling the waterways for days before its landing, damaging high winds and subsequently, devastating floods. The land on which we now stood had been completely underwater, the floods stretching almost to the ceiling of the first floor. The winds had pealed off part of the roof, allowing the winds and the rains to enter the rooms undeterred, leaving in its wake extensive destruction. Rather than rebuild, the owners had cashed out their insurance policy and had left the hunting lodge for the elements to overtake.

This meant that several years after the lodge was abandoned, my mother had traveled here. I pictured the computer equipment; they most certainly would not be operating after a flood had swept through that room. The stacks of computer printouts in the office could not have survived intact. Had they been moved here after the owners had abandoned it and hunters had gone elsewhere?

The focus now was more on my actions here and the crime I'd witnessed, so we started with my encounter with the mysterious woman and progressed to the location where I'd witnessed the murder.

It wasn't long before the room was lit up like a movie set, causing so many creatures and critters to run scurrying away from the light that I felt like an extra in a bad sci-fi movie. I described where I'd stood with the curtains barely parted, watching the scene unfold in the parking lot.

By the time we walked from the room to the center of the parking lot, a forensics team had assembled and was fanning out. I'd left my footprint in the victim's blood as I knelt beside him in the sandy soil, and our progress was slowed as the tech took photographs of the print and my shoe.

There were other footprints I hadn't noticed earlier; it appeared as if two people had dragged the corpse into the van and left their bloody prints in an area approximately four feet long. Part of me was relieved a dead man hadn't sprung to life and driven off, while another part shuddered to think of two people with shady backgrounds hauling off a body while I'd been in the office a few yards away. It also made me wonder if they'd been in the back of the van while I was checking out the front seat and visors.

I showed the agents the presumably fake drivers' licenses.

"All Latino," Derek noted wryly.

"Is that significant?" Steve asked.

"Possibly. We've had an influx of Latinos moving into North Carolina over the past decade."

"Oh?"

"Fifteen years ago, Latinos numbered around 25,000 in North Carolina. Latest statistics have them at over 600,000—and roughly two thirds of them are illegal." He shook his head. "My brother-in-law owns a construction company. Employs Americans. Makes sure every one of 'em completes the proper paperwork. But he's being put out of business by competitors who hire cheap labor—mostly illegal aliens. It's a damn shame."

I peered at one of the licenses. "So counterfeiting documentation to make it appear as though they're legal is a big business these days."

"I'd say so."

"That's just the tip of the problem," Steve said. "The Bureau's fingerprint searches are so backlogged, people are slipping through the system. And the problem is just getting worse."

We turned our attention to the tire tread marks, as the van drove directly through the blood, leaving a trail that grew fainter as it neared the road. An APB was issued on the white van, and I wished I'd had the sense to get its license plate number. I wondered if Steve was making mental notes of my inattention to detail.

Derek interrupted my train of thought. "We need to keep moving. What happened next?"

We retraced my footsteps from the lot to the office, and I led them around to the back window, where I described in detail how I'd managed to break in.

"Good thinking," Steve said curtly.

I wondered whether he was being sarcastic.

We climbed inside. I made my way to the door and turned on the light. We were immediately surrounded by hundreds of bats.

Derek was clearly unnerved.

I told them how I'd seen the doorknob turn and was just beginning to tell how I'd rushed up the stairs, thinking an axe murderer was hot on my tail, when he interrupted me.

"We can go through all this outside," he said, his face looking pale.

Before Steve or I could respond, he was at the window. I think he leapt through it in one motion.

We joined him in front of the office, where he was wiping perspiration from his brow. His hand appeared to be trembling slightly. He must have noticed my fascination, because he quickly shoved both hands into his pockets.

Between Steve and I, we filled in the gaps of my ascent upstairs, Steve's retreat back through the window and his movements around the building while following the sound of my footsteps overhead, until we finished with my leap out of the window, which I managed to make sound fearless and heroic. I noticed that Steve did not correct me.

Derek didn't seem as interested in my exploits after I checked the victim, except to ask how long I'd been inside when I heard the van leave. I told him it was under half an hour, maybe closer to fifteen minutes.

Dawn was breaking when we finished and made our way to Steve's rental car.

Derek handed his card to each of us. "I'll be in touch."

"I'm sure you will," Steve answered, reciprocating with his card.

"I don't have a card yet," I said apologetically.

"You can reach her through me," Steve said without hesitation. He opened his car door and then turned back toward Derek. "Do me a favor? Have one of these guys return Sheila's rental car? She won't be needing it."

"Sure," Derek said, motioning for a sheriff's deputy. "No problem."

"I don't know when I've been this tired," I said as I tossed my bag and laptop into the back seat of Steve's car.

He didn't appear to have heard me. He started up the engine as I climbed in beside him.

I didn't know where we were headed or when I'd get some sleep, but somehow I knew everything would be alright. I leaned back in the seat, wrapping my arms around me, the computer's hard drive now cold against my skin.

37

We checked into the only vacancy the hotel had left, which wasn't half bad. It was a two-room suite; Steve decided to sleep on the sofa and give me the bedroom. I don't think his offer was meant to be taken as chivalry, but as a way to prevent me from sneaking out without him.

And he was probably right, though I was less inclined to give him the slip now. For one thing, as my senses returned, I realized I really did not want to be kicked out of the Academy. I'd come too far and had too much to lose. I wanted to know what happened to my parents, and I wanted to shake these terrorists that appeared to be everywhere, but I needed to do it in such a way that I regained his trust.

I slept until late morning. Then I reluctantly climbed out of bed and pulled some fresh clothes out of my bag. I combed my hair with my fingers, and pulled my sweatshirt down to a more modest length. I opened the door slowly.

I didn't hear anyone, so I assumed Steve was still asleep. I headed for the bathroom.

Moments later, my hair was dry and I was dressed in fresh clothes. I opened the bathroom door and stepped into the hallway.

I heard Steve's voice from the sitting room; from the one-sided conversation, I deduced that he was on the phone.

"Just trust me on this," he was saying. "I don't want to give up on her just yet. Give me 48 hours, and let's see what shakes out."

I was caught between the honorable thing to do, which was to back down the hall and disappear into the bedroom until such time as he was finished with his call, or continue to stand there, my heart in my throat, and listen to a debate over my future. As I stood there in limbo, I realized the suite had fallen silent. I glanced up to see Steve peering at me.

I half-waved, and then slunk back down the hall to the bedroom.

The murmuring resumed. I pulled the hard drive out of my gym bag where I'd tossed it early this morning, and wrapped it carefully with the sweatshirt. Then I put them at the bottom of the bag and covered the bundle with my remaining clothes and other items. I was just zipping up the bag when I heard Steve's voice at my door.

"I brought you some orange juice and Danish," he said.

"Thanks," I said. "I'm famished."

"I thought you might be," he said, as I followed him into the dining area. "Thought this might tide you over until we get a proper meal."

I grabbed a Danish and poured a glass of orange juice.

"So what's next?" he said.

I sat at the table, and pulled my legs under me. "I'd like to go to some of the places my mother mentioned in her calendar. That okay with you?"

"I think that's an excellent idea." He poured himself a cup of coffee and seated himself at the far end of the table.

"So, your mom came to Lumberton and paid a visit to The Triple R," he said. "And where did she go from there?"

"A pawn shop, not far from Lumberton."

"Was she in any financial difficulty?"

"No. When they died, they left a sizable estate. They weren't rich," I added, glancing at him, "But they weren't hurting."

After a moment, I continued, "Anyway, in her calendar, she had a strange notation: Regina Estrada, paying a visit to Jess. I need a picture taken."

"Regina Estrada..." Steve repeated slowly. "Was your mother Latino?"

"Heinz 57," I said. "Her father traced their heritage at one point back to Spain, so that's where 'Estrada' comes from. But she was not a typical Spanish woman, not after generations of Welsh, English, Scottish, and Irish mixed in... and a little bit of Native American, or so I'm told."

Steve nodded as if absorbing this information.

"Anyway, my mother always went by 'Reggie'," I said. "Regina was her given name, but I never—not once—heard her called that. So why would she enter that name in her calendar?"

Steve set his coffee cup on the table. "Do you enter *your* name in your calendar?"

I could feel myself gaping. "Of course not," I said, my eyes meeting his. "You'd never mention your own name in your own appointments."

We both leapt up from the table at exactly the same moment. Without a word, we grabbed our coats and dashed from the room. We were down the steps, across the lobby, and headed for the car when I realized he'd grabbed my hand and was pulling me along. Or was I pulling him?

38

The pawn shop was located a few miles southeast of Lumberton, deep into Robeson County.

We found ourselves in an increasingly desolate area once we turned off Old Whiteville Road, until we encountered a jumble of homes and businesses that rose out of the midst of neat rows of farmland. One home even sported a tombstone between the house and the garage, which I found fascinating.

Steve slowed down as we approached the pawn shop on the corner, which was connected to a general store and a gas station. As we drove past, he said, "Program my number into your cell phone and put it on speed dial. At the first sign of trouble, call me."

I entered his phone number and set up the speed dial. I tested it—with one push of a button, I was dialing him with my hand in the pocket of my pants, and no one would be the wiser. On his phone, the caller id registered. We were ready.

It wasn't necessary to rehearse. I was simply a customer, dropping in to check out their merchandise. I was to go no further than that. Watch, look, and listen. Soak up all I could. Then report back to Steve. Just like an Academy assignment.

He pulled up to the gas pump and slowly prepared to fill up the tank while I wandered past the general store.

I hesitated outside the pawn shop as though I were browsing the window displays. It was a mishmash of items, mostly jewelry: some new, some old, none antique, and all appeared cheap.

The windows were old, single paned, with wrought iron bars running their length. Where the bars had been installed, the concrete and brick veneer were now crumbling. I wondered how difficult it would be to break into this place.

I wiped the perspiration from my palm onto my pants and turned the knob. Taking a deep breath, I stepped inside. I closed the door, noting it had a fairly new deadbolt.

The room was small, perhaps twenty feet square. A strong odor assaulted me of stale spices and peppers that intermingled with a musty smell, as though the building had been closed up for decades.

Dusty glass cases with hundreds of smudged fingerprints framed the room in a u-shape facing the door, the greenish tint to the glass long ago succumbing to dirt brown.

On both sides, the walls were paneled in a dark wood grain that was obviously one step up from particleboard, like the walls of mobile homes from the mid-70's. At the back was a heavy velvet drape that stretched the width of the store.

The floor was poured concrete, painted dark gray, worn smooth from years of foot traffic.

A squat, heavyset woman eyed me from behind the counter. As I approached, I noticed a name tag pinned to her blouse: Marilyn.

When I opened my mouth, the words tumbled out as though they had a mind of their own. "Regina Estrada sent me. I need to see Jess about a picture."

"Regina Estrada?"

The heavily accented voice jolted me. I hadn't noticed the man sitting behind the counter on the other side of the room. He blended in well with the dark walls; his black hair cut short around a swarthy face and small, dark eyes. His shirt was a dark brown plaid. Though I couldn't see much of his physique from this vantage point, from the looks of his head and shoulders, he must have been wiry. The total opposite of the woman in front of me.

"Yes," I said. "I need a picture." I hoped my voice didn't sound as raspy to them as it did to me.

"You look just like her," Marilyn said. It was spoken as an abrupt observation.

As I turned back around, I caught her peering at my facial features. I really wasn't sure how to respond. My heart began to beat rapidly and I became acutely aware that my mother had stood in this very store.

"Ningún ella no," the man said, rising from his seat. I immediately translated the phrase into "no, she doesn't". As he studied me from across the room, I could feel the heat rising in my cheeks. Who were these people?

I don't know why I chose not to speak Spanish; I knew I could hold my own with the best of them. Instead, I asked Marilyn, "What did he say?"

"He said you certainly do," she replied.

"Oh." Before I could say anything else, the man's voice penetrated the room like thunder.

"Why did you tell her that?" he demanded in Spanish. "She looks nothing like Reggie."

Reggie. I hadn't heard that name in such a long time. I hadn't realized how many times a day I'd heard it growing up until just now. *Reggie, do you know where my socks are? Reggie, what's for dinner? Reggie, I can't get this remote to work...* My father's voice came barreling back at me from the past.

The man was gesturing with his hands, describing her height, her weight, her coloring, her facial features. The woman's ire was rising as she debated him. This was something I never expected, and I didn't know how to progress beyond this point. For now, I felt the most practical thing to do was allow them to continue with their little dispute, not realizing that I understood every word they spoke.

"Shut up, you sow," he finally hissed. "I did it myself."

It was spoken with an air of dismissal, and it obviously had the desired effect. Marilyn fell completely silent.

My head was swimming. Did *what* himself?

"When was the last time you saw Reggie?" he asked me in broken English, as he walked around the counter, his beady eyes fixed on mine.

I hesitated. I knew they were both studying me.

I looked him straight in the eye. "It's been a long time. Too long."

"Yes," he said slowly. "Reggie would have known Jess is only here at night."

I swallowed. "She probably told me," I said, trying to look sheepish. "It's been awhile, and my memory isn't so good."

"Then you will have time to refresh your memory," he said.

My heart felt as though it was pounding in the side of my neck. "Excuse me?"

"She lives behind the Restaurante. You should get reacquainted while you wait for Jess."

39

I was standing in the FBI Resident Agency, known as the RA, in Fayetteville, about forty minutes from the pawn shop, though it seemed like it was a million miles away now. I felt oddly out of place amidst the desks, computers, and paperwork, as I peered over Special Agent Miranda Humphrey's blond tresses while she placed a piece of tape across the bug.

She stood back. I watched her pale blue eyes admiring her work.

"It blends seamlessly with your bra's underwire," she said.

I glanced down at the tiny microphone lodged between my breasts. I hoped when I arrived at my meeting with Jess that I would not be frisked. Steve, Derek, Miranda, and I already had an embarrassingly detailed discussion about it, arriving at the conclusion that this would be the most secure location for the bug.

Now I could hear Steve and Derek's voices from just outside the door as I buttoned my blouse and tucked the tail neatly into my slacks.

Miranda waited until I was presentable before opening the door. "Ready to test it?" she asked.

Derek nodded and motioned for us to follow him.

As we marched down the hallway, Steve said, "Derek was just telling me they've been unable to locate the body from the motel."

"What does that mean?" I asked.

He shrugged. "Could mean the body was dumped or he wasn't dead."

We turned the corner and followed Derek into a room filled with electronic equipment.

"I know he was dead," I said emphatically.

"There are a lot of sparsely inhabited areas around here, especially along the Lumber and Cape Fear Rivers and in the swamps," Derek said. "There are thousands of places they could dump a body where it might never be found."

A technician turned toward us. "Perfect," he said. "I heard everything."

"This is Agent Steve Moran and Agent Sheila Carpenter," Derek said to the technician. He turned toward us. "And this is Agent Jim West, our technology expert."

We shook hands, and then Steve asked, "What're the specs on the bug?"

"This particular device," Jim explained, "works on ultrasonic signals. It's less likely to be detected than your standard radio frequency bug. Where will the van be?"

"About two blocks from the shop," Derek said.

"No problem," Jim answered.

"Let's go over the specifics," Derek said.

Steve turned to me. "I'll be dressed as a hunter; the Bureau is providing us with a pickup. I'll drive you to within a quarter mile of the store. Then I'll pull into the gas station, fill up, and spend some time in the general store. Interesting place. Owners appear to be Pakistani, but they claim they make the best North Carolina barbeque in these parts."

"Yeah, right," Derek said as he walked to a map across the room.

After studying the map for a few seconds, he started to speak. "Steve, you're here," he directed, pointing to the intersection where the general store, gas station, and pawn shop were located, "while Miranda, Jim and I will be here, behind this school. The van is marked *Jason's Carpet Cleaning*. We'll be dressed in jumpsuit uniforms."

Steve turned to me. "If things go bad, the signal is 'Red River'. Then get out of there. If I don't see you walk through the door within two minutes, we'll assume there's trouble."

Derek stepped forward. "There shouldn't be any trouble. Not on this visit. Remember, all you're doing is getting a picture taken."

I nodded. That was all. And hopefully I would find out the significance of the picture.

It would be a well-run operation. I was wearing a bug. And two undercover vehicles would be within shouting distance. I did feel a bit like Barney Fife, though, since I wouldn't be permitted yet to carry a gun. Come to think of it, Barney had a leg up on me: at least he had a gun *and* a bullet.

As if in answer to my thoughts, Steve said, "I don't think this is such a good idea. Sheila's not even out of the Academy yet."

"We don't have another agent who speaks fluent Spanish," Derek said. "We don't have a choice."

Steve nodded, though I thought I detected some lingering doubt in his expression. "We've not eaten since breakfast," he said. "If it's all the same to you, Sheila and I are going to grab a bite. We'll be in position precisely at 6:45."

With that, we walked back down the hallway and down a flight of stairs. The wind was picking up, causing the trees to lean dangerously low, their naked branches scratching against each other in a chorus as though they were coming alive. The sky looked ominous now; heavy clouds were moving in from the southwest. I found myself wishing we could get this over and done with.

We'd crossed the parking lot and were getting into a battered white pickup before I realized we'd separated from the other agents.

We were silent with our own thoughts on the drive from Fayetteville to Lumberton.

"Where are we going?" I asked as Steve made several turns that led us through a beautiful residential area filled with stately homes and tree-lined streets.

"Derek recommended a restaurant," he said with a sideways glance. "It's away from the tourist places along the Interstate."

My curiosity increased until we reached The Black Water Grille in Lumberton's quiet downtown area, just a stone's throw from the Lumber River. As Steve parked the pickup in the graveled lot across the street from the restaurant, my attention was riveted to the end of the street and the river beyond.

It was early enough that the dinner crowd hadn't descended yet, so we were the only patrons in a restaurant that would have appeared right at home in downtown Washington, DC. In fact, I hadn't realized how hungry I was until I started perusing the menu.

I wondered if there was a switch of some sort on the bug I was wearing. I should have asked if I could turn it off until we were ready for the operation to begin. But then, I was sure we were out of range by now.

At Steve's request, we were seated in the back corner of the dining room, next to a corridor that ran between the dining area and the kitchen and bar. We were separated from the corridor by a partition, which we could easily see over. The location provided us with an excellent view of a goodly portion of the restaurant.

Steve sat with his back facing the wall, with a clear, unobstructed view of the front door, while I sat opposite him. I'd like to say I nibbled on a low-fat dish, but the truth was that I was chowing down on Pasta Primavera with fresh shrimp to die for.

Between scoops of food, I found my eyes wandering to the corridor, which was lined with framed covers of *Cigar Aficionado*. Beneath them was a long, narrow table set against the wall. I watched as an employee appeared from a back room and strode down the corridor toward us with a telephone book in her hands. When she was just a few feet from us, she tossed the book onto the table. My eyes rested on the lone telephone book for all of fifteen seconds before I switched into gear.

"I'll be right back," I said, rising. "Ladies' room," I added to Steve's inquisitive eyes.

I glanced back as I approached the rest room doors. I could barely see the top of Steve's head over the partition, his hair catching the dim light from an overhead light fixture. The brown locks seemed to play with the light, causing it to become more brilliant. His head was downcast while he dove into his steak.

I stepped to the side, grabbed the phone book, and disappeared around the corner, which turned out to be right outside the rest room doors. My fingers trembled as I flipped through the pages to the letter "E". There were several Estradas in the area, I mused, moving down the page. There it was: Regina Estrada.

The address was not far from the pawn shop. It had to be the same place the man spoke about. I glanced at my watch. I knew I had to go there. And I had to go now.

"Not thinking of giving me the slip, are you?"

I glanced up quickly. Steve was standing in front of me, his arm outstretched, the palm resting casually on the wall.

"Why would I do a thing like that?"

His eyes were penetrating as he made a point of staring at the phone book in my hands. "Regina Estrada, right?"

I nodded.

"I know. I'm one step ahead of you."

He reached in his pocket and pulled out a scrap of paper. On it was written the address I'd just seen in the phone book.

Despite myself, I laughed.

"You need to learn to trust me," he said. "It's called teamwork—try it!"

The Mexican restaurant was in stark contrast to the warmth and sophistication of The Black Water Grille. It was 6:15 as we circled it; it was situated on a quiet corner across from an old-fashioned drug store, its sign swinging violently in the increasing wind like a bad scene from a spaghetti western. It was the end unit in a row of businesses, some of which appeared to be vacant.

The sky was dark as we turned down a dirt road that cut behind the restaurant. At a bend in the road was one stick-built home amidst several mobile homes in varying degrees of decay.

A man stood in the window of the house, as if he was watching for someone—or perhaps he was just watching us drive down this rural road.

I detected movement behind him, but the dim light in the house did not enable me to see clearly into the room.

Steve pulled in front of the mailbox. "This is it," he said, slipping on his hunting cap.

I opened the door. "Be back in a jiff, Bubba."

"Remember I'm as close as your cell phone," he said, stifling a grin.

I fingered the phone in my pocket. Without Jim and his receiver close by, my bug was useless. "I know."

As I approached the house, I saw the front door was open, leaving only a glass storm door that easily gave me a clear view of the home from front to back. As I climbed the rickety steps, I realized the tiny house was divided into two apartments.

The door creaked as I opened it. I heard a baby crying and the sounds from a Spanish television station on the left side of the hallway. They might be living in a ramshackle, subdivided old house, but by golly, they had cable. I tentatively knocked on the door.

A petite woman with raven hair and olive skin cracked open the door. A tiny baby was latched with a tiny fist onto her pale blue dress. "Si?"

In my best Spanish, I asked for Regina Estrada. She nodded to the door behind me and then quickly closed the door. I heard the rattling of a chain as it was latched.

I knocked on the second door. There was no answer, but I heard the sound of feet rushing to the door. I could sense someone on the other side.

"I'm here to see Regina," I called out in Spanish.

No one answered. The seconds ticked past.

I knocked again; this time, louder. "Reggie? Are you there?"

I heard a chain sliding into place, and the door opened slightly. The chain was across the door opening at eye level, allowing it to part only a few inches. A man's angular, lean face peered back at me. He was undeniably Middle Eastern. I gasped, and then struggled to regain control. "You startled me," I said in perfect Spanish. "I expected Reggie. Is she here?"

"No," the man answered. It's hard to mess up the word *no* in another language; it's one syllable and it's the same in English and Spanish. And yet, this guy did. I felt every hair along my spine stiffen.

"Do you know when she'll be back?"

Someone said something in the background. It wasn't Spanish or English, but rather a language I didn't recognize at all. Then the door was abruptly closed.

As I made my way back down the dim hallway, I had to struggle not to turn around. I had the creepy feeling someone was watching me, their eyes boring into my back. I couldn't wait to get into the fresh air and in sight of Steve and the pickup.

A woman was approaching the house. As our paths crossed at the base of the steps, I said, "Regina Estrada?"

She shook her head and moved away quickly, her eyes downcast. She swung a filmy black, white, and red scarf across her face as if to shield herself from the dust—or me. I watched as she walked into the house and turned to the left.

I returned to the truck. Wordlessly, Steve turned toward the main road.

40

Marilyn was sitting in the same chair as when I'd left, as if she hadn't moved an inch.

"Jess will be right back," she said as soon as I entered.

"Wait in back room," the man said in broken English, opening a hinged door in between the display cases.

I wondered as I squeezed behind the counter if this was a trap.

The man swung the door back into place and motioned for me to follow him to the rear of the store, where he parted the musty draperies that separated the decrepit show room from the office and stockroom.

Boxes were piled in a haphazard fashion amongst monstrous steel desks and old-fashioned steel typing chairs, their vinyl seatbacks split, revealing thick yellowed foam padding. Mountains of paper were laid chaotically on the desks, some stacks dangerously close to sliding off onto the floor. I wondered if anyone would notice if they did.

There were two windows, one on my left and one on my right. The one on the right was covered with sheers that I could easily see through to the parking lot. I watched briefly as Steve took his time at the gas pump before I turned back to the room.

The window on the left was painted black. Near the corner was a door with a bar across it and the phrase "Emergency Exit Only" in faded red paint. Next to it was a microwave, surrounded by paper plates and plastic flatware atop a rickety homemade rolling cart. No doubt, I'd found the source of at least some of the odors in this place.

The telephone rang, breaking the silence. I heard Marilyn answer it just beyond the curtain. She called for the man by name—Luis—who excused himself and left the room. His rapid fire Spanish filled the otherwise empty air as he debated the documents required to obtain a driver's license.

In a whisper, I described the room, the windows, and the door. "Also a laptop computer and a color printer," I said as I surveyed my surroundings. "Three cameras. A laminating machine." I stopped at one of the desks and felt a sheet of blank paper. "Heavy card stock. At least a ream of it."

I wandered to the desk in the middle of the room. Scattered atop it were various documents that appeared to be related to items recently pawned. I slid my finger underneath the topmost paper and gently moved it aside. Beneath it were more pawn documents.

Out of the corner of my eye, I saw a vehicle pull up just outside the window. Through the thin fabric, I watched the shiny Lincoln Continental with New York plates stop in the parking lot. It appeared oddly out of place; this entire store was not much longer than the fancy vehicle.

I placed both palms on the desktop and leaned toward the window. "We've got company," I whispered.

The driver appeared, stepping smartly around the vehicle to the back door nearest the building, opening the door and standing aside.

After an agonizing moment, a man's pant leg appeared. Even from this distance I could see the high shine of his shoe. It was followed by another leg, and then the man stepped outside the vehicle, his back to me.

His overcoat was obviously expensive and appeared well tailored, as though custom fitted. It suddenly occurred to me that this was Jess. As he smoothed his clothes, visions of mafia newsreels raced through my mind.

My hand slipped, and a mountain of papers crashed to the floor. Madly, I knelt and grabbed them by handfuls. I went to toss them back onto the desk when my hand froze in midair.

There, sitting in the same sort of disarray as the papers, were stacks of driver's licenses and Social Security cards.

I came slowly to my feet and rifled through them. The licenses were from Virginia, North Carolina, Tennessee, Alabama, and Texas, but none of them had pictures. My eyes darted to the cameras and the laminating machine.

The room blurred around me as everything came rushing at me like a locomotive at full steam—Luis just outside the curtains arguing about documents, my mother's note of "seeing Jess about a picture", the driver's licenses and Social Security cards. The trail Mom was following was one of identity theft—hers—and it led her straight here, where another woman just blocks away had assumed her identity.

I grabbed a handful of the licenses and stuffed them into my pocket before burying the rest of them under the pawnshop paperwork.

My heart was racing, and I debated whether to leave now, while I still could. I had all I needed. I shifted my attention to the window, where I could see the man speaking on a cell phone, his back to me, running his fingers through his hair as if he were extremely agitated. Jet black hair, slicked back. As I watched, he punched the air with his finger in a wild gesture.

Abruptly, he turned in my direction and instinctively, I started to duck behind the desk, but something stopped me.

It was the man from The Triple R, the man with the long jacket and the greasy black hair, the man who'd reached into his pocket and pulled out a gun, firing shots into the other man, killing him before my eyes.

My quickened breath felt raw in my throat. Now I remembered where else I'd seen him: on Long Island, at Alex's cousin's wedding, arguing with her brother, Ricky.

A noise behind me startled me, and I jerked around. I hadn't noticed Luis had finished with his phone conversation, leaving the store in deafening silence. He stood in the doorway, staring at me with narrowed eyes. I wondered how long he'd been watching me and whether my thoughts were visible on my face.

My lips were so parched that my teeth were stuck to them. "Red River," I said.

41

There have been definite times in my life when everything appeared to unfold in slow motion, like the time I attended the county fair in the tenth grade. I'd been standing at the top of a rise, buying and dressing a hot dog. I'd just finished with the relish when someone shouted my name and I turned. To this day, I don't know what I slipped on, but it sent me sailing down the hill, past all my neighbors and friends and fellow students. As I slid down the hill on my backside, watching the bemused expressions of everyone I passed, I remember my only thought was to keep the hot dog held high so I could still eat it when I came to a stop.

The scene wasn't jerky, like watching a frame-by-frame display on a slowed down video recording. It was completely fluid, exactly as it felt at this very moment, as though all my surroundings were somehow connected.

I could see the rage on Luis' reddened face, could see the veins popping out across his neck like blue rivers overflowing their banks, as he charged across the room at me, narrowing the distance between us as though it were mere inches and not feet. His swarthy, work-hardened hands were outstretched; his eyes glued to my pocket. The small stack of drivers' licenses now weighed more with every second that passed, causing my pocket to gape open.

I could feel the air around me whirling with my movement as I lunged toward one of the steel typing chairs. My fingernails sunk so deeply into the vinyl chair back that I could feel the metal frame beneath the ancient cushion. Raising the chair chest high, a scream escaped my lips as I sent it crashing against Luis, the old fashioned steel castors striking him across the jaw in a left hook that sent blood spurting across the desk.

Luis fell backward, his skull crashing against the steel corner of the desk, his eyes rolling backward in his head, as he crumpled to the floor.

Marilyn charged into the room, her angry eyes taking on the appearance of a bull charging at a matador, the curtains that had been between us merely a piece of red cloth that only angered her further.

Somehow, I managed to grab the chair that now lay straddled across Luis, my eyes fixated on a chunk of his hair stuck to one of the castors. Turning back toward Marilyn, I slung it with all my might.

She ducked as her arm shot out, pushing the chair away from her as if it were only a pillow. Instead of finding its target, it crashed against the back window, sending shards of painted black glass across the room.

She began to lunge for me then stopped short. There was a commotion just outside the opposite window. Instinctively, I turned and followed her widened eyes.

The man I recognized was crossing the parking lot in great strides, heading directly toward the window, the cell phone clasped in a hand that now hung at his side, the other hand outstretched, a gray metal within his palm barely discernible.

The man's heavy black brows were furrowed, giving the appearance of a Neanderthal unibrow. Even from this distance I could see the steel expression of a killer.

As I stood there motionless, a beefy fist that felt like a sledgehammer landed on my cheekbone, knocking me completely off my feet. As my head shot back, Marilyn's right arm retracted and her left fist came forward like a freight train, cracking against my jawbone as I fell.

As my body twisted from the onslaught and I struggled against unconsciousness, another punch slammed into my back just above my kidney, pushing my body against the back door, where the words "Emergency Exit Only" screamed at me.

I sank to the floor, frantically grasping for anything to break my fall. I felt my fingers latch onto the coffee pot handle. With all the strength I had left, I heaved the scalding pot against my assailant, smashing it against her bulbous nose with a loud crack.

My knees buckled just as the man in the lot fired a shot through the window. I heard it whizzing and felt it pass just inches above my head, through the spot where I'd stood just a moment earlier.

Then another shot rang out, followed by a third. There were sounds of shouting and a simultaneous chorus of people yelling, *"FBI! Drop it!"*

Marilyn had stumbled backward but was digging in her heels like a wounded animal ready to fight to the death. As she redoubled her efforts and barreled forward, I remained pinned against the coffee cart where I'd fallen. I instinctively drew my knees against my chest. As she closed in on me, I planted my pointed Tony Lama in her belly. At best, it would only buy me precious seconds. As she doubled over in agony, I recoiled and kicked her again in her chin, causing her to reel backwards. My chest heaving and with blood covering my face and body, I forced myself to get up.

Like an animal who would have to kill or be killed, I continued kicking her, the pointed boot toe finding a fleshy target so many times I lost count. My hands are small; I've always been short and small boned and I knew my fists would be no match against this larger opponent. But my boots were in style, complete with pointed toes and steel shanks. I kicked her in the head and her belly, kicked her arm as it raised to defend herself, kicked her fists as they started to beat back at me.

She stumbled backward across the room, her eyes beginning to roll back in her head. I moved forward, afraid to stop, afraid to let up for even a second, lest she regain her footing and come at me again. In a brief pause that I was afraid would cost me the fight, I managed to grab the metal bar off the back door. I swung it across my body like a bat, hitting her against the side of the head. As she fell, I raised it high above me, ready to slam it down on her again.

Then strong hands grabbed the bar from behind me, wrestling it away from me as I fought like a madwoman.

I heard a voice as if the speaker were distant and not inches from my face, "Sheila, it's me. Stop, Sheila. Stop. She's down."

As if on cue, she fell with a final thud that echoed in the tiny building. Miranda rushed in, returning her weapon to her holster and bending over her. Within seconds, she'd handcuffed her still body and radioed for an ambulance, but whether she was calling it for Marilyn or for me, I wasn't sure.

I relinquished my hold on the bar and slowly turned my agonized body to face Steve.

"Are you okay?" he was yelling at me.

I started to answer but my head was swimming, my body wracked in pain. I felt my knees begin to wobble and he dropped the bar and caught me, his strong arms cradling my tortured bones. "What took you so long?" I managed to croak.

As I started to thankfully retreat into his arms, a movement caught the corner of my eye.

Across the room Luis was gaining consciousness. With a pop-eyed stare fixed on the back of Steve's head, he jammed his hand in his pocket. As he retracted it, I saw the unmistakable glint of a gun.

My lips were so parched that I barely managed to blurt out Steve's name in a feeble effort to warn him. And at that moment, I knew we were out of time. With what little strength I had left, I grabbed Steve's gun from its holster and fired it across the room as Luis pulled the trigger.

42

I rifled through my gym bag until my fingers hit upon
the computer hard drive. I carried it into the conference
room of the Fayetteville field office, where Steve,
Miranda, and Derek sat huddled in a circle. They were so
deep in conversation that they displayed only mild curiosity
as I set up my laptop and proceeded to connect the hard
drive.

I'd steadfastly refused transport to Southeastern
Regional Medical Center in Lumberton. Nothing personal,
but I'd had enough of hospital rooms. I'd already decided I
wasn't checking back into Vanderbilt, either. I reasoned if
my condition was all that serious, I would have been toast
in that back room.

Luis remained under guard in Southeastern. I found it
incredibly interesting that he had three bullets removed
when I could have sworn I fired only once. He'd gotten off
one round before Miranda and Steve simultaneously
overtook him, but fortunately for us, it hit the wall behind
us.

Marilyn was on her way to jail with an FBI escort. She'd
been checked in briefly at Southeastern; under FBI

supervision, she was checked out, doctored up, and released into the custody of the law.

"From what we can determine, Jesus Rios—aka Jess—was the ringleader," Derek was saying. "There's enough evidence in that back room to prove the pawn shop was simply a front for an identity theft ring. What we haven't determined yet is why."

"What do you mean? Isn't it obviously a fraud scam?" I asked.

"Not necessarily," Steve answered. "It could be identity theft for fraudulent purposes or it could be providing identities to illegal aliens. They're both crimes, but prosecuted differently."

My mind wandered to the wedding on Long Island, the argument between Ricky and Jess, and the conversation I'd overheard between Ricky and Alex. Could this have been what they were arguing about? Could Ricky have become involved in providing false identities to illegal immigrants? I'd not mentioned Alex or her brother to Steve. I cast a sidelong glance at him. If Alex knew about this, it would cost her a career in the FBI; if she was in deep enough, she could even go to prison.

What would happen with my own career, if I didn't tell them of my suspicions? Just as bad, what if I told them only to find out my suspicions weren't valid?

"Well, Sheila," Steve said, leaning back and propping his feet on the coffee table, "Looks like you've solved your mother's mystery."

Steve looked at the other agents. "Sheila's mom found out she was a victim of identity theft. She learned where the imposter was living, and came here—perhaps to confront her. Somehow she learned where the pictures were taken, and paid the pawn shop a little visit."

It seemed odd to be discussing my mother so casually. Despite the years since her death, I still felt a twinge of sadness. I turned back to the computer and entered the Windows Explorer. Once there, I opened the directory of the hard drive and thumbed through its contents.

"It's all here," I said.

"What's all where?"

I sheepishly turned to face them. "I forgot to tell you. I kind of borrowed the hard drive out of one of those computers at The Triple R."

I thought I detected a flash in Steve's eyes.

"They have templates set up for making drivers' licenses, birth certificates, even wedding documents. Funny," I mused, "some of them have a Mexican seal on them."

"Too bad we can't use it," Miranda said.

"Why not?" Steve asked.

"Fourth Amendment—Search and Seizure."

"You're kidding me, right?" Steve pressed. "Of course we can use it."

"But—"

"Under The Patriot Act, we can definitely use it."

"But there's no terrorism involved here," Miranda argued.

While they debated the finer points of what could constitute a terrorist threat and bypassing the Fourth Amendment, I turned back to my exploration of the hard drive. Something was gnawing at me. I couldn't quite put my finger on it, but—

"The beginning of the trail," I said so abruptly that I even startled myself.

They stopped talking and stared at me.

"My mother said the beginning of the trail was at the wholesale store," I explained.

"So, that's where she discovered who had stolen her identity," Steve offered.

I nodded, unconvinced. They returned to their debate, the arguments on each side gaining momentum. Now Derek chimed in, agreeing with Steve.

I pulled out my mother's cell phone and looked again at the pictures. The woman in the background was now of more interest to me than the man had been earlier. Was this the woman who'd stolen Mom's identity?

I turned back around. My eyes met Steve's.

With his eyes still locked on mine, Steve interrupted their conservation. "Derek, can we get surveillance at the house—somebody to wait for the fake Regina Estrada to show up and take her into custody?"

"Well, we've got bigger fish—" Derek stopped himself. He looked at Steve and then at me. "Sure." He pulled his cell phone out and began dialing. A moment later, he was dispatching Agent Jim West to the house behind the restaurant.

"So," I said, trying to sound casual, "you have bigger fish to fry?"

Derek cleared his throat. "Nothing personal. But identity theft is so pervasive that trying to apprehend every person who has stolen an identity is like trying to capture every fly at a garbage dump."

"But this—" Steve said, rising and crossing the room to the computer "—this is different. This is an identity theft *ring.*"

I was silent. He rested his hand on my shoulder, his eyes searching mine. "Sheila, do you understand what you've done? You've busted open an identity theft ring. That's pretty impressive."

"No," I said. "That's not all that's going on here."

"What are you talking about?" Miranda said, leaning forward in her chair.

"We're still at the beginning of the trail."

Derek laughed. "Maybe you don't understand the significance—"

"I went to Regina Estrada's home tonight," I said, glancing at Steve. "I spoke with a man in her apartment. And he wasn't Latino."

"Latinos aren't the only ones who steal identities," Derek said.

"These names," I said, reaching to the coffee table and picking up a handful of fake drivers' licenses, "are all Spanish in origin. They *sound* Latino."

"What are you saying?" Miranda asked.

I looked at Steve. "The men in that house were Middle Eastern."

"So?"

The significance of my own words hit me like a sledgehammer. I jumped up so quickly, I almost knocked over the laptop. "Jim is going to need backup."

Derek already had his cell phone in his hand and was hitting the redial button as he spoke. "Why?"

"They're Arabs," I said. "Arabs, masquerading as Latinos."

Each word hung in the air like the blade of a guillotine.

"My God," Miranda breathed. "Oh, my God."

43

Steve and I drove southeast past tobacco fields that were now relegated to a constant broad, flat blur with an occasional darkened structure or stand of trees thrown in against the midnight blue sky. As we careened around the corner, the truck's rear wheels slid dangerously across the double yellow line into the oncoming lane and I instinctively held my breath. Steve's knuckles were stiff and white as he hung onto the steering wheel, his hands locked on the ten o'clock and two o'clock positions, the green glow from the dashboard reflected in his eyes as they remained riveted on the pavement ahead.

Once around the bend, the road opened wide, allowing us to gain momentum as we sped toward Regina Estrada's house. I clutched the hand grip above the passenger window and held on as the truck accelerated toward eighty miles per hour.

Derek and Miranda were ahead of us in their Bureau car. The police radio mounted under the dash in the pickup came alive with the sound of Miranda's voice coordinating with the local sheriff's department. Any second I expected to hear their high pitched sirens on their way to assist us.

As Miranda directed, I dutifully turned the frequency on the radio to a channel dedicated to our mission, where I learned that two more agents were en route from Fayetteville and at least two sheriff's deputies were also on their way. Miranda directed them to silence their sirens as they neared, and pull into the parking lot at the Mexican restaurant on the corner until she and Derek arrived at the scene. Then we would surround the house before approaching the men inside. The adrenalin was starting to pump through my veins like a racehorse at the starting gate.

"Why would Arabs attempt to pass themselves off as Latinos?" Steve's voice broke my concentration.

"They wouldn't want to call attention to themselves," I answered, my hand tightening on the hand grip while we took another tight curve, in a desperate attempt to keep from sliding across the bench seat. A dump truck was approaching us from the opposite direction as we leaned into the curve, its lights so high it nearly blinded us. He leaned on his horn as we sped past him, missing the side of his vehicle by inches.

I glanced at Steve. His eyes were fixed straight ahead and if the close encounter unnerved him, he wasn't letting it show.

The pungent blended odor of manure and ammonia reached my nostrils through the truck's open ventilation, heralding our approach to a poultry farm. I could barely make out several sets of low-lying buildings on our right as I continued, "If Latinos are migrating here in droves, as Derek said, the locals are probably used to them. A couple of Arab men might arouse suspicion, but a couple of Mexicans would not."

"But the Latinos would know they're not one of them. How would they get around that?"

"You know," I mused, "My folks employed dozens, if not hundreds, of migrant workers over the years."

"On their tobacco farm?"

I nodded. "My dad paid minimum wage and only hired documented workers, while many of the other farms paid much less and didn't even ask for proof of legal entry into the country. Twelve or more would be tucked into vehicles that were built for half that many, the cars sometimes held together with bailing wire and a prayer. Most of them lived in shacks with no running water and no electricity, preyed upon by landlords who charged top dollar for accommodations an American would refuse to live in, rarely putting down roots as they moved from one locality to the next."

"Spare me the pity," Steve said.

"I'm surprised at you," I said. "It's actually little more than economic slavery. These people were looking for the American Dream inside a chicken house or a hog processing plant or in between rows of cotton, tobacco, or soybean."

"They can look for the American Dream," Steve said, "but they can do legally—just like the rest of us."

There was a long pause. "The Latinos won't turn them in," I said finally.

"Won't turn in the Arabs?"

"Most migrant workers are here illegally. You heard Derek's statistics. They won't do anything to bring attention to themselves."

We slowed as we passed the intersection where the pawn shop, general store, and gas station were located. Despite ourselves, we both turned to look at the ramshackle building that held so much drama for us just hours ago. Two men stood at the darkened front window, their hands cupped around their eyes, their faces pressed against the glass, in an attempt to peer inside the store. A large black and orange sign on the door announced "Closed/Cerrado".

"They won't be getting their driver's licenses today," Steve remarked. Then he chuckled. "Maybe we should set up shop there—pretend we're Jess. Bet we'd rake them in by the dozens." He glanced at me. "But then, we're not INS."

We'd long ago lost sight of the Bureau car, though we'd continued to roll through the countryside at speeds in excess of eighty miles per hour. The radio had fallen silent as well, which could only mean that everyone was converging at the restaurant in preparation for storming the house.

Traffic had increased from the opposite direction. More than one driver was sitting low in the seat as though he or she could drive undetected, while just their obvious hurry to leave the area was enough to arouse suspicion.

I was just about to ask Steve if we should throw up a roadblock or checkpoint of some sort when we rounded the last bend and I caught sight of the aged restaurant with the faded pink and lime green sign just up ahead, already surrounded by scores of law enforcement vehicles. No wonder the Latinos were fleeing. They thought it was an INS raid. No doubt, many of those who just passed us would never return.

Steve slowed to twenty-five miles per hour. We were no more than sixty feet from the entrance to the parking lot when an explosion erupted directly behind the restaurant, raining outward in all directions like a gray cloud filled with firecrackers. A split second later, we heard another explosion—one large crack that sounded like a bomb detonating, followed a split second later by another one, and then another. They were all coming from the location of Regina Estrada's house.

Now we found ourselves in a hail of debris that rained broken pieces of wood, shards of glass, and rusty nails down upon us. They hit the roof of the truck with such a force that I was certain in another moment the debris would penetrate the roof.

A fireball of brilliant red lit up the night sky, releasing a thick black cloud that reached skyward in the shape of a teardrop and the width of the entire block of buildings. Shingles and bricks were flying through the air as though a tornado had touched down.

Through the dust and debris, I could barely see the figures in the parking lot scrambling for cover anywhere they could find it—under the cars, inside them, or hiding in the alcove of the restaurant entrance.

The explosions kept coming, one right after another, like a spectacular Fourth of July fireworks display. The truck's side window exploded, spraying me with glass as a door knob crashed through, barely missing me as it slammed into the glove compartment door and bounced into the seat back between Steve and me.

Steve screeched to a stop, skidding the truck 180 degrees so the tail was facing the explosion. I turned and watched, horrified, as flames shot four stories high, turning the night into day. The noise was so deafening that I barely heard Steve shouting at me to get down. Before I could respond, he pushed me toward the floorboard and threw himself on top of me as the world around us erupted.

44

The sun's morning rays were still hours away. It would find us a quarter of a mile from the blast site, any sunshine muted by a thick fog that had rolled in overnight. It was impossible to differentiate between the smoke and the fog as the area in which the house once stood continued to smolder. Our vehicles, the surrounding buildings and fields, our clothes, and even our skin were covered in a fine white powder.

I glanced in the direction of the spot we'd deduced was Ground Zero, where dozens of high-intensity portable lights had the area lit up like the Las Vegas strip. A decontamination team in silver uniforms appeared otherworldly as they scoured the area, searching for signs of chemical contamination.

It had been Derek's call to bring them in, and it had been immediate. Ever since the 1995 terrorist attack in Tokyo, there had been increasing attention on chemical warfare.

Our first course of action while waiting for the decon team to arrive was to establish our three zones. The hot zone surrounded Ground Zero, the house that I'd visited just hours earlier. What the concussion hadn't torn into splinters, the fire had almost completely incinerated.

The warm zone was a larger area that extended northeast of the explosion. People to our immediate southwest might be in little danger, but those to our northeast could be in harm's way.

Beyond that was the cold zone, the area considered clean or unaffected by the blast—for now.

We were at the border of the warm and hot zones. We were considered, until proven otherwise, to be contaminated. It was in this location, on the front lawn of a farmer's stately ancestral home, where we established our first control point. No one could enter the hot zone without our express permission, and no one could leave without our clearance.

Miranda was coordinating roadblocks for miles around, extending several miles to our northeast, where another control point had been established.

As I peered through the fog to the northeast, I could barely make out the silvery gray metal rooftops above rows of commercial chicken houses.

"Any livestock will have to be destroyed if chemicals are present," I said.

"That's just the beginning of our problems," Steve said, turning to face wind socks that had been hastily erected. "The jet stream could carry any chemicals directly through eastern North Carolina and Virginia before heading out to sea. The damage and loss of life would be devastating." He nodded toward the helicopters that had transported the special teams, situated right in the middle of the road about a mile from where we stood. Jim was standing outside one of the aircraft, appearing deep in conversation with two first responders. "Our zone perimeters will have to be adjusted—and adjusted quickly—should the wind shift."

While the decon team worked on securing and assessing the area where the bomb blast had occurred, a special triage team was dispatched to examine each individual who had been anywhere near the explosion. I watched now as an attentive medic cleaned a nasty four-inch gash across a deputy's forehead, which had undoubtedly occurred from the flying debris. I wondered if they would stitch him up right there.

My eyes wandered over the farmer's front yard and into his tobacco fields, which now was beginning to look more like a battlefield. Others in our small group had varying degrees of cuts and scrapes, but some of the residents hadn't been so fortunate.

I watched as two men wandered into the yard as if in a daze, their clothes ragged and filthy. One had blood streaming down the front of his open shirt. A medic rushed to his aid, directing another to help him with a stretcher. A line of ambulances had already begun to converge, ready to whisk the wounded to Southeastern Regional Medical Center, where Luis was still convalescing.

We both were among the first to have been examined. I had only a tiny scratch dangerously close to my eye that was most likely from flying glass. I found myself picking debris out of my hair in much the same manner as I'd removed the debris from the mall blast.

"Agent Carpenter!"

I heard my name before I recognized the voice. I doubt if I would have been able to identify Derek on sight, his military-style dark hair covered in so much dust that he looked like Andy Warhol.

"The hot zone has come back clean," he said as he came within earshot. "We still need to check for casualties. You're the only one who speaks Spanish well enough to round up all the Latinos remaining in the hot zone."

I nodded. "Where do you want me to start?"

He pointed to the houses just beyond Ground Zero. "Anybody you find has to be directed here."

"I'll go with you," Steve said.

Before either of us could object, he was striding resolutely toward the houses.

Dawn was breaking as we cleared out two homes that didn't have four bedrooms between them, where at least thirty Mexicans were living. They could not have missed the drama unfolding right outside, yet they were all huddled in the dark as if they were clueless. I wondered how many were illegal aliens. I hoped none of them would make a run for it, placing Steve or I in a position where we'd have to stop them.

Eventually, we located an attractive Mexican woman who appeared to be in her 40's who spoke very good English. I ushered her across the fields to the triage area and to the front of the line, where she could serve as an interpreter while I rounded up more of the local population.

I felt awkward moving about the hot zone while the decon team was still suited up, even if they did just declare it "clean". I wondered if I was either expendable or they figured I would have shown signs if I'd been contaminated.

The Estrada house had burned to the ground, leaving in its place only a smoldering mass. I found myself drawn to it, marveling at the sight of an area where a house had once stood but which now didn't contain a piece of wood large enough for kindling. In its place was a depression that reached deep into the ground. I almost felt like I was studying a meteor crater.

My eyes followed the outline of the driveway until it stopped. I'd stood right there the day before, climbing the steps to the house, walking through the front door and into the corridor that divided the tiny house into two apartments.

And then I saw it.

It might have been a hundred feet behind the house: an ancient, burnt oak tree. And about thirty feet from the ground, tangled in its branches, was a woman's torso.

I hadn't realized my jaw had dropped until Steve asked, "What is it?"

"Come with me," I answered, grabbing his hand. I hoped I didn't get sick when I reached it, but I knew I had to identify it.

"Oh, my God," Steve breathed as he spotted it.

"It's her," I said shakily. The torso had no head, no arms, no legs. The clothes and skin were so blackened that it was difficult to tell where one ended and the other began, were it not for a single shred of pale blue fabric.

I turned away.

"Regina Estrada?" Steve asked incredulously.

I shook my head. "No, the woman who lived across the hall from her." I choked back my emotion. "She was carrying a baby when I saw her yesterday."

I heard Steve's voice as though it were far away, directing Derek's attention to it via our radio. "The crime scene techs will process it," he said to me as he walked the other way. I thought I saw him wipe perspiration from his brow, leaving a streak in the white dust that still covered him, though a chill hung in the air.

As we wandered now from house to house, building to building, I found myself looking into the trees and on the rooftops, looking for a sign of the woman's baby. What I found instead were structures with gaping holes where windows had once stood, a doorknob embedded in wood siding, and a toilet resting against a chimney. Anything that didn't disintegrate upon impact was thrown as much as a quarter of a mile away.

It was ominously silent. I realized as the sun rose higher in the sky, I should have heard the chirping of birds, the scurrying of animals. But I heard nothing. I knew the decon team would be searching for dead or dying animals. Their bodies would no doubt be tested for signs of poisoning, even though the hot zone had been declared clean. And for days, weeks, or even months, every unexplained casualty—every nervous system problem, skin eruption, or respiratory ailment—would cause another examination of this day.

We rounded up at least two hundred Spanish-speaking people, of whom there weren't ten who spoke even cursory English, and now there was a meandering line of them crossing the fields to the triage area. As I looked back, I could see additional fire and medical personnel arriving at the scene.

We were a good quarter of a mile in the opposite direction, near the southwestern quadrant of the hot zone, when Steve literally stumbled on a hand. We both stared at it for at least two minutes before either of us could speak. Then Steve radioed in, providing coordinates, so the crime scene techs could process it.

I bent down. It was a man's hand, roughened and calloused. My gut told me it didn't belong to the man who had opened the door yesterday afternoon in Regina's apartment. I shivered and stood up.

"Time to head back," Steve said.

I wondered as we crossed back across the field if my face was as ashen as his.

By the time we got back to the house, Derek was there, directing about a dozen law enforcement officers and crime scene techs. Behind us, it looked as though the entire Robeson County Sheriff's Department had converged on this rural area.

Derek waved us over to him.

Shaking his head as we approached, he said, "This is just preliminary, mind you, but my guess is the house was filled with dynamite."

"Ya think?" Steve said with a deadpan expression.

Derek continued, "I don't know how much we'll find." He kicked at the ground, now blackened. "What isn't on the other side of the county is vaporized."

I watched his foot, kicking the ground absent-mindedly, the toe of his once shiny shoe now covered in soot. Then my eyes traveled across the ground, still looking for the tiny body, though I knew it could not have survived.

A glittery object caught my eye. "What's that?" I asked, pointing.

The three of us stood there for a moment, attempting to identify it.

Finally, Derek shrugged. "Your guess is as good as mine."

"Can I take a closer look at that?"

Derek hesitated.

"I can do it," Steve said. "I have a longer stride than Sheila; I can get it in two steps."

"We need to preserve—"

"I know what it is," I said. "Get it, Steve, please."

I watched as Steve bounded forward like a cat on hot coals. From the expression on his face, he recognized it as soon as he bent down to retrieve it. He gingerly rocked it away from the surrounding debris, grasped it in his palm, and bounded back as though his original footprints were stepping stones.

"What is it?" Derek asked, his eyes shifting from Steve to me and back again, before coming to rest on the pocket sized, partially blackened metal device.

"It's a flash drive," I answered breathlessly.

45

The sun was beginning to set as we drove down Old Whiteville Road en route to Lumberton, its gradual disappearance serving as a reminder of a long and grueling day. I was looking forward to getting back to the hotel room and soaking in a good hot bath; every muscle in my body ached. It occurred to me that we'd had precious little sleep the night before and had been relying on pure adrenalin to get us through the day. A glance at Steve's face and the darkening bags forming under his eyes confirmed we were both running on empty.

A heavy fog was moving in, enveloping emaciated cypress trees that rose out of the swamps in a surreal mist that made them appear otherworldly. The wind was picking up, causing the marsh grasses and cattails to sway as though they were engaged in a hypnotic dance.

At Lennon Bridge, we came to an abrupt stop. We saw the flashing blue lights reflecting off the trees in a ghostly light show before we'd even rounded that last bend in the road. Between the haunting display of the swamps and the blue lights reflecting on the naked limbs in the dusk, I was beginning to feel more than a little vulnerable.

As if in response to my thoughts, Steve cranked up the heater. It did precious little with all the damage to the pickup's glass, and I involuntarily shivered as much from apprehension as the cold. It would have been nice to have borrowed an undamaged car, but every law enforcement officer was in need of theirs due to our present set of circumstances. I'd be glad to get this pickup turned into the Fayetteville office and be back in Steve's rental car. But right now we were focused on simply getting back to the hotel.

I peered past the cars stopped ahead of us to see two sheriff's vehicles. In the rapidly dimming light, I barely made out the outline of a deputy checking registrations. He shone a flashlight into the first vehicle in line, capturing a full carload in its harsh targeted beam.

The car, which appeared to be an old two-door hatchback with as much rust as good metal, slowly pulled across Lennon Bridge and stopped on the narrow shoulder, where a Highway Patrol Officer directed them out of the vehicle.

I thought of the description I'd given Derek of the Middle Eastern man, and wondered how many olive-skinned, black haired, brown eyed men of medium height and weight would be stopped and questioned.

We probably could have pulled out of line, shown our FBI identifications to the officers, and promptly been on our way, but I sensed we were safer staying in our seats until we approached our turn. Maybe it was the darkness moving in coupled with the knowledge that we had no idea where our suspects had escaped to, that made me feel as if we were all on edge.

The flash drive was secured inside an evidence bag that remained in a dash compartment just inches from me.

Despite my exhaustion, I could barely contain my excitement.

Steve rested his wrists on top of the steering wheel. If we waited much longer, I thought he'd be ready to rest his head there, too.

"What are you thinking?" he asked, glancing toward me.

My eyes met his. The lids looked heavy, but the color of his eyes was as intense as ever.

"You know perfectly well what I'm thinking," I said. "This tiny piece of metal can hold as much information as the hard drive I took from that hunting lodge. And if we were able to find thousands of identity theft records on the hard drive—"

"Who knows what this little baby will tell us?" Steve completed.

I opened the evidence bag and peered inside. Though it hadn't left my possession since I'd found it, it was somehow comforting to view it again. I was intimately familiar with the device, having used one as a data backup since I was in college. The exterior was now melted and blackened, only an occasional mottled blue casting a revealing glimpse of its original hard blue plastic casing. I knew the interior—the flash drive itself—would be metal. The question was whether the metal had survived the fire, and whether it would still be readable.

As if in answer to my thoughts, Steve asked, "Do you think you'll be able to read it?"

"I'm sure I can," I answered without hesitation. The excitement in my voice made me sound as though I was more fully awake than I felt. "It's just a matter of how long it will take. Technology has changed so much that we're now able to read drives that were erased, drives that have been under water, or supposedly destroyed in fires—"

"—just like this one," Steve said.

"Just like this one," I repeated.

The deputy waved us forward, and Steve and I dutifully displayed our FBI badges as we approached the checkpoint. I noticed the deputy peering curiously at the truck's windows and one hand slipped instinctively to his weapon. He leaned down and shone the flashlight into the truck, comparing our faces with those on our identifications. The plate on his jacket proclaimed his name as Alec Brodie.

"Either of you speak Spanish?" he asked.

For a brief moment, I considered pretending not to hear his question in the hope that he would just wave us through and we could be on our way back to the hotel and the comfort of a warm bed. I noticed Steve was conspicuously silent.

"I do," I heard myself answering.

"Sure could use your help," Deputy Brodie said.

"What've you got?" Steve asked.

Deputy Brodie nodded toward the car that had just been pulled off the road. "We're encountering a lot of folks who can't speak English. Wonder if you'd like to take a stab at communicating with them?"

I leaned across the seat so I could see the deputy's face better. "The blast site was declared clean."

"We're not trying to quarantine 'em," he answered. "Just ask a few questions."

I nodded, and Steve drove slowly through the checkpoint. As he pulled past the stopped car, we gasped simultaneously. There were at least a dozen more stopped on each side of the road. All of the occupants were seated on the ground outside their vehicles, while sheriff's deputies painstakingly searched each vehicle.

Steve maneuvered the truck onto the shoulder. I slipped the evidence bag into my jacket pocket and hopped out of the truck. As my legs stretched to meet the pavement, I felt the muscles tightening as if in protest. Hopefully, this wouldn't take long.

My hopes for a quick exit were soon dashed.

The word was out that INS was cracking down on illegal aliens and convoys of them were headed out of the area on every road for miles around. I peered into so many faces that I lost count, and frankly, I was beginning to be alarmed by the number I saw whose identifications appeared suspect or those who were lacking any identification at all. When one of the deputies informed me that he hadn't found a single driver's license among all these Latinos, it was difficult not to become sidetracked. Instead, I tried to remain focused on finding the man I'd seen one day earlier.

I couldn't group them all into one classification. Each had an individual story to tell. Some had weathered faces and roughened hands that told of long periods of time working outdoors, perhaps in construction or landscaping. Others had a distinct odor that reminded me of slaughter houses and processing plants back in Tennessee. The children clung to the adults as if afraid they would forcibly be taken from them. Some of the smaller children were barefoot, and many of the Latinos, both child and adult, wore only thin cotton clothes better suited for the summer.

I asked each person if they knew of someone living in their midst who pretended to be Latino but who definitely was not. Sometimes, they peered at their shoes as if they held a great deal of interest to them and I was unable to get more than a one-syllable negative answer from them.

Others, upon realizing I spoke their language, wanted to convince me they were here legally. Some of them wanted to distance themselves from others who they perceived as potential troublemakers, telling me they were Guatemalan, Mexican, or from any number of Central or South American countries. Some of them begged to be let go, telling me of the steady jobs they had and the number of people—both in America and in their native countries—who depended upon their income.

None of them admitted to knowing Regina Estrada, though I suspected several of them knew the name. And none of them wanted to admit that non-Latinos had been living amongst them.

Fighting to remain awake and tired of getting nowhere fast, I returned to the truck and leaned against its hood.

"Why are they protecting them?" Steve mused.

"I don't know that they are," I answered. "We had quite a few Latinos working on my folks' farm. Their culture is so different from ours… South of the border, they handle their own disagreements; they don't get law enforcement involved. And there are so many corrupt officials in their own countries that they don't trust them here, either."

I heard the sound of footsteps behind us and turned to see Deputy Brodie approaching.

"Any luck?" he called out.

I shook my head.

"We can't detain them all," he said. "We'd have half the Latinos in this county, and I doubt even that INS would be all that interested in them." He pulled out a cigarette pack and offered it to us. Steve and I declined. "It's a nasty habit," he said almost apologetically as he lit one.

In the glare of the lighter, his face looked deeply lined, his eyes drooping just a bit as if he had seen too much in his lifetime. His accent was not Carolinian, and I wondered what had brought him here to this part of the country.

"Let them go," Steve said, interrupting my thoughts. "We're looking for at least one—possibly two—Middle Eastern men. Not Latinos."

"I don't mean to sound ignorant," Deputy Brodie said, "but I don't know how to tell the difference."

They both looked at me, their eyes searching mine for an explanation. For once I was at a loss for words. Finally, my vocal cords constrained with the tension I felt inside, I said, "That's what they're counting on."

46

I sat at the table in the hotel room, picking at a warm chocolate chip cookie I'd grabbed from the hotel lounge. I could hear the water running in the bathroom. I'd taken my shower first and once I was done with my cookie and Steve was out of the bathroom, I'd brush my teeth and head to a nice warm bed.

I heard a door open and softly swing shut, and I instinctively turned to peer at the crack under the hotel room door. A shadow was clearly visible across the threshold before quickly disappearing. I rose from the table and moved silently toward the door. The shadow returned broader than before, which could only mean the person was closer to the door.

I stopped at the doorframe and pressed my ear to it. I could have sworn I heard someone breathing heavily on the other side.

Cautiously, I leaned across the door and peered through the peephole. I caught sight of the back of someone's head, as though he were leaning toward the doorknob. He was small, perhaps just over five feet, and had a full head of black, tousled hair.

I stared at the deadbolt, which remained securely in place. Once I flipped it, it would undoubtedly click, alerting the intruder to my location. I would have to be lightning quick.

I calculated my movements. I planted my right hand on the deadbolt thumb turn and took a deep breath.

Then with a movement as rapid as a snake strike, I threw the deadbolt, hurled open the door, and shouted "FBI! Freeze!"

I felt Steve's presence behind me even before I heard his voice. "Get your hands in the air!" he barked.

Petite, feminine hands rose high in front of me. Our visitor was a woman.

She was shorter than me and even with a heavy jacket on she was so small that if it weren't for her beautiful eyes under flawless, long lashes and her perfectly formed facial features, she might have been mistaken for a pre-teen.

I recognized her immediately; she had been at Lennon's Bridge when I was attempting to interview the Latinos. She had stared at me with a blank expression when I spoke to her in English, and when I'd switched to Spanish, she had studied her feet and murmured that she didn't know anything.

Now, as Steve led her into the hotel room, she nodded in my direction and pleaded in English, "I came to speak with her."

I closed the door behind them.

"Sit down," Steve directed, pointing at the sofa. He sat across from her in a chair while I walked around the coffee table and sat at the other end of the sofa.

"What are you doing here?" I asked.

"I was trying to get up my nerve to knock," she said sheepishly.

"Why did you act like you didn't understand English, when I spoke to you earlier?" I asked.

She looked down at her palms. I stifled a gasp when I saw the harsh calluses and dry, cracked skin. "Sometimes it is not good for others to know."

"You know the men I'm looking for, don't you?" I said quietly.

There was a long pause. She nodded. She removed her arms from her coat but kept it draped around her shoulders as if she were still chilled from the night air. Her hair, which had been obscured by her coat collar, now fell around her shoulders in beautiful, thick black waves.

And then in the pale light cast by too-small lamps, she told us her story.

Her name was Conception Rivera, but she was called Concha. She had come to this country almost five years ago from her native Mexico. She was born, the sixth of nine children, in a rural village northwest of Oaxaca. Her father was a construction worker, one of thousands hired to sweep through the region, clearing the trees and jungle in preparation for roads that would eventually stretch from east to west across Mexico. Her mother died when Concha was barely ten years old, leaving her to raise her younger siblings while her father was away for increasingly longer periods of time; then the time came when her father did not come home at all.

The children grew up in extreme poverty. Two of Concha's older brothers moved to northern Mexico in their early twenties. They occasionally visited, each time bearing more gold and silver jewelry, flashing large wads of cash, and wearing clothes such as Concha had never seen before. They ridiculed the village and its ways, but most of all, they ridiculed its poverty.

Eventually, when Concha was eighteen, they talked her into joining them in Ciudad Juarez, along the Mexican-American border.

It was a difficult undertaking for Concha, traveling northward to Ciudad Juarez, a town such as she had never seen before. On the one hand, it was filled with riches and American tourists and beautiful dancers, ornate buildings, restaurants and hotels. But it held another personality as well: that of crime and drugs, of corruption and poverty and pain.

On her first night with her brothers in Ciudad Juarez, they were gunned down in front of her. Their bodies were robbed of their jewelry, their cash, plastic bags filled with white powder, and all of their possessions right down to their American made leather belts and shoes.

Concha fled, but she didn't know where to go. She didn't have the money or the means to travel back to Oaxaca. She left Ciudad Juarez, traveling northeast, into an inhospitable desert.

She eventually stumbled onto a small village, which she would come to realize was a staging area for border crossings. It was there where she first saw groups of Middle Eastern men.

They spoke a different language and they always remained in clusters of four or more, always with one or two designated speakers presumably to serve as translators. Although their skin tone and hair color was not that different from theirs, they stood out from the Mexican population in their physical features, their mannerisms, and their cultural background. They seemed to have a never-ending supply of cash and yet never worked. They remained for days or weeks inside shabby motels, only showing their faces occasionally and never for very long.

Through listening and observing, Concha decided to risk everything to cross the border. It would be a dangerous journey, filled with the constant threat of smugglers and marauding, lawless mobs who knew the area between Ciudad Juarez and the American border like the backs of their hands. They would prey on the flood of illegal immigrants, knowing they carried all of their money and their worldly possessions with them. They particularly enjoyed abducting the women and committing unspeakable crimes on them.

But Concha decided it was worth the danger to cross the border and arrive in the United States, where she would no longer live in poverty, where the stores never went empty, where food was always plentiful, where she could get a job cleaning an Anglo's home and make more money than she could ever have imagined.

Her goal would take nearly a decade to achieve. She would work in various border towns as a barmaid, a cook, or even a prostitute—anything to earn money, which she squirreled away for her trip across the border. Every time she thought she had enough money, the price was raised— first due to the vigilantes patrolling the American border, and then due to American troop patrols.

It would be too risky for her to travel alone, across the vast desert or further west across the rugged mountainous terrain. She would have to pay for someone to smuggle her across, to guarantee her safety, and to help her realize her dream of becoming an American. She began to learn English in bits and pieces, never knowing if the words she heard were correct, but rehearsing them nonetheless.

She watched as groups of Middle Eastern men moved into the border towns, remained for weeks or months at a time, only to disappear during the night. She knew, and other Mexicans knew, they were using their country to gain access to the United States. The Mexican police took their money in exchange for silence. The government provided them with Mexican documents—passports, licenses, birth certificates—all containing the Mexican insignia. On paper, they were Mexicans.

Concha eventually realized her dream of immigrating to the United States, and eventually she would find her way across Texas and through the southern states, to North Carolina.

By the time Concha finished her story, the sun was beginning to rise. I hadn't slept for another night, but I knew I had to see this through.

"When you came here, you saw these same men again?" I asked.

She nodded.

"And did you know Regina Estrada?"

"There was no Regina Estrada. It was a name on a mailbox, yes. A telephone number, yes. But no woman lived there. Only four men."

I looked across the room at Steve, who was studying Concha.

"What did these men do? Where did they work?"

"They did not work. They stayed in the house."

"They never left? Never?"

Concha hesitated. "One time I saw one—a man they called Miguel—at a mall."

"A shopping mall?"

"Si."

"What was he doing, buying clothes or something?"

"No." Concha ran her fingers through her thick black hair. "He was just sitting in the food court, just watching."

Daylight was streaming through the windows by the time I said good-bye to Concha. I was confident she wasn't going to flee. She had a home in Robeson County better than anything she'd ever experienced before—a mobile home that had running water and electricity, a real bed, and a somewhat working kitchen and bathroom. She had a steady job cleaning homes, enough to pay for food and clothing. She had a driver's license and a work visa, though I suspected neither was in her real name.

After I closed the door and turned back to the room, I found Steve staring out the window at the parking lot below. I joined him there and we watched in silence as Concha departed the hotel and crossed the lot to a rusted Impala that I'd bet my last dollar had four bald tires. As she approached the car, Steve jotted down the tag number.

She hesitated after unlocking the door. Then she reached into her purse and pulled out a scarf, wrapping it loosely around her neck. As she slid behind the steering wheel, the early morning sun caught her in its sights, briefly displaying the flowing black, white, and red material. I recognized it immediately as the one I'd seen outside Regina Estrada's house but before I could react, she pulled away.

I turned to Steve. "I think—"

"I do, too," he said, pulling out his cell phone and calling the Lumberton Police Department. While waiting for them to answer, he said, "We just spent the night with Regina Estrada."

47

The industrial lights and hustle and bustle of the Raleigh Airport stood in stark contrast to the events of the past two days. Gone were the flatlands and the swamps with their sometimes-brackish waters and green algae slime, the bald cypress and wetland fields of cypress knees. Gone were the expanses of farmlands and pine forests, occasionally sprinkled with the low-lying metal rooftops of chicken houses or the taller and larger poultry and hog processing plants.

As I looked around me, gone also were the waves of immigrant workers. Yet as I sat at the gate waiting for our flight to be called, I knew I had not seen the last of Robeson County. I would be back.

Derek, Steve and I were huddled in a corner of the terminal, our backs to the wall, allowing us a full, largely unobstructed view of the terminal. The polished floors and industrial carpets were overtaken with a mixture of families, businesspeople and couples waiting for the next flight to Nashville. Sleet had moved in.

I'd tried my best on the ninety-mile drive here from Lumberton to convince Steve I should not return to the hospital. My headaches had subsided for the most part and

I really thought we would all be better served if we simply headed back to Quantico.

He'd agreed after a lengthy telephone conversation with Supervisory Special Agent Pippin from Quantico—too lengthy in my opinion—with one caveat: I would have to be cleared by a physician.

Derek telephoned us en route and agreed to meet us at the airport check-in.

I wrapped my fingers around a warm cup of cappuccino and breathed in the fresh vanilla aroma. I caught a glimpse of a neighboring traveler's powdered donut and wondered if I had the time to stand in line for one.

"So you know Concha Rivera was picked up by Lumberton Police just two blocks from our hotel," Steve was saying.

"Yes," Derek said. "Miranda is there now interviewing her."

"What will happen to her?" I asked.

Derek shrugged. "Depends on how much she's able to help us. We have a lot of unanswered questions."

I nodded. "It took a lot of courage for her to come to our hotel last night."

"We'll keep that in mind," Derek said. "Anyway, we're certain now that Jesus Rios—Jess—was not in charge of the operation."

"You'd initially thought he was the ringleader," Steve noted.

Derek raised one eyebrow. "He wants us to think he is, with his expensive clothes, bodyguards, and fancy limousine. He certainly acts like a big fish in a small pond."

"But?"

"But he doesn't have the smarts to put something like this together. Somebody else is calling the shots."

My mind flashed back to that windy day on Long Island. It was entirely plausible that Ricky was the mastermind.

Jess had certainly not acted like the big fish in a small pond as he'd struggled to catch the money Ricky had thrown at him.

But if I told them I suspected Ricky, Alex would also come under suspicion. She would have to. The Bureau wanted only squeaky-clean agents. And if Alex were somehow involved—no, she couldn't be. The conversation I'd overheard, pleading with Ricky and the concern for her career, told me she was not involved.

But Alex knew about Ricky's operation. And that alone would place her on seriously shaky ground. And if I didn't speak up now about my suspicions, I could end up right alongside her.

I took a deep breath. "There's something you both need to know."

My words were drowned out by the loudspeaker. "Ladies and gentlemen, your flight has been delayed due to bad weather. Please remain in the gate area, and we'll announce more information in the next few minutes."

The passengers let out a collective groan.

"I'll be right back," Steve said, hopping up and making his way to the gate attendant.

Derek turned to me. "You were saying?"

I hesitated as I watched Steve. We were a team now, and he was still an instructor. I couldn't tell Derek of my suspicions without Steve's presence.

Fortunately before the silence became awkward, Steve returned. He began speaking before he'd even reached us. "Our plane is delayed in Atlanta. Bad ice storm coming up from the south. We might be here awhile." He returned to his seat. "So do you think Jess is involved in terrorism?"

Derek shook his head. "There's nothing to substantiate that, at this point, anyway. It appears more likely that Jess was providing false documents to illegal immigrants—

mostly driver's licenses, stolen social security numbers and green cards."

"Any idea where he got the names?" Steve asked.

"The hard drive Sheila confiscated has been passed on to others. They tell me there are thousands of names, too many for each one to be stolen individually."

I nodded. "It wouldn't be all that unusual to obtain thousands of names by stealing one company's client records—a credit card company, internet service provider, bank…" I paused. "Remember the case concerning Teledata Communications?"

"Do I ever," Steve said. "To date, it's the largest known case of identity theft; information contained on the three national credit reporting agencies—Equifax, TransUnion and Experian—were stolen and sold to criminals. The FBI investigated that case and made the arrests."

I sipped my cappuccino. We sat in silence for a moment while I wondered if my moment of opportunity had passed. I decided to wait until I could talk to Steve alone. Instead, I asked, "Have you been able to identify the woman at The Triple R?"

"Not yet. We're still working on that," Derek answered.

Steve ran his hand through his hair. "My guess is she was involved in culling names. She then sold them to Jess and his outfit, who in turn, sold them to undocumented workers."

"But why set up shop in an abandoned motel?" I asked. "Why not do it in the comfort of your living room? With computer technology the way it is today, there's no need to travel to some remote location like that—"

"Maybe she wanted to obscure a trail," Steve mused. "If we could identify her and get a search warrant, we might find her own PC is completely clean."

"Jess maintains he doesn't know who she is, or what she was doing at The Triple R," Derek said. "But then, he also claims he was not there that night and he did not participate in any murder."

"Have you found the body?" I asked.

"Not yet. But we're looking."

I pictured the bayou-like wetlands surrounding The Triple R, enveloped by quagmires of rich black mud and batteries formed by decaying vegetation; nature itself providing a guarantee of inaccessibility. The cypress knees, set so close together, could snag a body in their craggy grasp and prevent it from ever floating downstream toward civilization, unless heavy spring rains or flooding would eventually flush it out. I glanced at the rain pounding the windows and involuntarily shuddered. "What happens if the body is never found?"

Derek shrugged. "Depends on how much evidence we can gather. It wouldn't be the first time the FBI has made a case without a body."

"What is Jess' connection to the men from the Estrada house?" I asked.

"He's denying everything. We have him on identity theft. We're investigating wire fraud and conspiracy charges and of course the murder charge… but we don't have anything to connect him to the other suspects."

"And the explosion?"

"We're working that scene, too. Looks like the explosion was intentionally set. Maybe they wanted to destroy any evidence."

Instinctively, I reached in my jacket pocket and fingered the flash drive, still encased in the evidence bag. I hoped by the time we landed in Nashville, I would know its contents backwards and forwards.

"I've been thinking about all of this," Steve said, leaning forward and rubbing his chin thoughtfully.

"Me, too," I said, "and I'm beginning to wonder if the men at my parents' house were really after me, or if they were after evidence my mother might have left. Or evidence they thought she had."

"Too bad we can't ask them," Derek said with a touch of sarcasm.

"Maybe we can," I said conspiratorially.

They both stared at me. I looked in Derek's eyes but I wasn't able to get beyond the mask he'd perfected that effectively hid his emotions. Then I looked at Steve.

"Let's flush them out," I said.

"It's too dangerous," Steve answered immediately. "You're not even out of the Academy yet."

"He's right," Derek agreed. "Besides, we have a lot of seasoned agents on this case now."

"But they haven't tried to kill any of them," I said, hoping the calmness in my voice hid my growing excitement. "They want *me*. To get these guys, I have to become the decoy."

There was a moment of stunned silence before both of them answered in unison, "Absolutely not."

Their cries of protest were drowned out by an announcement cancelling our flight.

The look on Steve's face and his exasperated sigh was priceless. I knew he was envisioning hours sitting on hard chairs that would only get harder and more unbearable as we waited, trapped here with cable news repeated every thirty minutes until we were ready to scream, trying to keep ourselves entertained with a hastily bought book or magazine.

"It's a sign," I said, hoping my excitement would be contagious. "We can drive back to Quantico. We're probably closer to the Academy from here than we are to Nashville. Who knows how long it will take for our flight to leave? We could be back in what, three hours, maybe four!"

An expression flashed across Steve's face that I could only interpret as hesitation: he started to say *No*; I knew his lips were headed in that direction, but the word never formed. He looked deep in thought.

"Put me back in the hospital, or have me interviewed by the media. Do something that puts the word out that I'm back, and that I can identify the suicide bomber. Let him come after me again. We can catch him."

"No," Steve said forcefully. "It isn't going to happen, Sheila. Not now. Not ever."

48

We drove northward on Interstate 95 in a rented dark blue Buick LeSabre, the Raleigh-Durham International Airport now only a fading memory. The storm that swept through Atlanta was tracking to the north, bringing with it colder temperatures, ice and snow. It was moving fast, the clouds and gray skies heralding its approach, the temperatures dropping steadily.

There was no doubt in my mind that had we stayed at the airport waiting for the plane from Atlanta, the minutes would have stretched into long, unproductive hours. I stole a glance at Steve, whose eyes were focused on the road ahead, and wondered if he realized yet that driving by car back to Quantico was indeed a great idea.

"So," I said, "you're from Texas?"

He nodded.

"Any brothers or sisters?"

"Two sisters, one older and one younger."

"A middle child, huh?"

He glanced at me. "And you're an only child."

"Yes, I am."

"And I take it that your great-Aunt Jo is your only relative?"

I nodded. "My mother had two brothers—she was a middle child, too—but one died from cancer and the other died from a heart attack."

"They all must have been pretty young when they died."

"Mom was not even fifty when she died. My uncles died a few years earlier..." My voice faded as I tried to remember their birth years to calculate their ages.

"And your dad? Did he have any siblings?"

"No... it was just him."

"And Aunt Jo is his aunt?"

"Yes. My grandfather's sister. She had a daughter once, a long time ago... She died from leukemia."

"I'm sorry."

I fell silent. The traffic became increasingly heavier the farther north we drove. I realized we were coming to the close of the three-day Veteran's Day weekend. It had been only three days ago that I was sitting in my dorm room, whiling away the hours until I left for Nashville, and only two weeks since the mall explosion. It felt like an eternity. I glanced at my watch. Quantico was roughly a four-hour drive from Raleigh on a good day. We'd left Raleigh two hours ago, but had made slow progress.

"What are tomorrow's plans for me?" I asked.

Steve hesitated before answering. I knew he'd had a rather lengthy telephone discussion with Phil before he'd agreed to cancel our airline reservations and head for Virginia. I'd been dying to know the details of their conversation, but Steve, true to form, held the information close to his chest.

"Eight a.m., you're to be in the doctor's office. If the doctor tells us you can resume the Academy, you'll go straight to class."

I started to ask, "What if he doesn't?" but bit my tongue. I would pass the exam. I was well. I'd had no more dizziness since—well, I guess since the fight with Marilyn. Maybe she knocked the concussion out of me.

And this meant I'd missed only one day of class.

I refocused my attention on the laptop, which was fittingly perched on my lap. Before we'd even reached the turnoff for Interstate 95 from I-40, I'd begun examining the flash drive in earnest.

My first course of business was to examine it physically. I wasn't even sure the connection would still fit into the USB port or if it was damaged beyond my capabilities. The flash drive had the typical connection, known in the industry as an A connector. It was a tiny rectangle about the length of my thumbnail and was probably made from steel. The outer rim appeared to be damaged, perhaps by the intensity of the fire; the normally white material that held the four prongs in place was now singed and blackened.

It took awhile for me to carefully clean the connectors; I improvised and used Q-tips and a soft wood cuticle pusher from my cosmetics case along with a cloth soaked with rubbing alcohol from Steve's first aid kit. Then it took several more tries and adjustments before I could properly seat the flash drive into the USB port.

Unlike a hard drive, the flash drive doesn't rely on moving parts, so in that respect, I was lucky. With a fire that intense, moving parts could have melted and would no longer function properly. Instead, the flash drive used solid state technology—the information was embedded in a microchip through a series of electrical charges.

Steve pushed down hard on the brakes, sending the laptop flying to my knees, where I grabbed it before it hit the dashboard. I was so intent on protecting the computer that I didn't realize he'd thrown his arm in front of me until we'd come to a complete stop.

Traffic ahead of us was at a standstill.

"Where are we?" I asked.

"Just south of Richmond," he answered, rather sheepishly removing his arm from in front of my chest.

"That's okay," I said. I started to tell him that my father always did the same thing, as if his arm could keep me from sailing through the windshield, but I thought better of it. I didn't know how he'd react, being compared to my dad.

I returned to the computer. It eventually recognized the flash drive, which was a step in the right direction. It should have recognized it immediately, but given the condition of the drive, I supposed I was fortunate that it recognized it at all. But I still was unable to read any of the information.

"I need a break," Steve said, breaking the silence.

I glanced at him and then at the road. I'd been so intent on reading the flash drive that I hadn't realized the traffic had begun moving again. "How long have we been moving?"

"About an hour," he answered, stretching his arms out in front of him and cracking his knuckles.

I caught a glimpse of a road sign as we whizzed past. We were approaching Chippenham Parkway between Petersburg and Richmond.

"Get off at the next exit," I directed.

"You know a good place to eat and take a break?"

"Do I ever!" I answered, closing the cover on the laptop.

It was dark when we entered Richmond and made our way to the Fan District. A flood of memories returned to me as Steve drove slowly along shady streets where protective trees met in the center like a majestic canopy.

"You asked about my relatives," I said. "Margaret is the closest thing I have to a sister. We're opposites in so many ways, but she—her whole family—rallied around me when my parents died."

"How did you meet her?"

"At Vanderbilt. We shared a dorm room. Became best friends. And when my folks died, the Reeds became my extended family."

When we turned onto Monument Avenue, the Reed's four-story home was lit up like Times Square on New Year's Eve. The front porch was already decorated for Christmas, though Thanksgiving was still over two weeks away. Garlands of holly were draped from the porch railing, wrapped festively with sparkling lights. The massive front door was open, revealing a giant Christmas tree through the glass storm door.

We had difficulty finding a parking space, which isn't that unusual in The Fan, but it appeared as though most of the cars' occupants were en route to the Reed's house. Steve finally maneuvered into a parking spot that opened up on the street.

We walked up six steps before stopping on a broad concrete landing bordered on two sides with decorated Douglas fir. Ahead of us, on a steep incline and at the end of a dozen more steps, was the house. Now that we were so close, the roofline of the wrap-around porch effectively blocked the upper floors from view. A front tower extended onto the porch, the tall, narrow windows covered in filmy white curtains that did little to conceal the silhouettes of a dozen people milling around a massive dining room table. Even from this distance, I could see the trays piled high with hors d'oeuvres.

The people spilled into the front hallway, where they lined the golden oak stairs behind the etched glass door, wine glasses clasped in their hands. The sound of laughter and gaiety reached my ears, beckoning me inside.

"Maybe this isn't a good time," Steve said, interrupting my thoughts.

I drew my attention away from the house and looked into Steve's face. He looked haggard. It had been a long trip from the Raleigh International Airport. Now North Carolina seemed a world away.

"I know you're tired," I said. "We'll only stay a few minutes. The Reeds would never forgive me if they knew we were this close and didn't come inside."

When I opened the storm door, the sound of laughter and conversation was at a high pitch. Above the fray, I heard the unmistakable sound of one person's melodious laughter.

"Is that Margaret?" I asked to no one in particular as I entered the house.

The crowd in the hallway parted as I made my way past the majestic staircase. At the end of the hall sat Margaret, two men on either side of her, looking like a modern-day Scarlett O'Hara at the Twelve Oaks barbeque.

"Sheila!" she exclaimed.

She was in a wheelchair. A thick micro suede blanket lay across her lap and draped almost to her ankles, where bandages encased her legs and feet.

As she steered her way toward me, I rushed to meet her, wrapping my arms around her neck. "Margaret, you're home!" was all I could think to say.

"Oh, Sheila," Mrs. Reed exclaimed, darting from the dining room into the hallway. "I knew you wouldn't miss this!"

I drew back from Margaret. "I'm sorry I didn't call—"

"Nonsense," Mrs. Reed said. "I told that nice girl from the Academy that you didn't need to call me back. I knew you would make it."

I hesitated.

"Sheila, she did give you the message, didn't she?" Margaret said, her eyes studying mine.

I glanced at Steve. "I haven't been at the Academy," I said. "I've been working in the field."

I could see Margaret's eyes as she looked past me to Steve. I placed my hand on his shoulder and drew him closer to us. "Margaret, this is FBI Agent Steve Moran, my instructor at the Academy. Steve, this is my best friend, Margaret Reed."

He went to shake her hand, but it was bandaged. Instead, he clasped it between both of his. "It's nice to meet you," he said politely.

I watched her eyes dart from Steve to me and back again.

"So, who's the new man in your life?" Margaret whispered conspiratorially.

I glanced at Steve, who was sipping a glass of ginger ale while he chatted with Mr. Reed.

"I told you," I said. "He's my instructor."

"He's more than that."

I tried to appear taken aback. "What do you mean?"

"Oh, don't try to kid me," she said with a sly smile. "He's smitten with you."

"Oh, please."

"He's completely immune to every other woman."

"We're working."

"Oh? The FBI has crashed my party?" Margaret pouted. "And what exactly do you expect to find here?"

Steve excused himself from Mr. Reed and came to stand by my side.

"So," Margaret said in a louder voice, "We shall have to go shopping again, Sheila. You simply have to make the time to go with me."

"You're kidding, aren't you?" I said.

She pulled back the blanket to show her bandages. "I'm told I will have these things on for awhile," she said. "And I just don't have the clothes large enough to cover them. Do you think I want to wear the same clothes every day?"

"I repeat: you're kidding, right?"

Margaret grew serious. "The truth is I'm terrified to enter a store. But I have to. The sooner, the better. Otherwise, I could spend the rest of my life afraid of venturing out in public again, for fear—for fear of what could happen."

"I understand," I said, my voice sounding softer to me. "Yes, I will go shopping with you."

"The day after Thanksgiving," she said with renewed conviction. "All the stores are going to have massive sales. Seventy percent off, I hear."

I glanced at Steve.

He nodded. "It would be good for you, too."

"We'll be off?"

"Four-day weekend. You should go."

"Okay," I said. "It's a date. I will be here to pick you up. Ten o'clock sharp."

"By then all the good stuff will be sold." Margaret pretended to pout. "The stores open at five, you know that."

"What?"

"It's the biggest shopping day of the year! At least pick me up at six."

I sighed. "Six o'clock it is. And we'll spend the day mega-shopping."

49

Darkness descends early in Virginia at this time of year. It means I leave the dorm when the sky is still black and I don't return until after the moon is ascending. I glimpse only snippets of light during the day, usually when I am hurrying through the glass corridors that lead from one Academy building to another. It's a bleak time of year, though I understand after Thanksgiving, which is only a week away, our class will be allowed to decorate for the holidays. I found my mind wandering to the festive atmosphere at Margaret's house and briefly looking forward to a holiday season filled with lights and candles and sparkling decorations. Then all too quickly, I found myself simply looking forward to spring and warm weather, the holidays and the bleakness of winter far behind me.

In the week since I'd returned from North Carolina, I'd fallen into the routine of being an FBI recruit, having escaped being ordered right back into a hospital bed. I kept my ailments to myself, slipping a few aspirins into me every now and then, for fear they'd tell me I was too sick to continue in this Academy class. And now that I'd come this far, I didn't want to turn back. I couldn't.

Graduation was still more than two months away.

I sat at the desk in my dorm room, trying valiantly to memorize more than two hundred laws I would be expected to know. Beside my computer was the flash drive, even now blackened and mute, its secrets still locked inside. Steve had arranged for me to keep it, at least for the present time, since my computer skills were on a par with those in the lab. But if I wasn't able to read it soon, I'd have no choice but to turn it in to someone else.

Alex had appeared nervous and somewhat distant since I'd been back, but I hadn't pressed her or tried to engage her in conversation. Fact was, I didn't want to know any more about her private life or that of her brother. If she confided in me, I would find myself in the unenviable position of reporting her.

In the evenings as I studied, I often saw Alex through the window, standing under the street lights. She appeared to have long and sometimes animated conversations on her cell phone, and my mind would flash back time and again to the conversation I'd overheard. When she finally returned to the room, she often appeared anxious and out of sorts.

The bathroom door opened. I could sense more than hear Alex entering the room, her small feet padding across the carpet.

I returned to my laptop and pretended to review today's lessons, though the words now seemed jumbled, my mind too full to grasp any more information.

"What's that?"

I looked up to find Alex standing beside my desk, busily drying her long dark hair with an already damp towel, the fresh herbal scent of her shampoo tickling my nostrils. I followed her gaze to the crippled flash drive.

"Flash drive," I said. I inwardly chastised myself for placing it in plain view.

She picked it up and examined it against the light. "What happened to it?"

"Aunt Jo accidentally tossed it in the drum with a lot of old papers."

"In the drum?"

She peered at me with narrowed eyes. I wouldn't have believed my story, either.

"You know, a fifty-five gallon drum. We burn leaves in it. Sometimes old papers. Anyway, this got in with the papers and got burned."

"Why are you keeping it?"

"It has some old pictures on it," I said, gently pulling the drive from her fingers and returning it to my desk.

"Like the pictures your mom took?"

I turned away from her and focused my eyes on the computer screen, where I hoped they'd be less visible. I was a terrible liar, and I knew it. "No, old family pictures. I thought I'd try to copy them onto my hard drive, if I can ever read this flash drive."

She sighed. Out of the corner of my eye, I watched her wander to her bed. She sat down heavily, ran the towel through her hair in a half-hearted effort to dry it, and then sighed again.

I resisted the urge to ask her what was wrong. The urge is powerful among women, and it wasn't easy to sit just a few feet away and pretend I didn't hear her.

After a moment, she spoke. "Ricky is visiting me tomorrow evening."

"Oh?" I tried to remain focused on the computer screen and attempted to sound nonchalant, but my stomach was performing somersaults.

"He's on his way to North Carolina. We'll probably just have dinner together and then he'll be on his way."

I'd said nothing to Alex—or anyone else—about my trip from Nashville to Robeson County. As far as anyone in the Academy knew, I'd been resting comfortably at Vanderbilt University Medical Center. While I was sure Steve

had informed his superiors of my activities, and while he
never instructed me not to tell anyone else about them, I
had a gut feeling that the less others knew of our side trip,
the better off I'd be.

She continued, "His business partner has run out on
him. He's going down there to try and find him."

"I didn't realize Ricky was in business," I mumbled.

Her voice sounded distant. "Yeah. Some sort of import
business."

I'll say.

"Anyway, his business partner works in North Carolina
while Ricky stays in New York. Looks like he might have
skipped town and taken a lot of money with him."

"Ricky's money?"

"Company money. The accounts have been cleaned
out."

My mind was racing. Could the FBI have closed down
the accounts and seized the money? Or was someone else
involved?

"What does Ricky hope to accomplish, if his partner
has already left?" I asked.

"It's a small place. Not like New York; it's the kind of
place where everybody knows everybody else. He's hoping
somebody will know where he went."

I tried to rise slowly, keeping my movements casual,
though my heart was pounding so hard in my chest that I
was afraid I would turn the desk over in my haste to get out
of there. I grabbed the flash drive and shoved it in my
pocket.

"I need to run down to the library," I said.

"I'll go with you," she offered.

"No," I said, perhaps a little too quickly. I added in a
softer tone, "By the time you get dressed, I can already be
there. It's only going to take me a few minutes to find what
I want anyway."

She appeared disappointed, but I shut down my PC and grabbed my jacket while it was powering down. Then I was out the door and racing down the hall. I had to find Steve.

50

I found Steve in his office, deep in conversation with Agent John Davidson, who was hunched over Steve's desk.

Steve glanced up and beckoned me inside, his puzzled eyes searching my face. Though I'd learned where all the instructors' offices were located during my first week at the Academy, this was the first time I'd ventured here—a minor detail that wasn't lost on either of us.

After our initial greetings and some idle chitchat with John about my fledgling FBI career, I turned to go.

"I didn't mean to interrupt," I said. "I can come back later."

"Actually," Steve said, "We were just talking about you."

"Oh?" I felt myself sink into the nearest chair.

"Have a seat," Steve said with a wry smile. "John has been investigating the mall bombing."

"I'd like for you to take a look at a few pictures," John said.

Lying on top of Steve's desk were pictures of eight men, four to a page. As John pulled them toward me, I gasped.

"You recognize any of them?"

I nodded. "This one." I pointed at one in the center. "He's the one who tried to kill me—and the one I saw in the food court, just before the bomb went off."

"That's Khalifa bin Hamad bin Fahad Hijazi."

"Khalifa bin who?"

Steve laughed. "Bin means 'son of'," he explained. "So he's Khalifa, son of Hamad, son of Fahad—his grandfather—and Hijazi is his family name."

"I see," I said, though it took another moment for this to sink in.

I leaned back in my chair. "So, you knew all along the suicide bomber wasn't a female?"

"Oh, it was a female, alright," John said. "Think, Sheila. *Suicide* bomber. This guy's still alive."

"But the dynamite strapped around him—"

"Most likely, he was a backup. My guess is, though, that he got too close to the other bomber. They should have been spread further apart, so when she detonated, he wouldn't be injured."

"But was he injured?"

"You tell me." John studied me with intense brown eyes.

"He knew I'd seen him," I said slowly. "And he was able to get to my room, almost was successful in suffocating me—" I raised my hand instinctively to my throat— "and he chased me through the hospital. My guess is he went down with the explosion but his injuries might have been similar to mine; no broken bones, no internal injuries."

Steve nodded. "Very good."

I returned to the pictures. "This man right here," I continued excitedly, "is the one I saw in Robeson County, the one in the house that was bombed."

"Aziz bin Mohammad Al-Fulani."

John took a magic marker off Steve's desk and drew a bright red "X" through one of the pictures. "This is the man that was killed in front of your parents' home."

"So they followed me to my parent's home," I mused. "When they were going through the house—were they looking for me?"

"We don't know yet," John said. "What we do know is all of these men are members of the same sleeper cell."

"And we don't know their plans," Steve added.

I nodded.

"Sheila, we want these men," John said, leaning closer to me.

"That's where you come in," Steve said.

I looked from John's brown eyes to Steve's green ones. "What do you want me to do?"

Steve leaned toward me so we were huddled together like players on a football field. "I'm going to take you up on your offer," he said. "We're going to use you as bait."

"Sheila," John warned, his brows furrowed, "this is going to be a very controlled operation. Don't go getting the idea that you're going to bust in by the seat of your pants and take these guys. This has to be planned out, every last detail. You got that?"

I looked back at Steve. "Will Steve be in on this operation?"

"Would it matter if he was?"

I didn't answer.

"Yes, Sheila," Steve said. "I'm in on it."

I nodded slightly. For some reason, my knees were beginning to knock together. I pressed them against each other tightly, hoping they didn't notice.

"Before we get started on the details of the operation," Steve said, pushing another piece of paper toward me, "this came in from the lab here at Quantico this afternoon."

"What is it?" I said, pulling it toward me.

"There's no easy way for me to say this," Steve said. I thought I detected a softness in his voice. "Your parents were poisoned."

"What kind of poison?" I asked. I was staring directly at the paperwork, but the words swam before my eyes.

"Nicotine."

"Nicotine?" My head shot up.

Steve reached across the desk and placed his hand on top of mine. His eyes locked onto mine; even if I had wanted to, I doubt I could have looked away.

"It's made by soaking tobacco for a few days. It turns into a brown sludge. Then you strain it, getting rid of the tobacco. Simmer what's left until the liquid is just about gone. What you end up with is a highly toxic substance."

"And that was added to the iced tea," I finished, my voice sounding distant.

"If it's any consolation, I don't think your parents suffered—not like they could have, with some other substances. The amount in the glasses was enough to put them into a coma within minutes of drinking it. They would have been alive when the gas line was tampered with, which would have caused the carbon monoxide poisoning. At least, we think the gas line was tampered with... Seems too much of a coincidence for the two to be unrelated."

I tried to absorb all that he was saying. I found myself trying to fight back tears; if I allowed myself to feel the pain, I might lose it right there in his office. I couldn't do that. I wouldn't do that.

"When they were found—why wasn't the home declared a crime scene? Why was there no investigation?"

"The carbon monoxide would leave tell-tale signs that any medical examiner would have recognized," Steve continued.

"If a medical examiner sees evidence as obvious as carbon monoxide poisoning, he's not likely to check any further," John added.

"So the deaths would be ruled accidental," I said, my voice starting to break.

"Even if an autopsy were performed, it's doubtful they would have tested for nicotine," Steve said. "Of course, this new evidence changes things and the case will be reopened."

I nodded. The three of us were silent. I felt a lone tear at the outside corner of my eye. Quickly, I removed my hand from under Steve's and wiped it away. "Thank you," I said. "Thanks for having it checked out."

"Sheila," Steve said, his voice still soft and calm, "this means someone was involved in your parents' deaths … As an investigator, this is the point where I'd normally ask you if you know anybody who would want to see them dead—"

"But given the circumstances, I think we both know who that is," I finished. Without thinking, I crumpled the pictures in my lap. "What about Concha Rivera?"

"The Fayetteville office—Derek and his staff—are interrogating her. If her story checks out, Middle Eastern men paid for her to come into this country," John said.

"Why would they do that?"

"In return for a cover. She works off her debt by running errands. It allows them to remain out of sight. Any arrangements they made—rental agreements, utilities, etcetera—would be done through her and her name."

"You mean, my mother's name."

"Yes, your mother's name."

"And Jess?" I said. "How does he figure into all of this?"

"He was selling false identities," John said. "I doubt if he is a terrorist; he doesn't fit the profile. But he made it possible for them to pass as Latinos."

I nodded, anger now swelling up inside me, pushing the pain aside.

"We're still interrogating him," John said. "So far, he's not telling who he gets his orders from. And the woman you saw at the hunting lodge—she's disappeared without a trace."

I looked into John's eyes. I stared hard for a long moment before turning to Steve. My own voice sounded hard when I spoke. "We need to talk."

51

If I never again inhaled the antiseptic air of a hospital ward, it would suit me just fine. Even now, as I reclined in the hospital bed, my attention focused again on the flash drive, the odor tickled my nose and made my head swim. I pulled the hospital tray toward me so it straddled my lap, the laptop securely seated in the middle, the flash drive protruding from the USB port. I'd been trying to read the drive for the past hour and had gotten no further than I had before.

A male nurse in a sage hospital tunic and matching pants popped his head in. "Pizza will be right up," he announced. "Do you want anything to drink?"

"How about a bottle of wine?" I quipped.

He raised one eyebrow.

"A Pepsi, then?"

He disappeared around the corner.

There were definite advantages to being a decoy. The "nurse" was actually Agent Troy Foster from the Washington field office. He would be manning the desk in the hallway off and on throughout the night, seeming to be engrossed in monitoring other patients or even catching a few winks, when, in reality, he would be keeping a sharp lookout for our expected visitor. At least, I hoped he would keep a sharp lookout.

Under the thin cotton gown that covered my torso, I wore a white shirt, while under the covers my legs were warmly embraced by dark blue slacks. Even my shoes were on. I was ready for action. The only thing that would have made me feel more secure was having a gun strapped to my side, but John and Steve nixed that idea with yet another reminder that until I graduated from the Academy, I would not be allowed to carry my Bureau weapon.

I glanced across the room, trying to appear casual. A huge bouquet of pink roses sat on the credenza, complete with a "Get Well" balloon and a card that expressed wishes for me to recover quickly. Somewhere in between the baby's breath and the long stemmed roses was a video recorder no larger than a tube of lipstick.

One room away, Steve, John and Agent Samantha Foote sat in front of a monitor with an unobstructed view of most of my hospital room. The only areas that were out of sight were a short hallway at the door, just around the corner from a private bathroom, and the bathroom itself.

I also knew additional cameras had been mounted at each end of the hallway; it wouldn't matter whether Hijazi used the elevator or the stairs—we'd have him long before he even reached my door.

It was the perfect setup.

Now all I was doing was waiting for him to materialize. If his last appearance was any indication, we expected him to arrive sometime during the night. I glanced at my watch. It was only six o'clock. I'd have at least another four or five hours before we could even begin to anticipate him.

I flipped on the television and tuned it to WRC-TV, where I was one of the top stories. It had been a local

NBC reporter who had been doing a story on the Academy on the day I fainted. So it was only natural that we'd use the same reporter to perform a follow-up interview and story. The interview appeared at noon as though it was live, with the reporter in my hospital room showing me suffering from a concussion far worse than I actually had. I managed to say a few words, but the reporter filled in the gaps—including the fact that I would never be able to forget the face of the suicide bomber's accomplice. The cameraman even showed the reporter passing the room number as they walked in.

It would air again during the evening news and again on the late night program. It was only two minutes, but we hoped it would have the desired effect. Just for good measure, I even vowed that once I graduated from the Academy, my top priority would be tracking down the suicide bomber's accomplice; the man who helped to send my best friend to the hospital, fighting for her life.

It had ended with the journalist announcing which hospital she was reporting from, and handing it back to the news desk.

I didn't mention Hijazi by name or show his picture. We wanted him to have a false sense of security so he would come after me again, here in this hospital.

"Ready for some dinner?" Troy announced as he entered my room, carrying a round plate with a metal top to keep the contents warm.

I moved my laptop to the side as he plopped it down in front of me.

"Pepperoni," he grinned.

"Thanks!" I said, pulling off the top. "I'm starved!"

Four slices of pizza were packed together on the plate. "Hey, a pepperoni's missing!" I moaned.

"You'll have to take that up with Steve," he said before disappearing again, the door swinging closed behind him.

While I ate, I downloaded some utility software I'd found on a hacker's web site. It was amazing what could be found in cyberspace, if you only knew where to look. The trick is always to select the software that won't send spyware hacking into your own computer, wreaking havoc and deleting or corrupting files. Sometimes I was lucky, and sometimes not. This time, I felt closer to unlocking the key as I read through the lines of code before running the program. When it didn't work, I tweaked the code, adding a few lines of my own, and continued to run it.

I'd finished the pizza and my soft drink was room temperature by the time I saw an old, familiar screen: the Windows Explorer was retrieving data from the drive.

I sat up straighter and watched the files as they transferred onto my laptop. Then I studied the resulting list.

Most of the file names were in a language that my computer could not decipher, resulting in square blocks where there should have been characters. But one of the files had a familiar extension—a database.

I heard a soft *thud*, and I stopped and looked up.

"Nurse?" I called out.

There was no response.

"What do you need, Sheila?" Steve's voice was almost a whisper in my ear.

"I thought I heard something," I whispered back, hoping the mike could pick up my words.

"We're watching your door. Nobody has come anywhere near it… Everything looks nice and quiet."

I held my breath and cocked my head. Then finally, I answered, "Must have been my imagination."

After a long moment, I returned to the laptop. Databases were one of my specialties. They were simply files that tracked bits and pieces of information. Now my fingers tingled with anticipation as I opened this database to reveal the information the terrorists had tracked.

Like the file names, most of the data was in another language, resulting in the familiar square boxes that were meaningless to my computer. But at least I had the file. I would turn this over to Steve or John, and their cryptanalysts and language experts would decipher it.

I scrolled through the list of more than a hundred lines before something caught my attention: a street address. I flipped over to the Internet and searched on the address; it was a mall located in Sardis, Nebraska. Nebraska? My only mental images of Nebraska were of corn fields and cattle. I googled the mall and quickly found it had a total of fifteen stores. Not exactly a flashy target.

I scoured the remaining lines. Several more addresses popped up, and I searched the Internet for each one—a shopping center on the outskirts of Washington, DC; a mall in Maine; another mall in rural Arkansas; a mall in a tourist area near Disneyland; Rodeo Drive… all shopping meccas of one size or another, some in heavily populated areas and others merely a blip in a rural field.

"Steve, can you hear me?" I said softly.

"What's up?" he answered, his voice soft and reassuring in my earpiece.

I looked toward the camera in the flower arrangement. "I retrieved the data from the flash drive."

"Great!"

"Steve, there's a list of malls and shopping centers in here."

There was silence on the other end.

"Steve, can you hear me?"

"Yeah… How many?"

"A hundred, give or take."

"Do you recognize any?"

"Some. You know, the big ones. But there are more in here in pretty rural areas, places that wouldn't be strategically located. And there's more than I can decipher because a lot is written in another language."

"Hold on." There was a long moment of silence. Then, "I'm sending Nurse Betty in with a blank CD. Can you copy it over?"

"Sure."

"We'll get it looked at, pronto."

I closed the database, brought up the Windows Explorer and waited patiently for Troy to appear.

"He's heading in now," Steve said finally. "Took us a minute to find a CD."

I rolled my eyes. "That was more than a minute," I mumbled.

I heard the door open just around the corner. In another second, Troy would be here, I could copy the files, and hopefully go back to deciphering them while the copy was en route to translators.

I waited but he did not appear. I thought I heard a sound like air escaping. Then there was the sound of a heavy thud, like something hitting the floor.

I threw the covers off me, dumping the laptop and tray onto the bed, and raced to the far end of the room. There, crumpled in the small hallway, was Troy, his face pale and his eyes rolled back in his head. Swiftly, I bent down and felt his neck for a pulse.

I heard the sound behind me at the same instant that a shadow crossed his face. Quickly, I turned.

I was staring into the cold black eyes of Khalifa Hijazi. As I peered upward at him, my lips parting to sound the alarm, I caught a glimpse of a ceiling tile pushed aside in the bathroom.

Then before I could make a sound, his face grimaced with the weight of a tire iron swinging straight for my head.

52

I was crouched beside Troy, my knees on the floor, my hand still resting on the side of his neck, my head turned almost 180 degrees as Hijazi's arm swung back with the tire iron.

Ducking was not an option. At the angle he was standing, if I ducked and he missed me, he could crush Foster's head. I couldn't allow that to happen.

A soaring shot of adrenaline coursed through my veins as I locked my hands together. With every ounce of strength in my body, I swung both arms around, striking him in both shins with the force of a baseball bat.

His body appeared to pulse in mid-air as his feet left the floor and he lost his grasp on the tire iron. It flew as though it had wings, one end catapulting itself over the opposite end as it sailed toward me. In a desperate attempt to deflect it, I threw my right arm high. The iron met the bones in my forearm with a deafening crack. It was futile trying to stop it, as if it were part of a thunderous wave hell bent on crashing into the doorframe. It hit the corner as the iron clattered onto the tiled bathroom floor.

Hijazi tumbled backward, his arms pistoning wildly as though he were trying to grab hold of anything to stop him from crashing to the floor. His head struck the edge of the sink and ricocheted onto the open door, spurting blood across the room.

Steve and John were at the hospital room door in an instant, guns drawn.

"FBI! Freeze!" they yelled simultaneously.

Steve remained semi-crouched in the tiny hallway with John a half step behind him, both their gun barrels leveled at Hijazi. Foster lay unconscious on the floor in front of him; a stream of bright red blood trailed across the floor from under his head. I was crouched on my knees, having swung around to face Hijazi.

Hijazi was leaning against the sink where he'd fallen. His right hand moved swiftly inside his billowing jacket.

"Freeze!" John, Steve and I screamed in unison.

I saw the grenade as soon as he pulled it from within the jacket pocket. I couldn't pull my eyes away from it. The safety pin ring was on the opposite side; even to my untrained eye, I knew it was Russian made. He held it under the fingers of his right hand, presenting it for a left hand pull.

We were all frozen in time. None of us dared breathe.

"Your rivers will run red on Black Friday!" he sneered in broken English.

His left hand jutted forward as a hail of gunfire erupted beside me. I hit the floor, afraid any upward jerking would put me directly in the agents' line of fire. The grenade dropped from his hand and rolled across the tile, stopping at my elbow. I grabbed it but as I turned to throw it, I realized there was nowhere I could toss it where we would be out of danger. It was then that I realized the pin was still secured.

When the barrage stopped, Hijazi lay dead, his bullet-riddled body propped against the toilet, a stream of blood coursing across the tile floor.

I slipped a sling around my neck and slid my forearm through the sleeve. I was now the not-so-proud owner of a fiberglass cast, which would have to remain in place for the next few weeks. I was just about to step down from the hospital bed when Steve stuck his head through the doorway.

"How's Troy?" I asked.

"He'll be okay. Took quite a blow to the head, and it's a miracle there are no broken bones."

"He's conscious?"

"He regained consciousness a little while ago. They're keeping him overnight, but it looks like he'll be released in another day or two."

I struggled with my jacket for a brief moment before Steve came to my rescue.

"So," I said, slipping my good arm through the jacket sleeve, "I hope this—" I lifted the broken arm slightly "—doesn't keep me from graduating."

"Oh, I don't think you're in any danger of that."

"So, it's over then." My words had an air of finality.

"Well, not quite. We got Hijazi, but we still have to round up the others."

I nodded. The others. Of course. For every fanatic we eliminated, ten more would pop up in their place, like a Pac man game running out of control. I looked into Steve's eyes. But we *would* control them; we would eventually eliminate or control them all. We had no other choice.

Steve lifted the other side of my jacket over my shoulder and pulled the collar around my neck. He paused as though he wanted to say something but couldn't quite find the words. His hand continued to rest on my collar, his fingers holding the fabric lightly, his eyes wandering from his own fingers to my neck and eventually upward to my eyes.

We were barely six inches apart. The faint scent of a slightly woodsy cologne reached my nostrils, and I found myself leaning into him. His eyes remained fixed on mine as his hand moved to my neck.

My cell phone rang, surprising us both. His hand flew off me as I mumbled my apologies and grabbed my phone from the jacket pocket.

"Hello?" I said nervously.

"Sheila!"

"Margaret... how are you?"

"Fantastic! I met the cutest guy—"

I smiled awkwardly, only half-listening to her latest conquest. When she paused to catch her breath, I managed to interject, "Can I call you back?"

"Sure... sure. Just don't forget. You're having Thanksgiving dinner at Mom and Dad's. And bring your walking shoes. Friday, it is Mega Shopping Day."

Steve had moved away from me and now stood with his back to the room, apparently looking out the window at the parking lot below. I wondered what he was doing for Thanksgiving, and whether he would be alone.

"I don't know," I said.

"What do you mean, you don't know? We're counting on you! Mom and Dad really want you here for Thanksgiving dinner. And you have to take me shopping on Friday. It's the biggest shopping day of the year—Black Friday!"

"What did you just say?"

"Mom and Dad—"

"No, after that."

"You have to take me shopping."

"What did you say about Friday—what did you call it?"

"Black Friday."

"Why did you say that?"

"Oh, for heaven's sake, Sheila. Really. You are such a non-shopper. It's Black Friday, the biggest shopping day of the year. It's the day that most stores go from red ink into the black—"

I was across the room in two seconds flat. I clicked off the phone and shoved it into my pocket and grabbed Steve's arm before he could turn around to face me. "We've gotta go," I said hurriedly. "You were right. It isn't over."

53

As long as I live, I don't believe I will ever forget the expression on Alex's face as I marched into Damon's Restaurant in Spotsylvania with Steve, John and Samantha. I assisted in frisking and escorting them to cars waiting to whisk them off to the local field office. They were separated immediately; I was along for the ride with Alex, while Ricky was transported in the vehicle directly in front of us. Though I sat in the front passenger seat, the side mirror was adjusted so I could watch Alex, hopefully without being too obvious. Her eyes were wide and teary, her bottom lip trembling. I didn't know if she would be charged with aiding and abetting or an accessory after the fact, but I felt it safe to say that her FBI career had just ended.

When we arrived at Quantico, Ricky and Alex were kept apart while they were ushered into separate interrogation rooms.

Alex was held in a room by herself for almost an hour while we conferred in the next room. We watched her through a one-way mirror as she struggled to remain composed. As the clock ticked on, her anxiety was obviously growing; she bit her nails, pulled at locks of her hair, and rocked back and forth. When the other agents took coffee breaks, I knew they were allowing her to feel the emotion of the situation to help break her down before anyone spoke to her.

It surprised me when John asked if I wanted to talk to her first. But as I studied his eyes, I knew exactly what he had in mind. As her roommate at the Academy, they thought she might confide in me. I was up for the challenge.

I walked into the room as casually as I knew how. I could feel her eyes riveted on me, watching my every move. I felt as though I were under a microscope; I knew Steve and the others were also watching me through the mirror, assessing my performance.

I pulled out a chair and sat beside her, not across the table from her. I leaned toward her and took her hand.

"Are you okay?" I asked softly.

She dabbed at her eyes. "Can I have some water?" she asked in a faint voice.

"Yes," I said, "once you're done in here. They're going to be sending an agent in to talk to you—"

"To interrogate me," she said, leaning her head back and looking at the ceiling as if it held some answers for her there.

"It won't be pleasant," I said, keeping my voice calm and quiet. "I thought, if you wanted to tell me anything, maybe I can talk to them. Maybe they'll go easier on you."

She laughed, but it came out forced and choppy. "What do I tell you? That while I've been studying to become an agent, my own brother has been breaking the law? I think we all know that."

"What exactly was he doing?" I said, tilting my head and looking her square in the eyes. I allowed my brows to knit together, and I hoped I looked genuinely concerned and empathetic.

She hesitated and for a moment I thought she would answer with a sarcastic retort. But when she spoke, her voice was almost whining. "He provided forged paperwork."

"What kind of paperwork?"

She waved her hand. "I don't know, birth certificates, social security cards, driver's licenses…"

"For what purpose?"

"I know you're not going to understand this. But there are a lot of honest, hard-working people coming into this country who can't work and earn an honest living without the proper paperwork."

"Are you talking about illegal immigrants?"

She shrugged. "Mostly. And they want to work. They build our roads, our houses, our businesses. They gather our crops, they raise our produce. They clean our homes, they mow our lawns, they cook our meals. They don't call in sick; they don't take breaks; they're not on drugs. They just want to *work*."

The clock on the wall ticked loudly as our eyes met. I knew she was waiting for me to respond, and for once, I was at a loss.

Finally, I said, "So you were just helping them out." I hoped my words sounded compassionate.

"I wasn't. Ricky was."

"So… how did Ricky get the information to falsify the documents?"

"I don't know," she wailed. "I don't know."

"Do you have any ideas? Look, Alex, I want to help you. I believe you, when you tell me that you weren't involved…"

"They were stolen, okay? He wasn't hurting anybody. It wasn't like the people were out there buying things on stolen credit cards. If anything, the people whose identities were stolen benefited from this."

I leaned back and wrestled against the urge to show the anger that was welling up inside me. "How were they benefiting?"

"These illegal immigrants worked real jobs. Jobs where employers withheld federal taxes, state taxes, social security, Medicare… But the immigrants could never expect to get a tax refund, even if they deserved one. They would never be able to get social security benefits, or Medicare. All the money taken from their paychecks end up in government coffers. They're supporting *us*."

I tried not to look at the mirror, but I wondered what the agents could possibly be thinking as they witnessed this conversation.

I leaned forward again. "How do you know that all the people Ricky gave paperwork to, are honest and hard-working?"

Her answer was immediate. "Because the dishonest ones don't care about paperwork. They'll drive cars without a driver's license. They'll earn their living through criminal means—drugs, robberies, burglaries, fencing—they won't work long hours for minimum wage, doing work that Americans are too good to do themselves."

"So, if I'm hearing you correctly," I said, trying hard not to sound like a psychiatrist restating their patient's emotions, "Ricky was only helping honest people get honest jobs and make honest livings."

She nodded.

The door opened and both of us turned our attention to John, who entering the room with a swagger I hadn't noticed in him before.

"Sheila," he said abruptly. Without another word, he pointed his thumb toward the door.

I rose silently, without looking at Alex, and made a quick exit.

I stopped on the other side of the door and leaned against it, a heavy sigh finally escaping me.

"You were great," Steve said.

I looked back through a mirrored window in the door. John was circling Alex like a hyena circling its prey. "You think?"

"That's an act," he said, following my gaze. "We all thought you did great."

I felt my face burning. "I'm glad John came in when he did. I don't know how much more I could listen to, without getting into a debate with her. But I'm afraid I didn't get much information out of her—just opinions."

"You got enough. The agents with her brother will tell him she's spilled the beans; told us what he was doing. If he wants to save his own hide, he'll tell us who was selling the identities to terrorists—and why."

We strolled down the hall and stopped at the water fountain. My mouth felt as dry as a summer drought. I took a hefty swig, and turned to face Steve.

"You and I both know that faked paperwork is the least of our problems," I said.

He nodded. "I'd say that's an apt observation."

"We have three days before Black Friday. We have a list of malls and shopping centers which will be bombed. And what scares me is, we don't know that list is all-inclusive. And we don't know if we manage to stop the attacks on Friday, that they won't happen on Saturday, or Sunday, or one week later, or one year later…"

"The FBI Director is briefing the President right now."

My jaw dropped.

"You can drink that on the way," he said, glancing at my water cup.

"Where are we going?"

"The President's waiting."

My knees were shaking as Steve led me into a darkened room. I recognized several of the agents seated around the long conference table, but my eyes were quickly drawn to the large screen monitor at the front of the room. I sat down shakily, my eyes riveted on the meeting unfolding on the screen before me.

Around a conference table as long as ours sat the President and members of the Cabinet. Though there were some in the room that I couldn't identify on sight, I immediately recognized the FBI and CIA Directors, and the Secretaries of Defense, Homeland Security, and State.

The President was talking. "This is a war plan," he was saying forcefully. "We have to protect the American people from these attacks on our soil."

"Yes, sir," the FBI Director agreed. "And we already have a plan in place, involving the military, intelligence, and law enforcement communities." He turned toward the monitor and appeared to be looking right at us. "Agent Steve Moran has been working on this."

Steve slipped me a piece of paper before he rose to speak. On it was the simple directive: *Don't say anything to the President that you haven't said to me.*

I stared at Steve. I had no intention of saying anything to the President. I was still in the Academy. I was still awestruck at the mere fact that I could be in the presence of the Director and the President, even if it was via remote conference.

"As you all know, we put together this plan to coordinate our efforts some time ago," Steve said. "The National Guard will be called in to assist local law enforcement in providing security to these malls and shopping centers, not only on Friday but for the foreseeable future. We've already started the notifications, so all of these locations will be checked thoroughly over the next three days. It's possible the terrorists may have planted something—bombs or bomb-making materials—so they could enter on Friday without detection.

"Every store will be thoroughly swept by both agents and bomb-sniffing dogs. We also have several comprehensive lists of suspected terrorists and sleeper cells, so within the next three days, we'll be conducting a large-scale operation, rounding them up all across the country. For every sleeper cell we have in custody, that will be one more location that likely won't be bombed."

"Good work," the President said. "I understand it was one of your new agents who broke the code."

All eyes turned to me.

"Yes, sir," Steve said, coming to stand beside me. "FBI Agent Sheila Carpenter."

I stood. "Mr. President, I really didn't break any code—it was just information on a flash drive that I happened to access."

"Well, you did a good job," the President answered with a half-smile. The smile vanished as he turned to others in his conference room.

"Mr. President," I said. All eyes returned to me. I approached the screen where I could look directly into the President's eyes. "This is just one list. The way that these terrorists generally work is, no one person—or team—knows everything. Chances are there are several lists and a number of additional targets that we haven't yet identified. We can search all of these and we can protect all of these, but this doesn't mean the American people can remain safe. We also don't know if they were referring to *this* Black Friday; it could be another one that has nothing to do with American culture—or it could be this year or any other year."

Both rooms were silent. I could feel the Director's eyes boring into me, along with every agent's eyes in the room. If a spec of dust had drifted onto the table at that moment, I'm sure it would have sounded like thunder.

"So, what do you suggest?" the President asked me.

The Secretary of Defense removed his glasses. "Mr. President, we already have a plan—" he said with more than a bite of sarcasm.

"Tell the American people," I said.

The Cabinet was completely silent for a few seconds before they burst into laughter.

"You can't be everywhere at once," I said loudly. "But the citizens will be."

"That's all," the FBI Director said. A button was pressed and the screen went blank. I turned and faced the group. They stared at me with the same uniform dumb-founded expression. As I made my way back to my seat, it occurred to me that people all along the hierarchy had probably thought of the same thing, but it was up to the Director to advise the President. I sat down while Steve pulled his note away from me and crumpled it in the palm of his hand.

54

I stood in the middle of the food court. I was just outside Washington, DC in one of the busiest malls in America. It was Black Friday, and my palms were drenched in perspiration. I checked my watch for at least the tenth time in as many minutes. It was after noon, and the food court was filling up fast.

I slowly turned 360 degrees. Neon signs shouted at me, tempting me with chicken, hamburgers, tacos, and pizza. The aroma lingered in my nostrils. My stomach growled, my sides feeling almost as if they were rubbing against each other. Though I was surrounded by food, I knew I could not eat. Not yet.

I would never again stand in another food court without the memory of the explosion, without hearing the screams and feeling the debris caving in around me, the dust filling my nostrils while darkness closed in.

And if I could help it, no one else would ever experience it. Not on American soil. Not on my watch.

Long lines were beginning to form at the food counters. Babies in strollers. Couples holding hands.

After studying each person in line, I continued to turn. In the center of the food court was a grouping of animal rockers. A little girl jerked back and forth on a giraffe as though she were galloping across the African savannah. Nearby were several young boys on a toy fire truck; one of them rotated the steering wheel so vigorously that if he'd really been driving, the vehicle would have been going around in circles.

A studious-looking young man carried a raven-haired child to the lion rocker. He placed her on it and knelt beside her, gently rocking the animal while he firmly held onto her torso, the child screaming with delight.

I continued to turn, taking in silver-haired women who clucked as they passed judgment on teenage girls whose mid-drifts were exposed even on this cold November day. A young man with pink spiked hair walked past me with talons protruding from pierced lips.

A din of voices floated past me, providing a menagerie of conversations on many levels at once, sometimes drowning out the voices in my earpiece.

As I came full circle, my eyes met Steve's. He stood about thirty feet away where the food court met the mall. Like the other agents, we'd been on our feet for six hours straight. We had ten more hours to go before wrapping up. Hopefully, we'd be able to fall fast asleep before an early rise tomorrow and the start of this process all over again.

The Virginia National Guard was posted outside the doors, their weapons at the ready as if we were in a war zone. And whether or not the American public realized it, we *were* in a war zone.

Members of the Guard, the FBI, State Police, and local law enforcement strolled through the mall, each wearing their distinctive uniforms, or like Steve and I, wearing our jackets with "FBI" emblazoned across them. Every person was scrutinized, every action followed.

Half a dozen large monitors displayed the latest music videos and holiday ads, the non-stop action visible from every point in the food court, the sound barely audible over the clamor.

Out of the corner of my eye, I noticed the screen changing, the rapid movement replaced by a solitary figure in a navy suit. I turned and peered upwards as the food court came to a hush and all eyes turned to the President seated behind his desk in the Oval Office.

My heart skipped a beat as I wondered, along with countless others, what announcement he would make, and if news was breaking that somewhere in America a mall had fallen under attack.

Instead, we found ourselves riveted to a repeat of the live conference the President had initiated two days earlier. Instead of looking away or continuing about our business, we all watched it as though seeing it for the first time.

"It is the goal of these cowardly fanatics," he was saying, "to disrupt the American way of life. To disrupt our economy. To create fear and confusion. But we will not cower. We will not retreat. We will not be controlled by spineless extremists. In this, the most powerful country in the world..."

Though I wanted to lose myself in his words, I knew I must pull myself away, to continue to search the crowd for anything out of the ordinary. So I reluctantly turned back to the food court, though his words still hung in the air.

As I surveyed the crowd, I felt their eyes migrate toward me as the President told of rounding up suspected terrorists throughout the country, of striking at them first before they had the opportunity to strike at us. He implored the American people to show their solidarity, their unwillingness to be influenced by thugs, and to continue about their business and their normal daily activities.

As he spoke, I watched one pair of eyes after another begin to search the crowd, looking for someone who would appear suspicious, someone not absorbed in the holiday spirit, someone who did not belong on our soil and in our midst.

In Operation Grinch, we were to preserve our way of life. And during this important holiday season that meant every mall and every shopping center across America had been alerted. Every store had been swept by countless federal and local law enforcement agencies. Every security precaution had been taken.

And yet as I stood there, one of many sworn to protect and to serve, I wondered if we had truly done everything we could.

My eyes fell on a lone wheelchair threading its way through the crowd, the occupant beautiful even though both legs were obviously bandaged. I nodded in greeting as Margaret and her mother made their way to me, Margaret's lap burdened with shopping bags from every major store in the mall.

"Look," Margaret said, pulling out a plastic garment bag, "I got you some new suits."

I glanced at Steve. I couldn't afford to be distracted. He nodded and moved closer to my position.

"You shouldn't have done that," I admonished, though I was clearly thrilled.

"Of course I should have. But they're not really Christmas presents. *Those* I'm not going to tell you about," she said, grinning from ear to ear. "These are for your new career. Look, a blue pin-striped suit, a solid navy…"

I wanted to tear the bag open and just stare at them like a child mesmerized by holiday lights, but I knew I couldn't. My eyes swept the surrounding area while she spoke.

"Anyway, you can try them on later. We're going to take all this stuff out to the car. Then we're going to grab a bite to eat. I'm famished."

"Do you want us to get you something to eat?" Mrs. Reed asked, her eyes wide with concern.

"No, I'm fine," I answered, though I was starving. Perhaps after the lunch hour died down and the food court was less inhabited, I could grab a quick bite to eat or down a tall glass of iced tea.

"Margaret looks like she's doing okay," I whispered to Mrs. Reed.

"She's had her moments," she said. "But she's putting on a brave face." Then, "We'll be back soon," she said, wheeling Margaret around.

I watched as Mrs. Reed pushed the wheelchair through the thickening crowds toward the exit, Margaret's lap burdened with a pile of shopping bags. I marveled at her determination to bounce back so quickly, to return to shopping even before she was fully recovered. And on this day, of all days.

A man was walking swiftly on the other side of her, weaving in and out of the crowd, appearing to be headed for the same door. He caught my attention and as I continued to watch him, I understood why: as he wound his way past the shoppers, his head was turned sideways, away from me, as if he didn't want me to see his face.

I began striding toward the door, keeping him in my line of sight, my eyes riveted on his beige overcoat. The crowds were growing ever thicker, the clamor returning now that the President's speech had finished. Christmas music fought to rise above the din.

A young child bumped into me—or me into him—and I gently pushed him back toward his mother. I'd glanced away only for a second, and when I returned to where the man had just been standing, he was gone.

Margaret and Mrs. Reed were moving through the handicapped entrance.

I turned around. I saw jackets and coats of every description, but no one was wearing a beige overcoat.

I turned around again. I caught Steve's attention. "A man in a beige overcoat, black hair, about five-foot-nine, 160 pounds. I just lost track of him."

"Coming to you," Steve answered, his voice almost drowned out in my earpiece by the hubbub around me.

I looked back at the entrance. Mrs. Reed was busily pushing the wheelchair down the parking aisle toward their car.

Then I saw him: his overcoat slung over his arm, a black shirt and black slacks now visible. He turned and glanced back at the glass doors.

"My God," I whispered. "Steve, it's the man from my parents' house. The one who tried to burn it down!"

I began to run. Steve's voice was lost in my rush to get through the crowd, to get out of the mall, to apprehend this monster.

I reached the doors. Where was he?

I peered down the parking aisle.

"Everything okay?" I heard the police officer's voice before I even noticed him standing just a few feet away.

"No," I said. I described the man as quickly as I could, my eyes continuing to scan our surroundings. By the time I finished, Steve was there, along with a half a dozen agents.

"He can't get far," Steve said as we fanned out. "National Guard's closing the exits." As I moved away from him, following the aisle where I'd last seen the man, I heard Steve continuing to issue orders. I knew a team was now closing off parts of the mall, looking for suspicious packages and securing the area, while attempting to maintain calm.

I stopped midway down the aisle. He could have crossed to other aisles just as easily as following this one. If he knew I was following him—and he had to have known— he would have zigzagged through the parking lot, possibly checking for unlocked cars. He might even be right under our noses, hidden in someone's back seat, buried under packages.

I turned back toward the mall. At least he was outside. He wasn't going to detonate in *this* food court. He would never get back inside. Not now, not ever.

I began to jog back toward the mall. I glanced up to see several National Guardsmen standing atop the roof, visually searching the area. Then one of them raised an arm and pointed in my direction.

I slowed just feet from the mall entrance, my breath coming so heavily and so fast that it sounded like a freight train.

Rising above my breathing was the sound of an engine. It was so loud and so insistent that it drowned out Steve's voice and the voices of the others. As I turned slowly around, I heard tires spinning on the asphalt.

At the end of the aisle was a black SUV with blacked out windows, bearing down on me.

I screamed and grabbed the rifle from a National Guardsman, raising it to my shoulder as the vehicle sped toward me. Everyone was yelling, but I couldn't comprehend even a single word anyone was saying.

I leveled the rifle. My breath was steady now, my breathing deep.

My finger found the trigger effortlessly, coming down on it in a steady, consistent pressure.

Everything around me seemed at once to be in utter chaos. Others were gathering around me, closing in, even as the vehicle gained speed.

It was forty feet away. Thirty feet. Twenty.

I squeezed the trigger. As the rifle recoiled, the air was filled with gunfire. It was only then that I realized a solid line of National Guardsmen and law enforcement agents had joined me, almost shoulder to shoulder.

The windshield was riddled with bullet holes. The vehicle turned suddenly and went airborne, crashing back down half an aisle over, directly on top of a jet black Aston Martin Vanquish S.

A fireball lit up the parking lot, reaching more than thirty feet in the air, the bright red and orange fire quickly replaced by acrid black smoke. I instinctively placed my arm over my face, shielding it from flying debris.

People were running in all directions—the National Guard rushing toward the fire but held back by the giant flames, shoppers fleeing, passersby in the parking lot screaming as they sought to escape the onslaught of twisted metal, smoke, and the intense heat of the fire.

Frantic, I realized Margaret and Mrs. Reed had been just feet away from the man when they left the mall. Now I searched frenetically for Mrs. Reed's distinctive black Lincoln Continental with the Ambassador license plates.

When I found them, Mrs. Reed was standing perfectly still at the trunk of the car, Margaret sitting calmly beside her in the wheelchair, their eyes riveted on the flames as fire trucks and ambulances raced toward the mall, their sirens wailing ever closer.

Steve reached me as I reached my friend.

We stopped for a brief moment and simply stared in each others' eyes. Then I heard myself saying, "Next time, let's use concrete barricades."

55

We could feel the excitement in the air as Steve and Phil Pippin strolled around the classroom, handing out envelopes. Some of the other agents joked and held the envelopes to their foreheads as if they could telepathically determine their contents.

It was the eighth week of class and the last day before the Christmas break. Though we had several more weeks before graduation from the Academy, today we would learn where our first assignment would be.

One by one, agents were called to the front of the room to open their envelope and announce to the class where they would be stationed. Most were going to the larger field offices—ideal locations for getting up to speed fast.

Adiva would be going to the New York office to serve in the Joint Terrorism Task Force. Christiane was headed to Los Angeles. It wasn't lost on any of us that one seat was empty, and I couldn't help but wonder where Alex would have landed if circumstances had been different.

When they called my name, I walked slowly to the front of the room. I held the envelope in my hand for a brief moment. My eyes searched the room for Steve. He was standing along the side wall; I thought I detected a slight smile.

I had mixed feelings. I truly didn't want to think about leaving here and leaving Steve behind, though I hoped our paths would cross some time in the future.

I opened the envelope. I took a deep breath, looked at the class, and announced, "I will be going to…" and then glanced at the paper. "Washington, DC." Despite myself, I broke into a wide grin.

On the way back to my seat, I caught Steve's eye. He smiled and winked. I would be working just a few miles from Quantico. I would be working with John Davidson, and I would still have opportunities to see Steve.

After class, I finished packing my gym bag and paused to survey my dorm room before leaving for Tennessee for the Christmas holidays.

My laptop was already in the car, along with the box of photographs, my mother's cell phone, and what was left of my aspirin.

My eyes fell on the desk where I'd spent so many hours. My new purse—a Christmas gift from Margaret—was zipped up and ready to go, my keys beside it. The room already had a different scent, a different feel.

Beside the keys was a small stack of paperwork: the deed to my parent's home. I'd purchased it from the Beards after the Thanksgiving break, along with almost a full acre that surrounded it. The fire had damaged the home, but it was recoverable. I'd already entered into an agreement with a contractor to make the necessary repairs. They were already behind schedule and over budget and the project was just beginning. But once I got back to Tennessee, I could oversee the repairs and get them on track before heading back to the Academy for the final weeks of training.

It had been agreed, after too much discussion and debate, that Aunt Jo would live there. It was a much larger home. It would be a dramatic change for her, one that had been a long time coming.

I wasn't sure yet what I'd do with her old house. It was ancient and tiny, and really should be razed, but I didn't know if I would have the heart to do that. Maybe, if I had any money left over, I would get it renovated and leave it there for posterity if nothing else.

A knock at the door interrupted my thoughts.

"Ready?" Steve's voice was light and friendly.

I grabbed my gym bag. "As ready as I'll ever be."

He started to take it from me, but I held onto it and he didn't argue. Instead, he followed me down the hall to the elevator.

"Why do I think you had something to do with me getting assigned to Washington?" I asked as we stepped inside the elevator.

Steve pushed the button for the lobby. "You'll like it there. There'll be a lot of opportunities for you to use your computer—and investigative—skills."

"They never did find out who that red haired woman was in Robeson County, did they?" I mused.

Steve stroked his chin. "She's apparently disappeared."

"Something tells me I'll run into her again."

"Don't know about that," Steve said. "But stranger things have happened."

We reached the lobby. The television set was on in the corner of the room, and several agents were standing in front of it, watching intently. I started to cross the room to the front door, but then stopped and looked back.

"We don't know for certain there was any dynamite in that vehicle," the political pundit was saying.

"So what are you insinuating?" his opponent said, leaning across the table to look him in the eyes.

"Just this: that the President's ratings were at their lowest, and now we're to believe that America is under attack? That people have infiltrated our borders by just walking across, unimpeded, and they wanted to stop Americans from celebrating the holidays? Oh, puh-lease... This is nothing more than 'wag the dog'—"

I took a deep breath and turned to face Steve.

He cocked his head. "Are you coming?"

I nodded. Let the politicians sort it out, I thought as I crossed the room. I had another adventure waiting.

A Note from the Author

This book is not meant to be a commentary on illegal immigration, though it was impossible to develop the plot without touching on the serious ramifications of porous borders.

The statistics presented by Derek Greville in Chapter 36 are estimates provided for 2004 and 2005 by the PEW Hispanic Center, North Carolina; the Employment Security Commission; the Center for Immigration Studies; and reported in various North Carolina newspapers.

Derek's personal views regarding his relative's construction business and the experience of Sheila's family tobacco business with regard to the employment of immigrants reflect the experiences and opinions of millions of employers, legal immigrants and Americans.

The view presented by Alex in Chapter 53 is a view shared by millions of Americans on the opposite side of the immigration debate.

Conception Rivera's story as told in Chapter 46 is a compilation of experiences provided by individuals who wish to remain anonymous.

I leave it up to each individual reader to form his or her own opinion.

About the Author

p.m.terrell is the internationally acclaimed author of the suspense/thrillers *Kickback* and *The China Conspiracy*, both published by Drake Valley Press. She is also the author of *Take the Mystery out of Promoting Your Book* (Palari Publishing) and several nonfiction computer books, including *Creating the Perfect Database* (Scott-Foresman), *The Dynamics of WordPerfect* and *The Dynamics of Reflex* (Dow Jones-Irwin), and *Memento WordPerfect* (Edimicro, Paris).

Ms. Terrell is the founder of McClelland Enterprises, Inc., one of the first companies in the Washington, DC area devoted to PC training, and Continental Software Development Corporation, which provides applications development, website design, and computer consulting services throughout the continental United States and its territories. Her clients have included the U.S. Secret Service, CIA and Department of Defense, as well as various local law enforcement agencies.

Ms. Terrell is the co-founder, along with Officer Mark Kearney of the Waynesboro, Virginia Police Department, of the Book 'Em Foundation, a partnership between authors and law enforcement agencies dedicated to raising public awareness of the correlation that exists between high crime rates and high illiteracy rates, increasing literary, and reducing crime.

She is also a staunch supporter of Crime Stoppers, Crime Solvers, and Crime Lines, which offer rewards and anonymity to individuals reporting information on criminal activity. She is proud to have served as the first female President of the Chesterfield County/Colonial Heights (Virginia) Crime Solvers Board of Directors (2003-2004).

Visit her website at www.pmterrell.com.

CB 3/08

MG 11/07

3/07

ML